WOLFSRE

ACADEMY

Wolfsreach Academy

The Kylnnar War Saga, Volume 1

Justin Waine

Wolfsreach Academy

Copyright © 2024 by Justin Waine
Edited by: Nick Hodgson

Cover copyright © 2024 Epsom Fantasy Press Limited
Cover design by: Lee Matthews

Published by:
Epsom Fantasy Press Limited
www.epsomfantasypress.co.uk

ISBN: 978-1-7391807-4-4 (ebook)
ISBN: 978-1-7391807-5-1 (paperback)

First Edition: August 2024

Dedicated to:
Master Rommel Bernarte

CHAPTER 1

Location: Wolfsreach Space Port, Wolfstar III
Date: 17 December 2196 CE, Earth Standard Calendar
Time: 10.38 Local Time 26.5-hour clock

The small space port hummed with life. The air was filled with the burning fumes of plasma engines. Shouts and exclamations rang out across the asphalt. The whole place had the horrible bustle characteristic of war about to arrive.

At the edge of the landing platform, Helen Murphy watched a squat, boxy space transport fire itself slowly into the air before throttling up and heading for the atmosphere. She stalked across the landing field, dragging her right leg behind her. She was cursing quietly under her breath – partly because the dust from this rocky dump of a planet had worked its way into her bionic right leg, seizing up the knee joint, and partly because of what she saw before her.

Wolfstar III was a craggy, grey sand world on the very fringes of human-controlled space, the third sphere circulating a yellow sun of the same name. Whatever dreams the original colonists had planned for it had not long survived their arrival. Instead, it had become home to a small military outpost. Its space port reflected its status as an afterthought in a big universe. The top of a large mountain had been blown off to create a flat plateau, which had then been asphalted to create a level usable landing platform capable of holding perhaps a dozen small transport vessels.

As it was now, only two transports sat on the pad. One displayed the blue and black colours of the Confederation Fleet. It was the type of barge used to shuttle people or supplies back and forth from a larger interstellar transport holding in orbit above. The other vessel was a small army planet hopper, large enough for a dozen people. It was painted in green and brown camouflage more appropriate to a jungle world than the ashen mountainous sphere on which it found itself.

There were no buildings on the surface; they were buried in the cliff below the landing platform. On the first level down was a small terminal, little more than a waiting room, for those cooling their heels before a transport ship was ready for them. It was empty now. Below that was the flight control centre that monitored the vessels leaving and arriving. It also controlled the protective shield that could be used to envelope the platform and protect it from the planet's frequent rock storms. A skeleton staff continued to work in the ambience of the artificial light. At the bottom of the cliff was the monorail station which connected the space port to the rest of the base.

Helen stopped in front of a Confederation Navy officer who was standing opposite the barge. The officer was staring at a tablet and exuding an officious air like only a born bureaucrat could. A dozen fleet ratings, together with their attendant service robots, were busily using magnetic gravitators to shift piles of crates into the vessel in front of them.

Helen looked the woman up and down: she was a petite, dark woman, her hair cut short in line with war regulations. Her eyes searched the woman's navy-blue uniform, finding her name on a plastic tag pinned to the left breast. She spotted the two bars on the shoulder indicating the woman's rank.

"Lieutenant-Commander Pandey, may I speak with you?" Helen asked politely.

The officer raised her eyes from the tablet, a look of mild distaste spreading across her face. The middle-aged woman in front of her was pale-skinned and freckled. Her long curly red hair must once have been lustrous, but the grey on the front and temples now made her look distinguished. Penetrating green eyes met the officer's assessing gaze. Helen was wearing a dark green boiler suit, pulled tight round her thin frame by a black plastic utility belt.

"Don't you know how to salute, soldier?" the officer barked angrily.

"I'm not military," the red-headed woman replied calmly.

Sonia Pandey reached down and lifted a small mask on her belt to her face to take a hit of oxygen from the short oval canister attached to her waist.

A new arrival to the planet, thought Helen. Not used to the lower oxygen level yet. Naval vessels ran with oxygen atmospheres slightly below Earth standard, apparently to prepare their crews for new worlds, though in reality it was to save money. On Wolfstar III, the level of oxygen in the atmosphere was nineteen percent, below that on a naval vessel and lower than was normally considered safe for humans. It took some getting used to. New arrivals used small oxygen tanks to help fight potential nausea, and were derisively called 'puffers' by the longer-term inhabitants.

"And it's *Commander*: battlefield promotion; still waiting on the new uniform," the officer sailed on, seemingly ignoring the response.

Helen fought back the urge to scream at the officious woman. *Battlefield promotion*, she silently demurred. She doubted the woman had been within two star systems of a battle.

"I am the matron of the academy. We are still awaiting evacuation," Helen explained.

The officer took in the tall woman's lean, angular frame and decided she was the least matronly matron she could imagine. "My understanding was that the academy had already been evacuated?"

"The children with parents were evacuated two days ago. The teaching staff and the orphans who are thirteen and under were taken off yesterday. When are the remaining children to be taken off?" Helen demanded.

The officer seemed perplexed. She looked down at her tablet and swiped her hand across a few times. "My records show that all civilian and military teaching staff and all the children have been evacuated. You should have left by now if you're a civilian. I can't find you on the civilian list?"

"I'm medical auxiliary; try on that list," the matron suggested.

"Oh, yes: here you are. It says you're overdue. We can take you?" the officer offered grudgingly.

"And the two hundred children back at the school?" asked Helen.

"What two hundred children?" The officer was looking at her tablet again, still perplexed.

"Two hundred orphans of military personnel aged fourteen to seventeen years old." Helen spelt it out slowly, as if talking to a moron.

"Oh! That makes sense. The Military Empowerment Act of March 2196 states that all orphans in military academies over the age of fourteen are approved for military service for auxiliary function and planetary defence," Commander Pandey stated proudly.

WOLFSREACH ACADEMY

A sinking feeling threatened to immerse the school matron. She was aware of the law change – all the staff at the school had been briefed when it had come into force. It was one of a series of measures to bolster the troop numbers of the Gaian-Martian Confederation in their battle with the alien Kylnnar. A war had raged between the two for nearly eight years; a war the Confederation was losing. It was odd to think of the teeming mass of humanity spread across the stars running out of people, but that was apparently the case.

"Look, Commander," Helen said, angry and desperate now, "There are two hundred teenagers in a school down there and the Kylnnar are on the way." Helen thrust her hand out down the valley in the direction of the half-buried school in the distance.

Commander Pandey recoiled at the outburst, but her face showed no concern, just annoyance at being argued with.

"It is not my fault; the military have provided no orders to remove their soldiers," she responded peevishly. "Yes, there is Kylnnar activity in nearby systems, but we have no reason to believe they are coming here. I suggest your students – sorry, *soldiers*," the commander mentally cursed her error, "hunker down, sit it out and wait for the Kylnnar to pass by."

"And if they don't pass by?" the matron demanded.

At that moment, a wheezing, crunching sound punctured the seriousness of the confrontation. Commander Pandey looked at the red-haired woman in shock.

"My bionic leg; it's temperamental," the matron explained sheepishly.

She was secretly glad it was working. It was weird; even though there was no sensor array in the leg, it still felt like it was alive. That was when it actually bothered to operate correctly.

She had lost the Commander's attention. The woman was now studiously ignoring her and had gone back to staring at her tablet.

Helen fought down the urge to attack the box-ticking officer; a glance at the Navy woman's finely polished sidearm gave her enough pause.

Her leg now working, Helen walked across to the army planet hopper and the dozen squaddies milling around it. They were dressed in grey camouflage drabs, more used for city combat, but the closest the Army had to the environment the men had found themselves in. It contrasted with the greens and browns of their transport, which stood out starkly on the arid dusty world.

"Hello, Gunny!" came a welcoming shout from the group.

"Don't call me that," Helen muttered angrily.

If the grizzled veteran who had shouted at her took offence at her response he did not show it. She seated herself on a long low plastic crate and started to weep. The old soldier patted her gently on the shoulder.

"The Navy said no," he said; it was a statement, not a question.

She looked up at Armoury Specialist Thomas. She called him Tommo – everyone did; she had never actually asked what his first name was, and it seemed pointless now. The look of concern seemed wrong on his weathered face.

"You can come with us," he offered.

She looked at his little planet hopper. She knew he meant only her. There was only room enough for his team, so even taking her would take the ship over capacity. That was not a problem for a short journey out of atmosphere, so it was a genuine offer.

"I can't leave them."

He nodded in understanding and squeezed her shoulder again.

"You know she lied to you?" He stepped back as if afraid of her reaction.

"You were listening?" she asked, wiping away her tears on her sleeve.

"I caught bits of it," he shrugged. "The Navy lost the third fleet to the Kylnnar."

"Where?"

"Outskirts of the Copernicus system three days ago?"

"That's two, maybe three, systems away." She stood up, worried. *That explained the Commander's battlefield promotion*, she thought nastily.

"How badly did we lose?"

"I told you – we lost the third fleet," he responded.

"What, all of it?" she asked incredulously.

"Down to the last life pod, carriers, cruisers, fighters, the lot. Why do you think we're bugging out with such speed?"

"Do you think they're coming here?"

"She didn't tell you?" Tommo looked sad now. "Yes, Helen, they're coming here. Battlegroups are detaching from their main Kylnnar fleet, cleansing planet by planet."

"Why haven't you blown the armoury?" she demanded.

Looking out from the platform, she looked towards the school. Roughly halfway between the platform and the academy was a squat building buried in the side of the sharp V-shaped valley. It looked like a small pair of towers, but behind this was a large complex of tunnels. It was an armoury filled with weapons for the Confederation Army, in the days when humankind had been expanding outwards across the stars, not retreating.

"They gave me an hour to blow it. I'm good, but even I can't mine it in that time and get me and my men off the planet. The Navy aren't messing around: we're leaving at 11.00 local time. Even me chatting with you means we're cutting it fine," he said with a smile.

She watched as the few remaining ground staff appeared on the platform and embarked on the Navy barge. While she had been speaking to Tommo, the Commander and her staff had finished their work.

"Isn't there a self-destruct or something?"

"You've been streaming too many vids again; it's not a starship," he chuckled.

She refrained from pointing out that starships did not have a self-destruct either, though you could get pretty much the same effect by bypassing the safety protocols and overloading the engines. She was glad that Tommo had not thought to try that on the base's own power plant. Maybe he had and then decided not to do it, perhaps to give her and the orphans at least a small chance of survival. She was not going to ask just in case it turned out he was inept rather than kind.

"Don't suppose you'd give me the key to the armoury, would you?" she asked Tommo cheekily.

"You don't need it," he grunted.

"What?"

"I didn't lock it."

"What?" She was incredulous.

"Why bother? If the Kylnnar want in, they'll just blow or cut their way in. Let them clear it out and take the weapons. If I leave it open, chances are that it will still be here when we come back this way for us to use later," Tommo explained.

"I like your optimism," she remarked.

He wanted to give her a hug, but felt he didn't know her well enough. Instead, he stuck out his hand. She took it and gave it a firm shake.

"Good luck, Gunny," he smiled, but his eyes were filled with sadness. "Right, lads, pack it up. Time to go." Tommo raised his hand in a circling motion, ordering his men to embark the planet hopper. "The posh folks in the Navy won't wait."

"Last chance?" He waved his hand in the direction of the transport.

"Get going, Tommo. I'll see you soon."

14

"Now I like *your* optimism," he grunted.

She watched him disappear up the gangway. Her gaze lingered until it closed in a hiss of hydraulic fluid. She backed away; she had no desire to be fried by the backwash of the plasma engine. The ship accelerated off the platform before dropping down across the valley towards the school. It picked up speed, circling up and away before climbing into the sky and disappearing out of sight towards the atmosphere.

Helen fought down the urge to wave. They could not see her anyway. She stood for a bit longer watching the skies, not sure for what. She knew she would not be able to see the starship breaking orbit. She half expected to see Kylnnar ships arriving, but she knew the Navy would not cut it that fine. Based on what Tommo had said, it would be hours, not days.

CHAPTER 2

Location: Wolfsreach Academy, Wolfstar III
Date: 17 December 2196 CE, Earth Standard Calendar
Time: 10.59 Local Time 26.5-hour clock

He was tall, blond-haired and blue-eyed, with immaculately tanned white skin. Muscular and handsome, with perfect teeth and a firm jaw, he was sixteen years old, though looked anything between that and twenty-five. Cadet Sergeant Travis "Sam" Ronin was popular with both students and staff, status that came with being an elite football player. It was just a shame he had been stuck in a military academy where the only sport that really mattered was astro-hockey, at which he was proficient, but not on the level of the school hockey star, Onesie Harper. Still, it was enough to guarantee him jock status. Despite that position, he was not a total idiot.

However, the fact he was currently carrying out the worst punishment duty any student of Wolfsreach Academy could be given suggested that he was at least occasionally an idiot. He grunted and sweated, baking in the mid-morning sun, the oxygen-thin air making the manual labour harder than it should have been.

WOLFSREACH ACADEMY

He had been at it for over an hour and his lungs were screaming. He was using a short-handled spade to scoop up the mounds of grey sand piled up underneath and around the metallic grid walkway on which he stood. It was a frustrating task: it was difficult to work the sand out from under the walkway and tip it off the roof, and it was rapidly being replaced by more sand blowing down off the pitched roof that the walkway surrounded.

The teenager stopped shovelling grey sand and straightened up; *his back should not hurt this much*, he thought angrily. He took a deep breath, his burning lungs trying to grasp oxygen out of the air. He stared off into the distance. He may not have been enjoying the task he had been handed – frankly, he would rather have been on latrine duty – but he did appreciate that the roof of the gym gave him a spectacular view. In one direction, he looked up the rocky expanse of Wolfsreach Valley towards the landing platform; on the other side was a sweeping vista across the rocky plain at the end of the valley. He could just make out what looked like a planet hopper leaving the space port; it swooped down the valley in his direction. *Definitely a planet hopper*, he thought, as the spacecraft passed over his head before climbing up towards the atmosphere. He gave a sigh and went back to shovelling sand. Not for the first time, he wondered which moron had decided to give the gym a pitched roof on a planet riven by sandstorms but almost devoid of rainfall.

Wolfstar III was a windswept grey rock. Its only previously habitable area had been near the planet's poles, where there was a small amount of ice and enough water to make it survivable. It was curious that the Confederation Military had decided to place its base so far from the poles. It also sat at a surprisingly high altitude, as if Wolfstar III's thin oxygen were not already a challenge enough for human respiration.

The military base had largely outlived its usage, though its large armoury still remained in use. Some years previously, its training centre had been converted to a school, grandly named

Wolfsreach Academy. A place to safely stash the children of military service personnel while their parents were engaged in resisting the ongoing Kylnnar invasion of Confederation-controlled space. As the resistance had become increasingly unsuccessful, the school had become an orphanage for the children of the many victims, both soldier and civilian, of the relentless if slow Kylnnar advance.

"You going to help?" He addressed the girl sitting a short distance away, dangling her feet off the corner of the gym roof.

Cadet Corporal Inaya Chandra was a tall, lithe Indian girl. She was beautiful with light brown skin and chocolate brown eyes, and her long black hair, tied tightly in a neat braid, stretched down her back to her waist. She stared at her tablet and ignored her boyfriend's peevish enquiry. She kicked her heels against the wall and trod the open air. Inaya was unbothered by the drop from the roof; she had even unclipped her steel safety rope from the grey harnesses that she and Travis wore. They had both been handed punishment duty, but only one of them had any intention of completing the task at hand.

"Hey, I'm not the one on report; why should I?" The voice came from the opposite end of the gym roof.

Travis, confused, looked back in that direction; Inaya did not even glance up from the vid playing on her tablet. He could not see anyone as the pitch of the roof got in the way. He tiptoed gingerly along the metal walkway that surrounded the gym. He pulled his short metal safety rope with him as he went. It was attached to a steel safety rail that ran round the perimeter of the gym roof. Normally Travis had a pretty good head for heights, but there was something about the gym roof and its safety system that made it feel precarious. It was not that long a drop to the ground below, but he knew how hard the rock was. It was still a large enough distance to mean broken bones if he fell and the safety harness failed, though the fall probably would not kill him. He had no desire to go through the painful process of bone repair.

He reached the corner and saw a figure squatting down on one knee, her arms resting on the rail. She was staring up across the school towards the landing platform.

"You're not supposed to be up here," he muttered angrily.

It was more an observation than a reprimand. He should have known who it was from her southern drawl: Cadet Private Julia Williams. The fourteen-year-old girl was dressed like Travis and Inaya in the uniform of a Wolfsreach Academy student: black, with a thin red stripe running down the sleeve and leg on each side, although her upper arm lacked the red rank flashes the other two possessed.

"What are you doing up here?" Travis demanded.

Inaya and Travis had a good reason to be on the roof. After all, they were on report. It was the third time in as many months, and as a result they had been allocated the Academy's least pleasant task. But Julia had no reason to be up here.

Standing on this side of the roof, Travis had a good view of the school where he now lived. In front of him was the astro-hockey pitch; on the other side were the dormitory blocks, and beyond was the long valley leading up to the landing platform. To his left were the southern mountains, sharp rocks of glistening razor-sharp glass that framed one side of the Academy site. On his right was the main school building – *the only two-storey building*, he thought, although, like all the buildings, the lower floor was half sunken in the ground. The gym roof was on a similar level, despite having only a single storey, due to its combination of a higher ceiling and pitched roof.

The pitched roof was the problem. Travis looked admiringly at the flat roofs of the buildings surrounding him and watched the small fans that gently wafted the planet's grey sand off their surfaces. The grey grit of the planet got everywhere, helped by the rolling winds, which varied from light breezes to raging rock storms. This grit could build up quickly; so fast

19

sometimes that the weight of it could be enough to bring the roof down. So, each roof had fans to blow it away. That did not work on the gym. Its pitched roof slowed the accumulation of sand, but meant there was no simple automated solution to get rid of it. Instead, students would be sent up to manually shovel the grey build-up away. The teachers with a malicious sense of discipline made it into a punishment for the more insubordinate students. It was a double disciplining: not only did the student have the hard labour of shifting the piles of earth, but also the chore of scrubbing out the grey stains that would permeate their jet-black uniforms.

"I asked what you were doing up here, Private Williams?" Travis barked.

"Alright, sergeant, no need to get snippy," laughed the pale, brown-haired girl. "Just practising."

She held up a metallic grey pulse rifle with a telescopic sight with her left hand before resting it back in the crook of her right arm.

"That should not be out of your quarters unless you are on exercise. I should put you on report," Travis indicated the plasma weapon and tried to sound officious, but it was not in his nature despite his rank.

"Trying to get me to do your punishment for you?" Julia smirked in response.

She flashed her rifle at him again, showing him the energy pack was missing – without that, it was just a lump of metal.

"Why are you even bothering?" she asked her fellow cadet.

"That's what I said." Inaya had appeared round the corner.

"Hey, Inaya," Julia said with a smile.

Inaya gave her the barest nod of recognition.

"You two get caught up in the northern hills again?" the younger woman demanded cheekily.

Travis glanced involuntarily at the northern mountains that framed the side of the school, rising up behind the main school building. Personal relationships were frowned on between the students – it was the military, after all. It was also a school full of teenagers, so there was only so much that the teachers could do to police such things, and the northern hills provided a good place for amorous teenagers to escape to. His relationship with Inaya was perhaps the Academy's worst-kept secret. That was not the reason, though: they had snuck alcohol from the teacher's supply store. It had been Simon's idea, but Inaya had jumped at the chance, and she had dragged Travis into it. It wasn't the first time they had done it, nor the first time they had been caught. The teacher who found them had been incandescent with rage at such a violation. Stuck on a rock in the far reaches of human space, the teachers were fiercely protective of their drinks supply.

"It's not like that. There were three of us. It doesn't matter," he muttered grumpily.

"Simon?" asked Julia. Everyone knew who Travis's closest friend was.

Travis nodded.

"Guess lieutenants don't do punishment duty," she observed. "Still doesn't explain why you're doing it. Who ordered it?"

"Instructor Simpson," the sergeant replied.

"He's gone; all the teachers are gone," she said.

"That's what I said. Why are we bothering when they can't be bothered with us?" Inaya observed caustically.

Julia raised her eyebrow quizzically.

"The teachers are gone, the younger kids, the teenagers with the rich parents. Leaving us behind on this windblown rock. Those who aren't worth saving!" Inaya shouted angrily.

Travis rolled his eyes, settling on Inaya with a frustrated look that indicated that was not the reason they were still here and that they had already had this argument. Given Inaya's contempt for authority most of the time, Travis had been surprised that she had taken the evacuation of the teachers and a number of the other students before them so badly. She seemed to see in it some sort of personal victimization of those left behind.

"You know that's not the reason," he countered.

"So why are we all still here?" she snapped. "Why don't we matter?"

"We only have one thing in common, Inaya: we're all orphans," Travis replied sadly.

"Still doesn't explain why you're doing gym roof duty, if all the instructors are gone?" Julia said, curious.

"Lieutenant ordered it," Travis explained.

"What, Simon?" Julia replied incredulously.

"No, obviously not Simon," Inaya shot back.

"Hakeswell?" asked Julia with an evil grin.

Inaya's gaze of white-hot anger answered her question wordlessly.

Julia started laughing.

CHAPTER 3

Location: Wolfsreach Academy, Wolfstar III
Date: 17 December 2196 CE, Earth Standard Calendar
Time: 11.45 Local Time 26.5-hour clock

The astro puck rocketed down the hallway, slamming off a row of grey metal lockers before skittering across to the other side of the hall. It thudded dully into the light-green-painted stone of the lower half of the wall, then came to a halt at the bottom of the stairway. Its sudden appearance came as a shock to the young woman who had just stepped off the last stair into the hall. A second astro puck came flying down the hall – this one much faster. It cannoned off the wall, dislodging some plaster before smashing into the metal of lockers and careering to a stop part way up the staircase.

Jo Hakeswell, crouched on the ground, stood up and looked behind her. The puck had landed on the fourth step up. She looked back at the dented locker and mentally calculated the trajectory. Had she not ducked, it would have taken her head off. She fought down the urge to use language unbecoming to an officer.

"Hakeswell!" She heard a frightened whisper from the other end of the corridor.

"Stand fast!" she roared.

She stalked down the corridor, balefully searching out her attacker. She spied him at the end of the corridor, astro-hockey stick in hand, looking sheepish. He was surrounded by half a dozen friends. Cadet Private Joseph Harper was fourteen years old but looked thirty. A muscular six-foot-tall West African, he loomed over Hakeswell. His look of panicked terror at the approaching young woman in any other situation might have seemed absurd, but it made sense within the confines of a military academy.

"Hey, lieutenant," he offered nervously.

Cadet Lieutenant Jo Hakeswell drew herself up to her full height, which at five foot seven inches did not help much, and straightened her uniform. They both wore the same black one-piece jumpsuit with a dark red stripe down the arm and side. A red plastic badge stitched to her breast showed her family name. On her upper left arm was the flag of the confederation, but rendered in charcoal and grey rather than in the normal red and blue. On her epaulettes a single gold bar indicated her rank of second lieutenant.

"Was that you?" She thrust her hand down the corridor at the dented locker for emphasis.

"The second one."

"You nearly took my head off!" she screeched in a very unmilitary manner.

Private Harper looked at the lieutenant's good-looking cappuccino-toned face, her dark brown hair straightened and braided neatly behind her head, and could not decide if that would have been a good thing or not. He decided that the question was rhetorical and wisely offered no observation.

"Who hit the first one?" Jo demanded, her glare sweeping across the assembled students.

Up to this point, the cadets had been enjoying Private Harper's discomfort, but now their smiles shrank away in the face of the officer's displeasure.

"Leave them alone; it was me," came a soft voice from behind the group.

A young Asian man stood up and pushed through the group in front of him. He was still holding an astro-hockey stick, which he handed to one of the other cadets. He was thin, belying the beginnings of a muscular strength, with spiky black hair, just a bit longer than the regulation short back and sides for male cadets. His uniform mirrored Jo Hakeswell's except the single bar on his shoulder was silver not gold.

Jo felt a huge well of frustration building. Simon Kim, the misbegotten child of a Korean father and a Chinese mother, she unkindly thought to herself. Of course, it would be him. She immediately regretted the thought; she had nothing against the Chinese or the Koreans for that matter. Nor did she have any reasons to cast aspersions on Simon's parentage. Like most of the orphans he was close mouthed about his background. It was just he was so infuriating, his slovenliness, his unruliness, his complete lack of discipline and most grating of all the fact he largely got away with it. There was something about him, something that the teachers and other students could see that she could not. An indefinable quality that meant his bad behaviour, if not actually ignored, was at least tolerated far more than Jo could understand.

"What the hell are you playing at?" she demanded. "Look at the damage! You're supposed to set an example."

The other cadets tried to slip away.

"Stand fast!" she ordered again.

The students stopped, watching the confrontation between the two older cadets with dreadful fascination.

"I should report you," threatened Jo.

25

"Who too? The teachers are gone," observed Simon. "Chill out, Jo Jo; Onesie was just showing me how to improve my shuffle swing."

Joanna Hakeswell's frustration was at boiling point. Simon Kim was the only person left in the school brave enough to refer to her by her old nickname, at least to her face. At sixteen she was a year younger than him, and he remembered her from before her current promotion. She hugely disliked the military habit of giving everyone a nickname; what was wrong with your birth name, after all? Private Harper, for example, was not named Onesie after the garment but because as a child he had lost his left eye, now replaced by a bionic one.

"I suppose I should be grateful you suck at astro-hockey. You should stick to Taekwondo," she retorted nastily.

"Tang Soo Do," he corrected quickly, as if it were a misunderstanding he had to clarify regularly.

She wanted to scream. He was so annoying. He was an insubordinate, rude troublemaker. While not exactly lazy, he was certainly not a hard worker. All that was forgiven because he was a martial arts champion. He was so good that it had garnered him a lieutenancy. She supposed she should be happy he did not show the same skill at astro-hockey, the Army's sport of choice. He would probably be a cadet captain by now if he were. The entire system drove her insane.

"I'm reporting you, first chance I get," she declared.

"Could be a long wait?" he observed.

His own annoyance was starting to counter her frustration. Why did she always insist on operating like the worst military pen pusher? They were at school, not in an army barracks.

"You should be packed and ready to evacuate. I'll file my report when we get off planet," she replied.

"We're not going anywhere. The platform is empty. We're not being evacuated," he informed her.

"Who told you that? That's rubbish." She did not sound convinced.

She tried to look confident, but uncertainty gnawed at her. She was not stupid: the teachers were gone, and the younger students and those with parents to take them had been evacuated. All that was left were two hundred orphans. Half of those, like Onesie Harper, had arrived last year from Talos IV, their parents killed in the Kylnnar's devastating invasion of that planet.

"The platform is clear, Jo Jo – the last transports left nearly an hour ago." Simon's tone was comforting; almost caring. Almost as if he knew she would struggle with this news.

"You can't be sure. No way you can be sure the platform is clear from this far down the valley," she said, grasping for hope.

"I can, though. Nothing there, trust me," Onesie Harper interjected. He tapped two fingers against the temple nearest his bionic eye.

"Lieutenant Kim, Lieutenant Hakeswell, report to the Principal's office immediately." The robotic voice pulsed down the corridor from the public address system buried in the ceiling.

Simon glanced up at the cameras that hung unobtrusively from the ceiling. *Maybe someone had been watching*, he speculated. Maybe he would be getting into trouble for his antics after all.

"Lieutenant Kim, Lieutenant Hakeswell report to the Principal's office immediately," the electronic demand came again.

The pair set off at a jog towards the Principal's office. They left the main building, the only two-storey building in the school complex. A transparent tube of glasslike plastic had been cut through a trench in the rock, so the sides up to five feet in height were protected by the rocky earth. The top of the transparent tunnel let in only a small amount of light, as it was covered by thin layer of grey dust that gave it a dark, enclosed feel. A line of stark white strip lights down the centre of the tube did their best to mimic daylight.

The tunnel opened into a single-storey building. Like the main building and the connecting tube, it was cut five feet deep into the ground of the planet. Its glass roof had special fans that blew away the grey sand that was constantly trying to accumulate on top of it, although this meant the room was filled with a constant whirring sound.

The pair arrived in a small reception area, with an open-plan office space behind a bar on the left. To the right was the staff room, the door to which was shut. In between the two was the Principal's office, the door to which was ajar. The place, usually bustling, was now deathly silent, the only sound from the fan motors above. Simon and Jo looked at one another, each reading in the other's eyes the realization that they had been left alone.

"Get in here!" came a shout from the office.

Simon pushed open the half-closed door and walked in, followed by Jo. He stopped halfway to a salute as he recognized the woman sat at the Principal's desk. It was not the Principal, and he wondered why he had it expected it to be when he knew he had been evacuated the previous day. Instead, Matron Murphy sat there, her black army-issue boots resting on a pile of papers, shoved to one side of the metal writing surface. She was lounging back in the beige swivel chair that the Principal had arranged to be expensively imported all the way from Earth.

She did not look up but continued to stare at the oblong tablet clutched in her hands. As a medical auxiliary she did not expect a salute, nor was she obliged to give or return one herself.

Between the two lieutenants and the desk was an oval conference table, made of pine – another expensive import made by the profligate former Principal. Its surface was strewn with maps. The one on top rendered the valley from above. It showed the space port and its landing platform on the left-hand side, stretching down the valley as it moved right, past the armoury in the valley wall and the power plant below it. The school was shown on the right-hand side, where the valley opened out onto a grey stony plain. To the right of the school, in the shadow of the valley wall and almost entirely buried in the ground, was the monorail terminus. A pair of underground tracks ran from the terminus to the school, up through the valley to the armoury and on to the space port. Two trains ran back and forth between the four stations, meaning that no one had to go out into the sandstorm-swept valley unless they wanted to.

She sat up swinging her legs off the desk and then righting herself in the chair. Her bionic limb gave a pneumatic hiss as she did so. Helen focused her eyes on the two young cadets standing before her. The casual demeanour of only moments before was replaced by something far more serious, her matronly role underpinned with a military firmness.

"Astro-hockey in the corridors?" Her voice was a weary rasp, as if berating them was more a formality, rather than something than came from real conviction.

The two lieutenants said nothing, following the unwritten military rule, that a question that sounded rhetorical was best left unanswered.

"I have children crying, others going feral and that is only in the hour since the last transport left, you two should be showing leadership, not joining in," she snapped.

Helen went back to staring at the tablet grasped in her hands. The pair of cadets said nothing the words, *last transport*, rolling around in their heads. Whatever, they may have suspected, its confirmation from an adult gave it a grim certainty.

"I have a tactical exercise for you," declared the matron as she stood up. She placed her tablet face down on the desk and circled around so she was standing by the conference table.

"The medical staff are setting tactical exercises now?" enquired Simon with a raised eyebrow.

"Well, I'm the only member of the teaching staff left, so indulge me," Helen smiled at him.

The young lieutenant stared at the map. "What's the set-up?" he asked.

"A Kylnnar battlegroup is on its way to 'cleanse' the planet. You have two hundred military cadets who you need to protect. What do you do?" Helen asked, setting the scene.

Jo still stood to attention just in front of the door.

"You want to look at the map, Lieutenant Hakeswell?" the matron asked politely.

"No need; it's a distraction. No way we can defend the valley?" she responded, her eyes straight ahead and her boots still snapped tight together.

"Stand easy and explain, lieutenant?"

Jo's arms slipped from her sides to behind her back and she widened her legs into a more comfortable stance. Her eyes sought out Helen.

"A battlegroup is a Kylnnar main battle formation. At full strength, it will have four thousand soldiers embarked on it. It will comprise a light cruiser, three to four transport and supply barges, and at least one fighter wing. It will also have one bomber wing and drop ships if required – which in this situation is likely. The battlegroup will first bombard us from orbit. If that does not achieve their objectives, they will risk the fighters and bombers. Once they have achieved their objectives, they will deploy their troops to clear up any survivors," explained Jo.

"Clear up?" queried Helen.

"*Exterminate*," replied Jo coldly.

"So, you have set up what the aliens will do. What would your response be?" questioned the matron.

"With two hundred humans, we would be outnumbered twenty to one, and we would be heavily outgunned. Staying put is not an option: we would simply be wiped out by the orbital bombardment. I would split us into twenty skirmish groups of ten.

30

I would hike north; the Colonials have a small number of settlements nearer the pole where it is cool enough for them to manage their herds. We can get food and water and await rescue. The Kylnnar would find the valley empty. I expect they would raid the armoury and then move onto the next world," Jo said, setting out her plan with calm confidence.

"It's four hundred miles to the nearest settlement," observed Lieutenant Kim without looking up from the map.

"How can you be sure the Colonials will help us?" asked Helen, ignoring Simon's observation.

She had met the Colonials only a few times in the three years she had been stationed here. They were isolated seminomadic folk who occasionally came south to trade. They were notionally human, but they had been here for close on a hundred years, long before the Confederation had reached its hand out this far. They had adapted to the inhospitable environment, and while still recognizably human they were tall, all of them comfortably clearing six feet in height, and lean to the point of emaciation. They had an oddly expanded chest cavity, making it easier for them to breathe in the oxygen-thin environment. It was far too short a period to be describing them as evolving into a new species, but she could not help feeling that they were resting right on the line between environmental adaptation and evolution. They had shown little interest in the incomers. She also did not know how they felt about the Kylnnar – or, for that matter, how the Kylnnar felt about the Colonials.

"We just have to hope they help us," offered Jo lamely, prising Helen away from her thoughts.

"The Kylnnar are wiping planets clean of human life: why would they give the Colonials a pass?" observed Helen.

Jo shrugged helplessly at that. "This isn't an exercise, is it; this is real?" she asked, her eyes searching the older woman's face.

It took all her breeding, the centuries of military service by her family, to stop Lieutenant Joanna Hakeswell from collapsing into tears of terror. She was too young to die. They were all too young to die. It wasn't fair. She fought to keep it from her face, but only half successfully. Helen, who had gone through a similar realization only an hour earlier, watched her struggle with sympathy.

Simon Kim had found his own way of dealing with his mounting despair; he had realized from the outset that Matron Murphy's question was not just theoretical. He was staring at the map, going through scenarios, keeping some and discarding others. The blood was thundering in his head screaming at him to panic, but he also knew it would do no good.

"Any thoughts, Simon?" asked Helen.

He looked up from the map.

"We can't flee to the Colonials. Even if we could trust them – which I'm not sure we can – it's impossible. It's four hundred miles, over rough but largely open territory, in an oxygen-light environment. We could never carry enough food, water, and oxygen. Even if we don't suffocate or starve, chances are the Kylnnar could pick us off from the air before we got anywhere near the Colonials' settlements," Simon countered.

"What other option do we have?" demanded Jo; she sounded desperate.

"We defend the valley; more particularly the school," he replied.

"That's insane," Jo snapped.

Simon ignored that. "Have you got a pencil?" he asked Helen.

Helen found one and handed it to him. Jo abandoned her position by the door and joined them around the table.

"There are shield generators here, here, here and here." Simon drew rings in sweeping motions around four areas on the map: the space port, the armoury, the academy, and the monorail terminus. "We should be able to calibrate the three above the armoury, the academy, and the terminus to overlap to create a single shield strong enough to resist a bombardment from space, assuming they want something left of the valley when they're finished. That should be enough to keep the fighters and any bombers off us at the very least."

"You don't see the problem, do you?" Jo exclaimed. "The shields are designed to protect the installations from winter rock storms. They are like dropping a cup over each installation. If you recalibrate them to overlap, then they'll be more like plates."

"So?" Simon looked annoyed at his idea being dismissed.

"So, the shield will be fifty feet in the air. We might not have to worry about flyers, but we'll have four thousand Kylnnar coming at us with no shield to stop them."

"One problem at a time, Jo Jo," he said with a smile.

She threw up her arms in annoyance. "You can't be listening to this?" Jo demanded of Helen.

The matron ignored her. "So, your decision is that we stand and fight?" she asked Simon.

"You're not serious; you can't put him in charge?" Jo shouted angrily.

"I'm not, lieutenant: the interaction of Military Empowerment Act 2196 and the Confederation Army Regulations as updated 2194 are putting him in charge."

"Come again?" Simon asked.

Helen reached forward to the desk and picked up the tablet.

"The Military Empowerment Act of March 2196," Helen started reading. "All orphans in military academies over the age of fourteen are approved for military service for auxiliary function and planetary defence."

"That means we are obliged to fight, not that he's in command," interjected Jo.

Helen shot her a black look that said *listen*. "Confederation Army Regulations as updated 2194," she continued. "In the event of a planetary defence, command will be allocated irrespective of service branch based on Confederation Combined Military Rank Code."

"So, what: we're both ranked CFCC-1, we're both lieutenants; I can take command," Jo argued.

"You are a second lieutenant, and I'm a first lieutenant, so I outrank you, Jo Jo," observed Simon, though he didn't seem happy to point it out.

"Sure, your army rank is higher than mine, but our Confederation Combined Military Rank Codes are the same," she shot back.

"Will the two of you stop bickering and let me finish!" Helen was annoyed now. She carried on reading: "In the event of two commanding offices being of the same code rank, preference will be given to those commissioned into the Confederation Army over the other branches of the Confederation Armed Services. If this still does not resolve the issue of command, it will be based on the date at which the officer was promoted to the coded rank."

A look of horror spread across Lieutenant Hakeswell's face. She remembered when she had first been promoted to Cadet Second Lieutenant a year ago, a month after her fifteenth birthday. It was an unprecedented honour at the academy as the rank was usually restricted to sixteen-year-olds, but her sterling discipline and hard work had secured it. Simon Kim had been away at the time, competing at some Confederation Combined Armed Services interplanetary martial arts competition. He had returned interplanetary champion.

His victory had nearly not happened. It had turned out the competition had been for cadet officers only, something the school had only discovered on the way there. So Private Kim, the high-kicking troublemaker who no one in their right mind would promote to corporal, let alone lieutenant, had his promotion rushed through on the starship just so he could win a trophy. He'd taken off a private and landed a lieutenant. Even more insultingly, the paperwork had been so rushed they had promoted him straight to first lieutenant by mistake. Jo had been so outraged by this abuse of the system – partly because she felt it diminished her own achievement – that the date was emblazoned in her mind: it had been two days before her own promotion.

"What is she saying, Jo Jo?" asked Simon Kim.

"What she is saying, *sir*," Jo replied, using the honorific to Simon for the first time she could remember, "Is that you are now Military Governor of Wolfstar III and Officer Commanding Wolfsreach Academy."

Lieutenant Joanna Hakeswell snapped to attention with all the precision for which she was renowned and saluted smartly.

"What are your orders, sir?"

CHAPTER 4

Location: Wolfsreach Academy, Wolfstar III
Date: 17 December 2196 CE, Earth Standard Calendar
Time: 16.40 Local Time 26.5-hour clock

Green light flickered from the bank of computer screens, giving the control room an eerie ambience. A pair of strip lights hung from the ceiling. They were supposed to provide the room with light, but one was dark, while the other cast only a pale yellow hue over the side of the room furthest from the computers, trying to compete with the green luminosity and failing.

Sat in a battered swivel chair, a young man busily tapped away at a keyboard in front of the screens, a headset with a spindle mike wrapped round his neck. His keystrokes were answered by a series of approving beeps, which he acknowledged with a grunt. He kicked the floor, shifting the chair to his right, and started tapping away on another keyboard. This time he received no answering beeps, and he let out a stream of invective at the computer, some of which was highly unlikely to be true given the machine had never had any parents, and certainly not a mother.

WOLFSREACH ACADEMY

Fletcher "Flex" Lynch in any other situation would have been regarded as a prodigy. At fifteen, his knowledge of programming, particularly the more esoteric languages, far surpassed that of the teachers of Wolfsreach Academy. Short for his age, at only five feet four, he was patiently waiting for a growth spurt that might never come. His geeky aspect was punctuated by his round black spectacles, a rarity in an era when eyesight problems could usually be fixed with a simple operation. A life spent growing up on space freighters had meant that had never happened. It had been due to be sorted following his arrival at Wolfsreach seven months ago, but he had still been waiting when anyone capable of performing the surgery had been evacuated.

His computer skills had been learned on the freighters of his youth. Great rectangular ships, they were often little more than a large bucket with a control room and living quarters on the front and a giant engine at the back. Often kept running long past their prime, they used antiquated systems, which needed coaxing and coddling to keep everything running. His mother was a planet-to-planet pilot for a mining company; who his father was, he had no idea. With no one else to look after him, he had lived on the ship with his mother, his online education supplemented by lessons from the sailors and engineers onboard. His mother had been called up for the Army, as they had run short of pilots for their drop ships, and he had been sent to Wolfsreach Academy to finish his tuition.

Three months later, news had come that his mother was listed as missing in action. No details had been given for reasons of operational security. He had cried initially, but the news had created a strange warring feeling in him. If he gave into grief, then maybe that would make it true that she was dead, not simply missing. If instead he clung to the idea that she was simply stranded on a planet somewhere or comatose unrecognized in a military hospital, then maybe that was true. The one thing he knew for certain was that she wasn't a prisoner of war. The Kylnnar had no such concept, as they killed everyone they captured.

"You got it working, Flex?" Simon demanded, striding into the room.

"Give us a chance, sir," muttered Flex. "It's working fine for the school; I'm just trying to rig it so we can control all of them from here."

Each of the four installations on Wolfstar III had its own shield generator and control room. This had been by design. The planet was subject to rock storms, like a desert dust storm, but instead of sand it was detritus that was gravel-sized and bigger. If the winds got particularly strong, great slabs of rocks would tumble across the arid planet's surface with enough force to smash through even the most solidly built structure. The use of multiple shield generators instead of a single generator was justified on the basis that it was safer from a redundancy perspective. In reality, it had been cheaper to install smaller, older shields with separate control rooms than to pay for a single large generator for the whole base with all the required failsafes.

Flex tapped on the keyboard a few more times. When he didn't receive the answering beeps he wanted, he let out another stream of colourful language.

"I'm sure you're inventing some of those words," winced Simon. "What's the problem?"

Flex swung round and looked at Lieutenant Kim. "I'm routing control of each of the shields into this control room. That way we can control all of them from here, so even if we lose control of the other installations, we should still have the shields. At least until they blow the generators, or they blow the power cables to the energy plant."

Simon nodded, understanding. "So, what's the problem?" he asked.

"I can't get control of the landing platform shield; it's still locked down to the local control room. Without control I can't calibrate all of them properly to create one overarching field," Flex explained.

"I didn't think we needed the landing platform shield to overlap the other three shields?" enquired Simon.

"We don't, but if we don't calibrate them the same, there is a risk – a small one, I grant you – that the whole thing will feed back and could blow one of the generators or the powerlines," explained Flex.

"Surely there are failsafes to prevent that?"

Flex gave his commander a withering look. "You mean the failsafes I have to bypass to get this crazy plan of yours to work?"

"Is there a solution, cadet?" demanded his commanding officer. He was anxious.

Before Corporal Lynch could reply, his headset chirped. He swung round in his chair and hoisted his headset on his ears.

"That you, Onesie? You there? I'm putting you on speaker."

A voice crackled through the speaker on the desk. "I said, I'm in the room. The computers are running. I've asked it for access, but it said 'denied'. It looks like the Navy locked it out before they left."

"You try the keyboard?" asked Flex.

"The thing with the buttons?" Onesie's voice hissed through the comm.

"Yeah, that thing," responded Flex, rolling his eyes in frustration.

"One sec."

Rustling and crashing sounds came through the speaker.
"Got it."

"Try and log in with the keyboard," ordered Flex.

There came some muffled clacking sounds.

"Nope: access denied."

"You think you should go over there?" asked Simon.

"Doesn't work like that, Lieutenant: we need someone at each end to make this work," replied Flex. His attention switched back to Onesie. "Is the auxiliary computer to the right switched on?"

"There is one, and no, it's not switched on," came the electronically stuttered reply.

A smile played across Flex's face. "Got you," he mouthed quietly. "Dig out its keyboard," he instructed.

There was more crashing and banging; electrically distorted through the communication system, it sounded almost musical.

"Got it," crackled the response.

"Boot the computer," ordered Flex.

A distant whirring, followed by a series of beeps, came through indicating the system booting up.

"Before it finishes, hit ctrl and alt F12," commanded Flex.

"Done. Okay, it's saying something. 'Boot safe to start rollover'. Then there's a command prompt," Onesie read down the line.

Flex was quietly surprised that Onesie – a man who only interacted with computers by speaking to their artificial intelligence – actually knew what a command prompt was.

"Type in YROLL, all capitals, and hit return."

"It's asking for a password?" came Onesie's voice.

Flex cursed. "What would a grunt do? What would a grunt do?" he mused.

He looked around the desk in front of him, lifting up tech and staring into cubby holes. He opened a drawer and rummaged around in it, coming out with a little black book. Could it be that easy? He flipped through the pages until reaching a blank one, then flipped back to the one before.

"Type in stokesswitchover19, all lower case, then the number in numerals."

"Hey, that worked," came Onesie's surprised reply. "How did you know that?"

"I'm a genius," came Flex's cocky reply, as he silently thanked the Army for being even more careless with their security than the Navy.

"What do I do now?"

"Nothing; just leave it to me. I'm in the backdoor now; I'll fix it remotely," said Flex.

Simon listened as the cadet corporal tapped away furiously at the keyboard, looking from screen to screen, before tapping away some more. He was answered by a series of rapid pings.

"Nearly there," Flex muttered under his breath to no one in particular.

Green dotted lines appeared on the screen, slowly drawing out four circles on the glowing computer terminal. Three overlapped, while the fourth, which was over the landing platform, sat apart from the others.

"I'm going to take a look," declared Simon, hefting his hand-held communicator for emphasis.

The young lieutenant left the small circular confines of the shield control room. He ran up the concrete steps, taking himself up to the surface. Like much of the lower floor of the school, the control centre was half buried in the earth. It was located near the entrance to the academy's underground monorail station, at the north-west corner of the academy site. The young man looked out across his school, which it was now his job to defend. The science block was in front of him, with the main school building beyond, blocking his view of the astro-hockey court that lay on the other side.

He looked up at the blue sky, tinted its usual strange orange hue, looking for the tell-tale shimmer of the shield. The shield itself had been calibrated by its designers to appear a similar colour to the sky, so as not to feel oppressive to the people living under it. The phasing of the barrier gave off a slight fug in the air, which was clearly visible if you looked for it. And it clearly wasn't there.

Lieutenant Jo Hakeswell rounded the science block and approached her commanding officer. She executed a smart salute. Simon continued to stare up at the sky, his face a picture of worry. When she realized that her salute was unlikely to be returned, she dropped her hand.

"Is it working?" she asked.

Simon shot her an angry look. Then he understood she was not criticizing but genuinely concerned, and felt bad. In truth, Simon only had a mild personal animosity towards his number two, a pale reflection back of the obvious dislike she had for him. He mostly just found her annoying and stuck up. It did not matter now, whatever ill feeling there was he needed to bury it if there was to be any hope of them surviving this.

"No," he replied tersely.

He flipped the speak switch on his communicator. "What the hell, Flex, it's not up?" he said sharply.

"Give it a chance, sir," came the reply through the transmitter.

"How long?"

"Normal warm-up time is twelve minutes. With the calibration changes, maybe fifteen. Then probably another ten minutes to reach full reflective strength," crackled Flex's voice.

"How long?" This time there was a tinge of desperation to Simon's question.

"We're a school, not a starship; it takes some time, sir," came the narky reply.

Twelve minutes when you were busy doing something – chatting with your friends, staring at your tablet – went in a flash. That had always been the case when the shield was raised due to an incoming storm. Twelve minutes when you were waiting for it to pass, doing nothing else, took an eternity.

Simon looked at his watch, tapped his foot, looked at his watch again, kicked some dirt with his boot, looked at his watch again. Only three minutes had passed. He started pacing.

What felt like several ice ages later, there was a buzzing sound. Simon and Jo both glanced at their watches: fourteen minutes. A shimmer of light spread across the sky, casting a smoky blanket across the school. The pair of officers stared up at it. The longer they stared, the harder it became to perceive, but it was definitely there.

"Has it worked?" Simon asked into his communicator.

"Yes, sir," came Flex's proud response.

"How long will the power last?" asked Lieutenant Kim.

"We're on geothermal." Flex sounded puzzled down the line.

"What does that mean?" demanded Simon.

Jo could practically hear Corporal Lynch's eye roll at the other end of the communicator. She struggled to keep her own face impassive.

"It means that we have effectively unlimited power," she explained to her commander.

A similar response followed from Flex, crackling across the airwaves.

Simon gave a nod of acknowledgement; not that Flex could see it. The lieutenant's mind was on to the next thing.

"We're going to have to keep the shields up from now," Simon declared. "It takes too long to get the shields up to leave them down."

"The Kylnnar are going to know we're here. It's going to be like lighting a beacon for them to see," observed Jo.

"We could try and hide, but chances are they already know there's a Gaian military facility on Wolfstar III. They'll jump in and sensor-sweep for lifeforms. Then chances are they'll open up from orbit before we can get the shield up and then we're all dead."

"And you think the shields can take an orbital bombardment, when they're designed for withstanding storms?" enquired Jo.

"What do you reckon, Flex?" asked Simon.

Corporal Fletcher Lynch had just appeared from the top of the steps leading out of the control room, blinking like a confused mole seeing sunlight for the first time.

"Urg," he grunted.

"Will the shields hold against an orbital bombardment?" Jo asked.

"Probably," Flex responded.

"Wow, that's comforting," Jo observed sarcastically to Simon.

"Look, lieutenant," countered Flex, "It's an old system but adapted from a small starship type, so it's designed to keep out weapons, not just flying rocks. Given where Kylnnar tech is supposed to be, three shields overlapping should be able to resist even their best weapons. Assuming they haven't got something we don't know about or that hasn't been shared with us, at least."

"That still leaves the platform. We only have a single shield over the space port," Jo said.

"I told Simon – sorry, *Lieutenant* Kim, that, ma'am. He said it wasn't a problem."

"Not a problem?" Jo turned on Simon, arching her eyebrow the way her grandmother did when she wanted to intimidate someone.

"Look at the topography, lieutenant," replied Simon, gesturing expansively up the gorge towards the space port.

The space port was at the end of the valley on a flattened mountain top. It dropped precipitously to the valley floor below, as if it had once been the greatest of waterfalls – though Jo found it hard to believe there had ever been that much water on a planet this arid. The valley itself was lined on either side by mountain-sized cliff edges, before flattening out at the valley entrance where the academy had been built. Beyond that was a wide open plain. It would have made a perfect landing site except it was scattered with rocks, varying in size from astro-hockey puck to small lander. The space port aside, there was no clear ground to land any spacecraft larger than a small planet hopper for many kilometres.

"If they want to get their troops on the ground, the Kylnnar needs the space port," Simon explained.

"What if they don't see it that way? What if they destroy it just because they can? What if they do it by accident?" Jo demanded, panic creeping into her voice.

"Then it saves us having to do it ourselves," came Simon's cold reply.

"But then where will the evacuation ships land?" she asked.

"Lieutenant, let me be clear." Simon was angry now and struggling to keep his voice even. "No one is coming to rescue us; we are on our own."

CHAPTER 5

Location: Wolfsreach Armoury, Wolfstar III
Date: 17 December 2196 CE, Earth Standard Calendar
Time: 18.22 Local Time 26.5-hour clock

The monorail train swooped round the underground loop, banking slightly on the curve. Despite the otherwise empty carriage, the two lieutenants stood by one of the sets of electric double doors. Each grasped on to a separate metal pole, their bodies swinging with the motion of the train. Neither was speaking, both lost in thought.

The transport pulled into the wide expanse of Armoury Station, a single wide central platform enclosed by platform doors of metal and glass with the rail lines either side. The train juddered slowly to a halt as the computer controlling it matched the train doors to the platform doors. The platform doors swished open as the train came to a full stop, followed by the carriage doors a second later.

In contrast to the train, the platform was bustling. Two dozen cadets were busy carrying and dragging heavy crates of myriad sizes across the marble-effect surface towards each of the train doors. The students' black and red uniforms were partly covered by body armour, dark grey vests, and armoured helmets of the same colour. The helmets had built-in headsets with full communication equipment, computer arrays that dropped down over the right eye, made of what looked like red plastic. Some cadets had pulse rifles slung round their necks and tucked behind; others had stashed them in easy reach against the faux tiles that covered the walls of the concrete chamber.

Jo felt a sense of sadness. Although some of them looked the part of military men and women, others did not; they just seemed like children playing at soldiers. What made it worse was that some of those who seemed like real soldiers were younger than the ones who looked like kids.

A private nearest the door from which they had disembarked placed the box he was carrying on the floor and snapped to attention before executing a salute to the two officers. Simon returned the salute with the dismissive laziness of a four-star general.

"As you were, soldier," he ordered.

Looking around the platform, Simon realized that the rest of the cadets had stopped work and were saluting too.

"Back to work, all of you; we don't have time to waste," Simon commanded sharply.

He strode off across the platform, aiming for the central escalator that led up to the armoury. Jo, caught unawares, broke into a jog to keep pace.

The armoury was built into the side of the cliff wall. It could be accessed from the monorail station, which was dug into tunnels fifty feet below the surface of the valley floor. The only indication the armoury was present were two towers above the surface flanking a cargo entry door in the cliff wall, designed for accessing the arsenal in the days before the monorail had been completed.

The pair reached the top of the escalator and walked out of the tunnel into a wide cathedral-like atrium, large enough to accommodate a cargo lander. The giant reinforced doors to the surface were behind them, leading to three large tunnels almost big enough to drive a tank down. Simon had studied the plans only a few hours ago, so he knew where they led. He had never been in this place before: it was strictly off limits to students, though a few had tried to sneak in over the years. He had never been one of them – more because he deemed the risk of getting caught too high than because he was well behaved.

The tunnel to his left he knew led to a complex of rooms: barracks, a refectory, even a small bar that the teachers sometimes used for recreation. The tunnel to his right led down to the geothermal power plant and electrical management system for the whole complex. It was also the location of the armoury's shield generator. The tunnel in the centre led into the armoury proper, the place where the weapons were kept. A trickle of students was moving up and down the central tunnel, using mag-gravs to move large crates. A few were even using manually operated pallet trucks to move equipment.

Simon stopped one of the cadets, who saluted smartly. The lieutenant returned it wearily.

"Where is Travis?" he asked.

"The sergeant? Up there with Miss Murphy," replied the cadet, pointing up the tunnel from where he had come.

"Thanks."

There was a crashing sound as one of the hand pallet trucks collided with a mag-grav, throwing its contents all over the tunnel. Grenades spilled from the boxes, rolling out across the floor. Several cadets dived for cover.

"Stop mucking around, you idiots!" roared Lieutenant Hakeswell, with all the command for which she was renowned.

She started picking up grenades and tossing them back into the crate from which they had come as if they were tennis balls. The others followed suit, though they collected the scattered armaments with a good deal more caution.

Simon hadn't stuck around to find out what the chaos was behind him. He continued up the tunnel until it opened out into another wide circular space. It lacked the towering ceiling height of the previous hall, but there was still enough space here to comfortably manoeuvre a small transport. Three hangar-size halls, each with a large sliding metal door, ran off the central circular room. Two of the doors were pulled back. Simon skirted more cadets milling around with equipment in the centre of the hall, ignoring the occasional salute that they threw at him. He reached his target – a tall young man standing with a tablet in the open entrance of the centre hangar.

"Sergeant Ronin." Simon addressed his friend with uncharacteristic formality.

The man looked up from his tablet. Seeing his commanding officer, he quickly clipped the tablet to his belt before executing a salute. Lieutenant Kim returned the salute and gave his friend a big smile. Simon was surprised that Travis remained a cadet sergeant; his friend was much more suited to military life than he was, and he looked so mature he often forgot that Travis had only just turned sixteen. Simon did not know that his friend had been on the point of being promoted to cadet officer before the evacuation. Despite this, as the senior cadet non-commissioned officer, Sergeant Travis was third in command after the two lieutenants.

"How good is the news?" Simon asked, waving his hand to encompass the soldiers and equipment spread out around them.

"Very good, sir," said Travis with his perfect all-white-teeth beam. "We have pulse rifles, sidearms, grenades, mines, body armour, helmets and sniper rifles. It's like Christmas and birthday all rolled into one."

Simon nodded politely; he wasn't at a military academy by choice. He could fire a weapon, but that didn't mean he shared Travis's borderline odd love of them.

"And this you have got to see," said Travis, smiling even more broadly.

He beckoned Simon to follow him as he walked to the hangar to the left of the hall. A willowy Indian girl stood in the doorway, clasping a tablet in the same manner as Travis.

"Hey, Sam; hey, Simon," Inaya said with a smile.

Simon did not even think to berate his friend's girlfriend for her informality; despite the amount of time the three of them had spent hanging out, simply to be acknowledged by Inaya Chandra, the school's best-looking girl, was enough for Simon. She was approaching her eighteenth birthday and, given her charisma and intellect, she should have made lieutenant by now ahead of both him and Jo. She had done two things that had left her stuck at cadet corporal. The first was to get caught too many times breaking the school's unenforceable rule about relationships between students. She and Travis had been together for over a year, from just after their arrival here. Unfairly, it had not affected Travis as much. His jock status meant everyone cut him a lot of slack, even the teachers. It was Inaya who had coined his nickname 'Sam' – a joke she found hysterical, but refused to explain to anyone else. Her relationship could have been overlooked, as it had largely been done for her boyfriend, except for her other problem. Her tendency to insubordination when it came to anyone in any position of authority counted far more against her. She had only made corporal because of her age and her school record when she had first arrived, before anyone was aware of her antisocial tendencies.

"So, what we got?" Lieutenant Kim asked.

"You're not going to believe this," she said. Simon had never seen Inaya this happy; she was positively giddy with excitement. "Look."

Simon looked, but all he could see in the clinically lit room was grey tarpaulins thrown over what he guessed was either large bits of equipment or piled-up boxes of smaller equipment.

"We have four multiple-launch rocket systems!" declared Travis.

"Five pulse cannons," chimed in Inaya.

"Three…" Travis's voice died in his mouth.

Simon did not need to look behind. Only one thing could silence the lantern-jawed jock like that: Lieutenant Joanna Hakeswell.

It was absurd to the point of being tragic. *He was actually going red*, thought Simon. It was not just Simon who found Travis's obsession with Joanna ridiculous. Everyone who knew about it did – and that meant *everyone*, except Lieutenant Hakeswell herself, who was completely oblivious to it. One person who was definitely aware of it was Inaya Chandra, who looked down on the female lieutenant from her statuesque height with baleful hatred.

"Three military lasers," Miss Murphy finished for Travis, stepping from behind a tarpaulin-covered weapon.

"So, what did I miss?" asked Jo.

"It looks like we have heavy weapons," said Simon, turning to talk to Jo and deliberately blocking Inaya's look of loathing. "Let's see what we have in the other bin," he continued excitedly, starting to enjoy this situation.

He stalked across the central hall towards the remaining hangar. The others scampered after him, trying to keep up. Helen brought up the rear, her bionic leg wheezing and grinding. Simon stopped in front of the metal door. Unlike the other two hangars, the door was closed. His gaze wandered across the ample collection of luminous yellow and green health and safety stickers.

"Do those mean what I think they mean?"

"Yes," replied Helen.

"Anyone look in here?" asked Simon.

"We did," Helen said.

"So, it's safe?"

"Very," she replied.

Simon hit the round red button to the left of the door. It swept back with a reassuring swish. Trying to conceal his excitement, Simon took in the storage bins' contents. There was nothing. It had been stripped clean. Not even a hint of what it had contained. No empty containers, no forgotten tablet. It had been completely cleared out, then vacuumed afterwards.

"You seem disappointed, Simon?" Helen asked quietly at his shoulder.

The lieutenant looked to his right; the metal door had slid that way to open up the hangar. His eyes ran across the health and safety symbols, which spoke to him of weapons of mass destruction, chemical weapons, atomics.

"Were they ever here?" he asked, turning to Helen.

She looked at the immaculately cleaned room; not even a hint of dust.

"I can't say for sure, but I suspect so. That was probably what the fleet was so keen to transport away."

"So, they took their weapons rather than us?" Simon sounded bitter.

She nodded.

"Shame. We could have used them," he observed, brightening from his introspection.

"You only took command a few hours ago, and now you want to upgrade straight to being a war criminal," Helen observed coldly.

"You know, a military academy is a really dumb place for a pacifist to work," he shot back.

Helen Murphy fixed the young cadet lieutenant with the frostiest gaze she could muster.

He ignored it, already moving back towards the bin with the heavy weapons. He stopped in front of the hangar, his eyes playing across the tarpaulin-covered heavy metal in front of him.

"Travis, we need to get this stuff into position as fast as possible. Get the multiple launch rocket systems to the academy; I want them positioned in the four corners of the school. They have a three-hundred-sixty-degree field of fire. I want four of the pulse cannons at the academy three facing out over the rock plain and one up the valley," ordered Lieutenant Kim.

"You want me to take the other one to the space port to defend the landing platform?" asked Travis.

"No point. I want it on the Armoury Station platform, pointing down the tunnel towards the space port," ordered Simon.

"We're giving up the space port?" queried Travis.

"Were my orders in anyway unclear, sergeant?" barked Simon.

"No, sir," a chastened Travis replied, drawing himself up almost to attention.

"Right. Anyone know how to use a military laser?" asked the lieutenant.

This prompted a chorus of "No, sir" from the assembled soldiers and an insolent "Nope" from Inaya.

The students were trained in live fire exercises on pulse rifles and sidearms, but none of them had ever fired one of the three types of heavy weapons. That said, simulator training was the norm, the school had its own sims in the gym complex, and each student would have practised firing a pulse cannon and the multiple-launch rocket system on it. Their training might have been more theoretical than practical but, in their hearts, they believed they could use those weapons. The military lasers were another matter. Originally a weapon designed for starship combat, they fired a single consistent beam, which could then be swung like a rapier blade, scything through enemy vessels. It was only in the last four years that ground-based units had been issued to the Army to allow them to target drop ships trying to land. No one had thought to train military students on them.

"So, they're useless?" Jo muttered sadly, fingering the equipment wistfully.

"I'll show you," Helen sighed. She sounded reluctant.

"You know how to fire a military laser?" Simon's tone was incredulous.

She nodded slowly.

"Okay, great; get them to the school. I want one pointing up the valley towards the space port, the other two pointing in the other direction across the rock field," commanded Simon.

"We'll have to calibrate the phasing so they can pass through the shields," declared Helen.

"Who do you need for that?"

"Flex should be able to programme it."

"Right, all of you, get to it," ordered Simon, receiving a loud barrage of "Yes, sir" in response.

Simon and Helen were left standing together.

"How do you know how to fire a military laser?" Simon asked her.

"Misspent youth," she replied.

"I thought you were a pacifist?" he asked.

"No, not really; I just don't like guns," she explained. "I'll teach your soldiers to use them, and I won't stop you killing, I just don't plan on doing it with you. I plan on being somewhere saving lives, not taking them."

Simon mentally cursed; he had not thought about medical provision. The small infirmary at the school was never going to be big enough.

"Lieutenant Hakeswell!" he shouted over to his colleague, who was currently preoccupied with the military lasers. She trotted over. "We need more space for medical treatment; the infirmary will be too small. Convert the dining hall, get the ten best-trained medics we have. Once Miss Murphy has finished the training on the lasers, she will take over the medical facility."

"Yes, sir," confirmed Jo, who set off about her duty.

"You're getting better at this," observed Helen.

"I just hope it's fast enough," he replied.

Helen watched him stalk away in the direction of the monorail.

CHAPTER 6

Location: Wolfsreach Academy, Wolfstar III
Date: 18 December 2196 CE, Earth Standard Calendar
Time: 07.22 Local Time 26.5-hour clock

The small oval blob blipped onto the screen of the computer terminal, the sound answered a moment later with a ping. Flex stared at the screen, which was casting an eerie green light over his face. Another small blob, then a larger one, appeared on the screen, followed by further screeches from the speaker.

"Lieutenant?" he shouted over his shoulder.

Jo Hakeswell looked up from her own screen and came over to Flex. She leaned over his shoulder, her face now bathed in the same green ambience.

"You run a diagnostic?" she asked calmly, showing no signs of the mounting terror she was feeling inside.

"Running now, ma'am," he answered, his gaze never leaving the screen.

In a window in the top right of the screen, a diagnostic programme was operating, code blurring as it checked and checked again. It finished and flashed up: no issues found.

Jo stood back from the screen and flipped open her communicator.

"Lieutenant Kim, it's Hakeswell," she said sharply. "Get to the control room; we need you now."

"Understood," a voice hummed back at her through the comm.

Jo flipped it shut and leaned forward again, looking intently at the screen.

"You're sure the diagnostic is clean?" Jo asked Flex.

"Yes, ma'am; what we're seeing is real."

A large blob, flanked by two smaller blobs, appeared on the screen. This was followed seconds later by half a dozen smaller blobs. The pings of the speaker had become a staccato rhythm. It felt like gun fire to the lieutenant.

"Can you tell what's out there?" she demanded.

"I'm working on it," he shot back angrily.

"Work faster."

The planet had an external sensor array, allowing it to scan what was going on in its solar system. It was powerful enough to detect ships arriving at the edge of the system, not just the vessels that were sitting in orbit above the planet. It had two problems. The first was the mountainous valley walls that surrounded them. It was not so much their size as their geology that was the problem, laced with odd metals and refractive rocks, electrical and radio signals would be bounced around or even totally lost. This had the effect of throwing off sensors, confusing electronic signals and generally causing false or misleading readings. That meant the array itself had to be sited several miles away from the main base. It had its own shield, but the defenders of Wolfsreach had chosen not to activate it, in the hope its presence would be less obvious to any Kylnnar scanners. Its single shield would be strong enough to resist a rock storm but probably not an orbital bombardment. The second problem was the computer itself. Normally, the array was linked to the more powerful system in the space port, which was designed to monitor incoming space traffic, but Simon had ordered the feed to be redirected to the control room at the school. As had been the case with the shield control, Flex had managed to do this, but at a cost. The computer system in the school was older and it was creaking under the pressure of maintaining a shield while running a deep space scan.

Simon crashed into the room, breathing hard.

"Is it them?" he demanded.

To Jo he sounded more excited than worried. "We know it's something. That's all we know at the moment, sir," Jo muttered.

"Data coming through now," explained Flex apologetically.

The teenaged corporal tapped the screen, aiming for the largest blob. It popped out, flowing into the silhouette of a Kylnnar ship.

Flex whispered a profanity.

"That's a heavy cruiser," Simon said quietly, all excitement gone from his tone.

The three stared at the silhouette.

"What else have they got?" asked Jo quietly.

Flex tapped the screen rapidly, hitting green dot after dot. The computer pinged in frustration, unable to keep up with his demands. Flex pulled the keyboard towards him and tapped away for a few moments. The diagnostic window was replaced with a list of ship designations.

"One heavy cruiser, two destroyers, six transport vessels, a wing's worth of bombers and three wings of fighters, and something else," Flex read out the list.

"That's the heaviest battlegroup I've ever heard of," Jo observed.

"You said a battlegroup was four thousand soldiers?" Simon addressed Jo. "So how many in a battlegroup that size?"

"I don't know, but at a guess, a minimum of six thousand, and possibly as many as ten thousand, sir."

"So, taking an average, we're outnumbered not twenty to one, but forty to one?" he asked.

"I can't fault your math," she grunted darkly.

"Hang about," exclaimed Simon. "What do you mean 'something else'?"

Flex was still tapping away.

"Flex?" Simon griped.

"I'm working on it, sir."

Why were officers so demanding? he thought quietly. Like they knew how to do what he was doing. Why couldn't they just be patient?

"Flex?"

"Best guess is it's some sort of transport. The computer is confused: it's never seen the like before. It thinks it should be a frigate, but it's not got anything like the right number of heavy weapons. So, it looks like some sort of supply or transport vessel based on the same hull design as a Kylnnar frigate," explained the corporal.

"What's in it: more troops, more weapons?" Lieutenant Kim asked urgently.

Jo and Flex looked at each other, then back at Simon. They both shrugged in ignorance.

"Well, can you at least tell me how long till they get here?" he asked.

"Ten minutes; maybe less," replied Flex.

"What?" exclaimed Simon and Jo in concert.

"They didn't jump in at the edge of the system; they did it directly next to the planet. They'll need to lock into a matching planetary orbit so they can bombard us, but that won't take them long."

"Our naval protocols direct we come in at the edge of the system to minimize the risk of being surprised," observed Jo. Even Army cadets knew that rule.

"Guess they got cocky," said Simon. "Can we use that against them?"

"Target them with the military lasers?" Jo queried.

"No," replied Simon. "At this distance, their shields will recalibrate to deflect them."

"You sure, sir? I mean, it is literally light speed," Jo countered.

"I want to keep the lasers secret. If we survive the bombardment we'll need them for the next phase," he explained. "So will the shields hold?"

Flex looked up at him, at a loss for an answer.

"Corporal?"

"I don't know, sir: it was fine the last time I used a rock storm shield to protect a school from a Kylnnar orbital bombardment led by a heavy cruiser," Flex snapped at his commander sarcastically.

Simon looked down at the seated teenager. He looked young for his fifteen years, but Simon did not have time to coddle him.

"Corporal Lynch, I don't like your tone. When this action is complete, you will be on report," snapped Lieutenant Kim.

Flex looked at the normally laid-back officer's harsh face and swallowed. "Yes, sir!" he replied.

"Keep monitoring," Simon ordered Flex. "Lieutenant Hakeswell, with me."

Simon marched out of the control room across the open space towards the main school building. Jo followed him, looking up to check for the haze of the shield, taking reassurance from it.

Lieutenant Kim had disappeared into the building where the Principal's office and the staff room were located. Jo found him standing in the staff room. The white wood chairs and low coffee tables had been stacked up against the wall. A couple of cadets, stood by the high windows, were perched on the rough pile of furniture, pulse rifles in hand, scanning the open yard between the school and the monorail station and shield control room. Strewn across the room's floor were harnesses attached to small tanks. There were ten of them.

"You know what these are?" he asked Jo, indicating the packs at his feet.

She squatted down to inspect them.

"You trained on them?" he followed up.

She looked up.

"I trained on assault harnesses – well, in the simulator, not the real thing."

Simon nodded in understanding.

"But you know these aren't assault harnesses?" Jo continued.

"No, they're drop harnesses," he supplied.

Assault harnesses were used by army special forces and the naval marines to get above the enemy, using a jet pack to fly soldiers for a short distance so they could drop down on an enemy from above or behind them. They had evolved from the simpler drop harness, which itself had been designed as a replacement for the parachute. Soldiers dropping from above would be slowed by the jet packs countering their descent and cushioning them on impact. They came with cannisters of propellant that were one use only, and certainly not strong enough to fly anyone. You pulled a cord as you were about to land, causing the fuel to fire, usually resulting in a comfortable landing.

"I want you to find ten of the lightest students," Simon ordered. "I'm guessing they will probably all be girls. Take these packs to the upper floor of the main building. They are to be our roving support force to block any gaps. They'll need a commander," he mused.

"Well, it's not going to me; I plan to be out front with you," Jo replied stubbornly.

"No, I want you underground at Armoury Station. If we lose the armoury, we lose our power plant and our shields. That's where I need you," he explained. "Who to put in charge?"

"Corporal Chandra," she suggested.

"Inaya, are you crazy? She's the tallest girl in the school. She's practically the height of a Colonial," he exclaimed.

"Yes, sir, but she's thin and weighs next to nothing. She also has the best assault harnesses scores of anyone."

"But she's so insubordinate," he sighed.

Jo suppressed a smile; she was tempted to point out that many would have said the same about him. She decided it was not the right time: he had the fate of two hundred and one lives weighing on him.

"Well, if she's in command she can hardly be insubordinate," offered Jo lamely.

Simon was about to continue the argument. Then he stopped; he was listening. He could hear rain. He looked at Jo, perplexed. There was no rainfall on Wolfstar III, except for occasionally near the poles. The base had its own reservoir located under the school, which was renewed monthly from water sources near the pole, though at any one time there was a year's worth of water. There were also small sewage treatment and urine reclamation systems in all four facilities to derive drinking water should the reservoir fail. It was the one thing Simon had not worried about. Rain was another thing he had not thought to worry about.

The perplexed pair walked out into the school yard. Students had gathered on the large open space of the astro-hockey court. Others were looking or even hanging out of windows to see what was going on.

There was no rain.

WOLFSREACH ACADEMY

Light sprayed in rainbow colours across the shield as munitions rained down on the school.

"They're firing on us!" Flex's crackled notification came through Simon's communicator.

"I noticed," replied the lieutenant before clicking it off and staring back up at the sky.

A cluster munition hit, shattering on impact with the shield and releasing its multitude of anti- personnel mines. They bounced upward, exploding in a spray of white phosphorous, before dropping back onto the surface of the shield and vaporizing in little pools of blue fire.

A great beam struck out of the sky and hit the shield in a swirl of prismatic light. It seemed to be screwing downwards, almost as if it could drill through the screen of blue light in its way. All of them watched nervously, some muttering prayers under their breath. The blue shield started to turn white, bubbling and churning as light seemed to battle with light. Then, as soon as it started, the attacking laser beam flashed out of existence. Seconds later, another laser beam flashed down on the shield in another burst of prismatic colour. It went through the same drilling, churning process before winking out.

Simon looked down the valley. Munitions were hitting the planet surface in the areas not protected by the shields. Pulse shells capable of punching through a starship's armour slammed into rocks, spraying earth and splintered shrapnel into the air. Without the shields, they would have lasted barely minutes, mused Simon. He watched the space port and its platform carefully. As he suspected, the Kylnnar were largely avoiding it. The odd hit bounced off its shield, spraying fire into the sky. A laser beam crashed down in front of the space port, boiling the sandy ground to glass as it swept towards the landing platform. It caught the shield at its edge, cutting through the single-skin barrier in a froth of sharp burning white light. It touched the rockface and the edge of the platform, creating a fall of rocks and asphalt. The beam winked out of existence. This confirmed what Simon had expected: first, that one shield was not enough, and second, that the Kylnnar wanted to keep the space port intact.

"How are we holding up?" he asked Flex through the communicator.

"Good, sir," came the crackled reply. "Really good. Some issues on the edges, but almost nothing is getting through."

Simon switched his communicator from talk to broadcast.

"Everyone, back to your positions. Enough of enjoying the light show!"

His order blasted into the ears of the students, who rushed to obey.

CHAPTER 7

The grey flyer swooped low over the arid rock floor of Wolfstar III, banking left, heading for the space port. Flex watched on the scanner, though to him it appeared as a tiny green pinprick. He could see it had support from four more Kylnnar bombers coming in behind, but they were holding back, running spirals as they prepared for their own attack run. What were the aliens playing at?

Simon and Jo had taken up position on the roof of the two-storey main school building. Flat-roofed, it allowed those on it an almost complete three-hundred-sixty view of the school site. Only the gym, with its pitched roof, partially blocked their line of sight across the rock plain. The view up the valley towards the space port was unencumbered. Lieutenants Hakeswell and Kim were crouched behind a low wall that ringed the top of the flat roof. The wall had been further reinforced by sandbags – or rather, rock gravel bags – filled from the rough surface of the rock plain and the valley floor. It had been Jo's idea to keep cadets busy who were not otherwise engaged, keeping their minds off the terrifying prospect of the Kylnnar attack.

It was an old idea. No one had used sandbags in a hundred years since the first pulse rifle, firing a high-explosive piece of plasma, had replaced projectile weapons. A direct hit from a modern pulse rifle would go straight through a bag as if it were not there; it would go through a brick or concrete wall with the same ease. Thankfully, the school, as a military building, had been built to withstand such weapons, with a double skin of concrete with a triple polymer layer in the middle. That meant the school walls should provide some protection against lighter weapons. Thirty pupils, mostly fifteen- and sixteen-year-old new arrivals from the Talos IV evacuation, ringed the roof. Their red and black uniforms were covered with dark grey flak jackets; grey helmets were plopped awkwardly on heads; pulse rifles were clasped nervously in sweating hands. The shield protecting them was directly above their heads. It felt almost close enough to touch if one stood on tiptoe, though in reality it was well out of reach.

Jo and Simon stared out across the valley towards the space port. They used electronic field glasses that scanned the terrain, picking out and zooming in on anything untoward. In the arid valley there was little to focus on; only the occasional sighting of a scraggy fox-like creature chasing a hapless smaller mammal. They had swapped their hand-held communicators for the built-in headsets of their military helmets, receiving a constant buzz of updates from Flex as he tracked the bomber across the planet surface.

The soldiers on the roof could not see it yet. It was flying low, over the rocky outcrops beyond the flattened mountain that was now the space port. If it were going for the landing platform then they would only see it after it had dropped its bombs, as it banked upwards. Simon did not think that was likely, though: the orbital bombardment that they had to endure for two hours had focused its fire on the reinforced overlapping shields above the school, trying and failing to punch through. It had largely avoided the single shield above the space port, which they could have penetrated with sufficient sustained fire. The Kylnnar seemed to be leaving their options open, so it was unlikely the bomber would be targeting it.

Simon's field glasses picked up the grey shape as it banked over the mountain range at the end of the valley. It was flying high; the space port's shield meant it had to climb higher than it would like, showing its underside and wing expanse to the cadets at the bottom of the valley.

"Shall I give the order?" asked Jo.

"No, wait!" Simon's bark was harsh. Nerves were getting the better of him.

He watched as the bomber dropped down, trying to flatten out across the valley floor as quickly as it could. Simon knew it was flying higher than it would have liked, but with the shield still up over the space port it had little choice.

"Every third cadet open fire, pulse rifles only," he ordered.

Jo raised an eyebrow at that but said nothing.

A withering fire of plasma sprayed up the valley from the roof of the main school building, the three dormitory blocks, and the roof of the science block. *This had to look convincing*, he thought, but he did not want to tell the Kylnnar too much about the number of defenders. The bomber shrugged off the fire: most of it missed, and it was well enough armoured to resist the rest.

It dropped two bombs, aiming for the Principal's office and the monorail station entrance. The first caught the edge of the shield, which flipped it in the air as it exploded, sending a spray of yellow fire and white light across the sky above the cadets. All of them braced as the shrapnel rained down on the shield, vaporizing as it hit. The thunderous sound of the explosion reverberated across the school. The second bomb, aiming for the monorail station entrance, missed both it and the shield in its attempt to direct it under the barrier. Instead, it caught the side of the mountain, scattering rocks and shrapnel across the valley. Fire and rock sprayed across the corner of the school, smashing against the reinforced wall of the monorail station entrance building. Luckily, any damage was superficial.

The bomber pulled up from its run, skimming above the shield and down across the rock plain, before banking right out of sight.

"We could have taken that down," muttered Jo to Simon. She had switched her helmet comm to mute. She had no desire to share her disagreement with the rest of the cadets.

"Patience, Lieutenant Hakeswell," Simon grinned in reply.

"We've got a second run coming in!" Flex's urgent voice blurted over the comm.

"How many?" demanded Jo.

"Four bombers, two by two," Flex replied.

"Just like the ark," Jo said under her breath.

"Huh?" asked Simon.

"Nothing," she returned.

The first two bombers had made it over the landing platform shield and were dropping in a steep angle to the valley floor.

"Launchers one and two, light them up, track and launch!" Lieutenant Kim barked down the communicator.

The two launchers pointing up the valley came on, immediately tracking the two incoming bombers. Each sprayed out six small high-explosive missiles. Several made contact with the incoming bombers or exploded around them. The wing of the left side bomber was ripped off, sending it spiralling sideways and downwards into the valley wall. It disintegrated in a ball of white fire as its engines ignited. The second bomber battled desperately for control as the pilots fought to keep its nose up. It did no good: it cleared the school and the shield above it, but could not stay in the sky. It plunged to a crash landing across the rock plain, flipping and turning over as it caught on the boulder-covered surface. It did not explode, so the cadets poured pulse rifle fire into it.

Simon's attention moved back to the remaining two bombers coming down the valley. It was too late for them to pull out of their run, but they had long enough to take counter-measures at the unexpected presence of missile launchers.

"Launchers one and two, light them up, track and launch!" shouted Simon again.

"On it, sir," came the response.

Another barrage of missiles filled the air. The bombers slammed on their acceleration, using their armoured frames to smash past the projectiles before most could explode. The sky filled with fire as the missiles detonated, but the two bombers, moving at speed, burst out unscathed from the sea of flame the missiles had created. They dropped their bombs, four large devices, on the school, but they were moving too fast and overshot their target. They impacted on the shield, and a thunderous boom rocked the school, but the explosion and shrapnel dissipated harmlessly across the barrier.

Simon silently cursed that he had not been able to put at least some of the missile launchers on the roof. There had been no way to get them up there, and their weight might have collapsed the roof anyway. Besides, the shield would have limited their angle of fire even more than it was doing already. He was going to have to give away his other two launchers.

"Launchers three and four, track the bombers on the flip side and launch," the lieutenant ordered.

"Acknowledged," came the response from the gun teams.

The two launchers facing down in the direction of the rock plain open fired as the bombers passed over. A barrage of high-explosive missiles jetted out, twisting and spiralling up to avoid the shield, catching the bombers in the rear. One was almost vaporized as the projectiles caught its rear tail gear, setting off a fuel fire through the aircraft. The second was disrupted by the sudden high heat of the air and the exploding shrapnel of its fellow. Its engines gave out and it glided to a sickening crunch on the planet's rocky surface.

"Any more aircraft on track?" Simon asked Flex over the comm.

"No, sir."

Simon switched his comm to broadcast.

"Alright, people," the lieutenant said over the comm, trying his best to sound heroic, "Good work. We have won the first fight: four bombers. Any casualties to the dining hall. Keep alert."

He clicked off the broadcast.

"Very inspirational, sir," said Jo.

Simon Kim searched for sarcasm in that statement but could find none.

"Lieutenant, I need you to take over command of the armoury now; you have to hold it," he ordered.

"Understood, sir." She saluted and left.

Simon Kim did a quick round of the young men and women on the makeshift battlement, trying to gee them up. That done, he found the stairs at the far end of the roof and trotted down, heading for the dining hall on the ground floor of the school.

He stepped through the double swing doors where it joined the school building into an immaculately clean room. The smell of bleach stung his nostrils. The former comforting odours of cooking had gone, replaced by a hospital-like astringency. The tables and chairs had been stacked against the wall nearest the rock plain, partly to clear space and partly to provide extra protection against incoming pulse fire. Forty camp beds had been lined up in three rows, two of fifteen beds and one of ten, with wide alleyways left between them. The central row had fewer beds because a makeshift operating theatre had been placed in the space created, using medical equipment stripped from the infirmary surrounded by green privacy shields. A walkway from the double doors had been left so patients could be easily delivered there.

Helen was standing in the centre of the temporary operating theatre, giving orders to a collection of cadets. She looked up as Simon walked in and gave him a reassuring smile.

"I hear the initial attack went in our favour," she said.

"You heard?"

She tapped the small communicator pip in her ear.

"This looks good," Simon said with a wave across the room.

"This will be the best it looks for a long while," she replied, slightly harshly.

"You trained the crews on the military lasers?" he asked, ignoring her barb.

"As much as possible, given you wouldn't let us fire them and we have only a matter of hours for what should take three months," she observed.

"I need the element of surprise; besides, the time we had is the time we had," he replied.

His tone was slightly pleading, as if seeking approval. She had none to give him. She was angry at the whole situation they had been left in. She looked across the bare antiseptic room, all carefully arranged, and knew what it might look like soon.

"You sorted the other thing I asked you to?" he demanded, confident again.

"I showed Harper and his team how to place them. I took Lieutenant Hakeswell through the arming and detonation process."

He nodded.

The double doors pushed open with an ominous bang. A child, a fourteen-year-old boy who looked twelve, staggered in, half carried between two friends. Blood, recently clotted, covered half his face. His left arm lay limply across his front. Simon did not recognize him.

"Where was he?" Simon asked one of the cadets carrying the injured boy.

"We were dug in – the rocks near the station, sir. We caught some shrapnel when the bomb dropped," she replied.

"He the only one injured?" he asked.

"No, sir."

As if to punctuate the response, a further four injured cadets shuffled into the room, mainly flesh wounds and broken bones. Simon scanned them.

"Walking wounded. Patch them up and get them back out," he ordered.

The medics were already fussing around them, cauterizing wounds and bandaging them up.

"So you're a doctor now?" observed Helen sardonically.

Lieutenant Kim shot her an angry glare. He did not have time for this.

"Why is there only one theatre? It won't be enough," he snapped at Miss Murphy.

"No, it won't," she replied.

Her tone was matter of fact. She could see the strain he was under. She hated war, loathed it, but that wasn't his fault. He was doing what he had to.

"I'm the only one with any surgical training. We have two surgical tables, we will need two surgical tables, but for that we need two surgeons. We have only me, and I know only the very basics. Kids are going to die who should be saved, and there is nothing we can do," she explained wearily.

The plastic window high in the wall shattered suddenly, spewing debris across the room. Heavy pulse fire thudded into the wall.

"Flex!" he shouted over the comm. "What is that?"

"Five fighters are hovering on the rock plain; do we open fire?"

"Wait," the lieutenant ordered.

He could hear sporadic pulse fire coming from the roof above.

Simon ran down the hall, heading for the fire door at the end that led into the yard beyond. He opened the door and crouched down. He fell to his belly and crawled out up the steps to the level of the ground. Pulse fire was pouring at head height and above into the school. The higher shots were skittering in a spray of light on the shield. The rest were slamming into the dining hall he was lying next to, as well as the officers' mess to his left and the gym to right, gouging out great chunks of concrete.

He pulled up his field glasses, not that he really needed them. Five space fighters were hovering above the wreckage of the bombers, pouring a constant stream of plasma shots into the academy. They did not seem to have a target. A Kylnnar lander was on the ground; Simon could see their hulking alien forms milling around the destroyed bombers. The fighters were trying to cover its activity.

"What the hell are space fighters doing in atmosphere?" he demanded to no one in particular.

"They are evacuating their dead."

Helen's reply surprised him. He looked to his side; she had crawled up the steps, so she was lying next to him.

"Launchers three and four, prepare to fire, wide dispersion – you'll never get a lock with this fire screen going!" he shouted down the comm.

"Wait," cautioned Helen. "Save the missiles."

He looked at her; her eyes said *trust me*.

"Wait for my command," he ordered down the line.

He watched the lander retract its ramp and take off. The screen of pulse fire slowed and then stopped as the fighters swooped away after the lander.

"Launchers stand down for now," Simon ordered down the link.

"What was that?" he asked Helen.

She had stood up, her bionic limb wheezing.

He clambered to his feet, trying to fight a sense of embarrassment.

"They were evacuating their injured and dead," she explained.

"You don't think about the Kylnnar doing that?" he offered lamely.

She shrugged in response.

He looked around. There was just the two of them; his communicator was off.

"Why did you do it, Helen? Why did you put me in charge of this last stand?" he demanded.

Was it rude he had not called her Miss Murphy? He had never called her Helen before. Who cared in a war zone? Besides, he was in charge, not her.

"I'm from the Isles. We don't do last stands," she said with a grin.

"What does that even mean?" Simon grumbled exasperatedly.

"It's only a last stand if we all die, so let's not do that," she continued.

"Sure, no problem," he muttered angrily and rudely stalked off.

She watched him go, the grin broadening on her face, and decided she had made the right decision.

CHAPTER 8

Location: Wolfsreach Space Port, Wolfstar III
Date: 18 December 2196 CE, Earth Standard Calendar
Time: 21.17 Local Time 26.5-hour clock

Travis crawled hand over hand across the rocky surface, wincing as the sharp rocks bruised and scraped him. His mop of blond hair had been hidden carefully beneath a black beanie. His face was covered with grey greasepaint, allowing him to blend seamlessly with the mountains and the dark of the night. To Private Julia Williams he sounded like an elephant blundering through the bush – not that she had ever seen such a creature outside of vid streams. The fourteen-year-old private swung her night scope back from Travis's direction and clipped it back on her sniper-grade pulse rifle, resuming the prone position she had held for the last hour. She was watching the space port's landing platform through the green night light of her scope.

A few minutes later, Travis Ronin crawled into position beside her, and let out a long breath. She hid her annoyance at him, putting her off her own breathing.

"Hey, sergeant." Her voice burred with the deep south tone of her ancestors.

"Hey," he muttered back. "What are you doing up here?"

"Watching the landing platform, as per Lieutenant Kim's orders," she replied, her gaze never shifting from her objective.

"He ordered you to perform overwatch from the armoury tower?"

Julia fought down the normal human inclination to look to her left at the pair of towers that rose out of the cliff-like mountain side, where the two towers marked each side of the entryway for transporters seeking to reach the armoury from the air.

"Yeah, well, with respect, the lieutenant isn't a sniper," she replied.

"What does that mean?" Travis demanded, his voice creeping above the whisper the pair had both been using up to that point.

"Don't be where the enemy will expect you to be," she observed, not raising her tone to match his. "Besides, the view is better from here."

"Tom is in the far tower," the sergeant countered.

She fought down the urge to express her contempt. Julia and Tom were the two best-ranked markspeople at Wolfsreach Academy. Well, that was not quite true. She was the best, Tom was sixth, and the other four had been evacuated, she thought bitterly. Of those who remained, she and Tom were the two best. During their inventory of the armoury, the students had found two Mark VII advance grade pulse sniper rifles; the most accurate rifle available to anyone within the Confederation Military. Not unreasonably, Simon had issued them to the two best shots he had left. He had ordered them, via Travis, to take up position in the two towers above the armoury, giving them an excellent field of fire across the whole valley. To a sharpshooter like Tom Bolton and an officer like Simon Kim, this made perfect sense. To a sniper like Julia, it was a way to get killed. Travis had his orders, and he knew the opinion of the seventeen-year-old Tom on the matter, but his gut told him to trust the young girl next to him.

The snap of small explosions came from what appeared to be the direction of the landing platform. It was hard to tell exactly; the valley made sounds reverberate and echo back. In the air fifty feet above the space port there were momentary puffs of light as what looked like grey fireworks were going off.

"We have activity," Julia purred.

Moving for the first time since Travis's initial appearance, the sniper moved her eye from the scope and with her head slightly raised watched the darkness with her naked eyes.

"I can't see anything," muttered the sergeant, looking through his field glasses.

"Neither can I," she commented, tapping the night vision scope.

"Why?" Travis demanded.

"No idea!" came the teenager's petulant reply.

The sergeant adjusted the settings on his field glasses, trying to get the electronic system to pierce the murky blackness in front of him. It was as though a pall of smog had fallen over the landing platform. The field glasses were spluttering at readings, picking up some sort of metal in the air. He could not be sure, but it appeared that the explosions had created a metallic dust haze above the platform, almost like an old-fashioned barrage of smoke. The dust seemed to be unconcerned by the shield from the way it was cloaking the platform – that or the Kylnnar had somehow managed to get the charges in just under the shield.

Judging by the low chatter over the communicator bead in his ear, this mist was confusing both Julia's night vision scope and the night-time targeting systems of the heavy weapons further down the valley.

"They've covered the platform with some sort of metallic fog," muttered Travis.

Julia nodded her understanding and unclipped her scope. She pointed it up into the night sky above the space port, searching for a gap in the metallic blur in front of her, looking for landers.

"There they are," she said to herself.

Through the blur she could make out small Kylnnar landers: blocky, rectangular things. They were coming in low across the mountains behind the landing platform, using the higher mountain on which it rested to shield themselves from the heavy weapons position around the academy below. Through the blur, she could just make out the rough shadow of a lander contacting the platform. It had sneaked under the protective shield above the landing area – *a very neat bit of flying*, Julia thought grudgingly.

"They're on the platform," she whispered urgently to Travis.

He pushed himself up slightly and pulled out the communicator stashed in his belt. It was then she noticed Travis was travelling light: no flak jacket, no helmet, easier for him to move on the rocky outcrop above the valley. Her respect for him went up a notch.

He flipped open his communicator. "Ronin to Kim, Ronin to Kim," he breathed.

"This is Kim," came the response.

"We have landfall. I repeat, we have landfall."

"Understood," came the commander's voice before it clicked off.

Moments later there came a roar from the Academy end of the valley. Missiles coursed through the air, slamming into the cliff wall below the landing platform or exploding in the air above it as they came into contact with the metal mist. It was joined by fire from the pulse cannons. Julia noted they were holding back on the military lasers, at least one of which was pointed down the valley in the direction of the landing platform.

"You know we're not going to do much to them as long as they keep their landers on the far side of the platform?" she offered.

"Huh?" asked Travis, who was not really listening, but watching the light show in front of him.

"At the firing angle from the Academy, as long as they keep their landers on the far edge of the platform, you can't see them with the pulse cannons. The missile launchers can't get a lock due to this metallic fog, so you'll only hit if you get lucky. Chances are they'll just hit our own shield above the platform. We're just wasting ammo!"

"We're making sure their landing is contested," replied Travis. "We can't hold the platform; we just need to look as though we're trying to fight them off, to keep them cautious."

"We could have rigged it with explosives," she declared.

"We only have enough for one big job, and it probably wasn't enough for the space port anyway," he replied, his eyes focused on the landers. In the dark all he could see was the intermittent burn of their landing thrusters.

A flash of plasma struck near one of the bursts of engine flame. A small explosion hiccupped out the back of the transport, sending it pitching upwards and across the flat asphalt; it came to a halt in the centre. Lit by the flames, Kylnnar foam projectors could be seen spraying fire-retardant material across the engines before the fires could take hold and blow the plasma reserves.

"Idiot," muttered Julia angrily.

"What was that?" demanded Travis. "One of our missiles?"

"No," she answered. "It was Tom."

Her scope scanned the edge of the platform, as the fog was starting to clear. She could see figures, small at this distance and resolution. She recognized the lizard-like figures of Kylnnar troopers, which she had only seen in news reports before. They were setting up tripods on the edge of the platform.

"Oh no, tell Tom to get gone," she urged Travis.

She knew he was still there. A sniper would have moved after that shot, but Tom was not a sniper.

"What?" The sergeant looked confused.

"Just do it?" Her whisper felt like a scream.

"Tom, this is Sergeant Travis?"

"Hey, sergeant," came Private Bolton's response. The same far too easy-going tone that had kept him from ever climbing the ranks.

"Tom, you need to move," Travis ordered.

"Get out, Travis," Tom laughed. "You see that shot? I took out a transport. This is a great spot, I'm going to get…"

A roar filled the air, discombobulating both Julia and Travis as the sound came from both in front of them and from the communicator in Travis's hand at almost the same time.

"Tom? Tom?" Travis demanded of his communicator, but it gave no response.

Three Kylnnar rotary pulse cannons were pouring fire down the valley at the armoury towers from the landing platform. The first hits had smashed into the far tower where Tom had taken up position. It was vaporized. Masonry was blown out across the valley floor. The second tower had initially got off easier, with only one cannon hitting it, reducing it to a pile of flame. It joined the other in being obliterated as the two other rotary cannons turned their fire on it.

"They must have been built for show; military-grade buildings should not fall like that," Travis said, shocked. "How did you know?"

"I didn't," replied Julia, a sole tear trickling down her face.

"But Tom?" Travis was still trying to process. They were on the astro-hockey team together. They stole whisky together once; memories flooded him.

"Shut up, sergeant, and let me work."

Julia was lying down again, her scope plugged back into her rifle. She vectored in on the clearest of the rotary pulse cannons. Her scope followed the tripod, up to the barrel and along to the power unit at the rear. She let out a slow breath and pulled the trigger. At this range she did not need to try that hard. Half a mile out with a Mark VII, this was easy. Her mind was not as calm as it should be, her breathing was off, and her trigger had been a bit more pull than her normal squeeze. But it did not matter, as the plasma pulse slammed through the centre of the power pack, which exploded in a cascade of fire. The weapon and its two-man crew were engulfed in chemical fire.

She started to count. She hit ten when the fire from the other two rotary pulse cannons raked the rocks behind her, sending up a rain of sharpened shrapnel. She heard Travis grunt with pain next to her.

She hit twenty on her count and started to strip down her weapon so she could pack it over her shoulder, taking the scope off the rifle and placing it in front of her.

She hit thirty on the count, as a second wave of plasma flame slashed across the rocks behind her. It was no closer; if anything, it was further away.

She stopped her count and use her sniper scope to view the platform. The two remaining rotary cannons were packing up. Pulse and missile fire coming up the valley were getting precariously close to the Kylnnar gunners.

"We move now," she hissed to Travis.

The pair crawled hand to hand across the rocks. It took them ten minutes to reach relative safety – a rocky outcrop weathered from the mountain sticking out above the bare stone escarpment across which they had just crawled. It gave a place of temporary respite for the pair to sit up and breathe, out of sight of the space port. Travis took a swig from his silver metallic water bottle and handed it to Julia. She held it to her mouth, but she waited for a moment before drinking. Maybe she was sobbing; it was hard to tell in the darkness.

"Lieutenant Hakeswell, this is Travis," the sergeant said into his comm.

"This is Hakeswell: go ahead."

Even on a communicator she sounded so confident and in control, thought Travis.

"Standing orders all fatalities are to be reported to you," he said.

"Go ahead." Her tone sounded quieter.

"Cadet Private Tom Bolton reported KIA," Travis informed her.

"Are you sure, sergeant?" the comm unit crackled back.

"As I can be, ma'am," came his sombre reply.

"Understood. Any enemy killed or injured?" Hakeswell asked.

He looked at Julia, and she leant forward and held up two fingers close enough in front of his face for him to see.

"Two Kylnnar, probably dead, one transport damaged, degree unknown, one pulse cannon destroyed," he answered.

"Understood," Hakeswell replied before the communicator clicked off.

"So that's what it takes for you to talk to the love of your life?" Julia chuckled.

"What are you talking about?"

"Oh, come on, sergeant. Everyone knows – well, everyone but her," she observed. "Make sure you tell her before we all die. You should at least do that."

Travis looked at her, lost for words – not that she could it appreciate it in the dark.

"Maybe leave it until near the end," she said with a grin he could not see.

"Why?" he asked cautiously.

"Less embarrassing when she rejects you," laughed Julia. "Also, less time for Inaya to kill you."

Chapter 9

Location: Wolfsreach Academy, Wolfstar III
Date: 18 December 2196 CE, Earth Standard Calendar
Time: 23.32 Local Time 26.5-hour clock

There was a confident knock on the door.

Simon Kim looked up from the map in front of him.

"Come," he ordered before staring back at the map.

The door opened and Helen Murphy slipped quietly into the room. The wheeze of her prosthetic leg told Simon who it was. He looked up again and gave her a broad, almost childlike, smile.

It was nice to see him, she thought. Despite the smile he looked exhausted, as if he had not slept the previous night, clothing crumpled, dark shadows round the eyes, and a hint of stubble on a chin that normally struggled to grow any hair. She suddenly remembered how young he was; how young they all were.

Lieutenant Kim had taken over the Principal's office as his own. Most of the furniture had been removed, leaving only the table, a couple of chairs and a camp bed against one wall. A pulse rifle was propped in one corner, and a sidearm in its holster was on the table, holding down the corner of a large map. The map was the same one Simon had confidently drawn circles on only the previous day. That seemed like a long time ago now; that was before the Kylnnar had started their main assault.

A series of explosions and flashes lit up the room through the plastic glass of the windows high in the walls of the office. Mostly they sounded like distant pops, though a few were louder and probably closer.

"Drones again?" asked Helen.

"That would be my guess," Simon replied.

He looked up to the windows as if that would somehow confirm it. He could not see out from them; they were above his head. Besides, it was dark outside, as night had settled across Wolfstar III. The Academy was in blackout, though the blue light of the shield above cast an eerie light across the buildings.

"That will be the fourth wave," he declared. "They've sent two up the rock plain towards the gym, and now two down the valley from the space port. They're trying to get in under the shield."

She nodded in understanding – not that she was an expert on drone usage in military combat.

"They're trying to use smaller flyers to bomb us?" she offered.

"Maybe; the shield prevents them dropping anything from above, and bombers struggle to get their payload in under it. At least not without being shot down," he smiled wolfishly.

"The drones are small enough that they can fly them in under it," she countered.

"That's one possibility. The gap between the top of the buildings and the shield is pretty tight. You can't really fly them at high speed, or you risk losing them in the shield. So, you have to slow them down to get them in under it and then we can shoot them down with pulse rifles," he explained.

"The missile launchers are no use?"

"We have the wrong ammo, or rather the wrong launcher. We have missiles designed to blow through armour. We need stuff like an old-fashioned flak gun, which fills the air with metal. There are missiles that fragment in the air to create a blanket of burning shrapnel that would do, but we just don't have them."

"You said one possibility," she asked, realizing there was more than one.

"I think my opponent is counting guns," he said darkly. "I think he wants to know how many we are; cheaper for him to find out with drones than with Kylnnar lives. It's probably a bit of both: the Kylnnar find out what they're facing and if they get lucky take out a few of us into the bargain. So far, it's only been minor injuries."

"So, they'll know there are two hundred and one of us," she sighed and took a seat at the table. Her bionic limb wheezed and coughed as she seated herself and she rubbed her knee where the prosthetic joined the flesh.

"Two hundred. You heard about Tom?"

"I heard," she replied. Word of their first fatality had rippled around the school.

"He was a good friend of mine; did you know him?" continued the lieutenant.

She thought for a moment: there had been so many kids over the years, some memorable, most not. She could not put a face to the name. The student population had been over a thousand before the partial evacuation, now less than two hundred remained.

"Yes. Nice kid," she lied, hoping that would be the end of it. No one wanted to know their friends would not be remembered, that they too might not be remembered when they died. Orphans were particularly sensitive to the fear of disappearing from the memory.

"I don't really have two hundred people anyway; at least not to defend this Academy," Simon sounded out his frustration.

"How so?"

"You have ten working for you as medical orderlies, Travis has a dozen with him in the rocks to the north – well, eleven now – and Lieutenant Hakeswell has four ten-person squads and some weapons specialists to defend Armoury Station. Add in Flex and the others on communication tasks and the four sick in the infirmary, and that is less than one hundred thirty troops to actually defend the school."

"We're down to two in the infirmary," she responded.

She meant the old medical building of the school, not the temporary field hospital that she had established in the dining hall.

"How so?" asked Simon.

"We had one with a broken leg and one with a broken right arm. I injected them with calcium rebuild serum. They are healing up rapidly. They can fight, just don't ask them to go rock climbing," she said with a smile.

"And the other two malingerers?" he demanded nastily.

"They have Lantern's disease," she said, as if that explained everything.

"So," he barked wearily.

"They're sedated. If they weren't, they would be hallucinating."

"Really? Could it spread?" Simon cursed to himself in case this was another thing to worry about.

"Very unlikely. Humans are generally immune to it. Those who are unlucky enough to get it suffer quite badly for a couple of weeks, but after that recovery is pretty much one hundred percent."

The lieutenant let out a giant sigh of relief. At least that was one thing he could ignore.

Helen sized him up. He looked even more exhausted as the enormity of the situation weighed upon his shoulders.

"Are you getting any sleep?" she asked.

"I have ordered for a one third rotation of personnel every eight hours and fifty minutes to give people some downtime to sleep and eat. That leaves us with fewer than ninety people to defend the school, though."

She nodded, grasping immediately that the odd choice of shift time was due to the planet's twenty six and a half hour day.

"I understand that, Simon, but are you personally getting any rest?" Helen was concerned; she did not need their young commander collapsing. He was fit and strong, and she knew from his reputation as a martial artist that he was fast, but like all teenagers he lacked that stamina, that ability to pace yourself and keep going that seemed to come in those a decade older.

Lieutenant Kim gave the camp bed an odd look: half hatred, half burning desire.

"I've tried to sleep, Miss Murphy, honestly, just to get an hour to refresh myself, but I can't. I just think about what will happen next. It's the adrenaline."

Helen had nothing to say to that. He was not the first to say the same thing. Anticipation was building across the school. It felt so palpable you could almost chew on it.

"So, what will happen next?" she enquired.

"They've got the landing platform, so next they will target the armoury," Simon said, prodding at the locations on the map.

The Kylnnar had captured the platform only a couple of hours earlier. They had now taken the shield over the space port offline and were bringing in large troop transports straight from space – the defenders of the academy could pick out hints of their outlines in the night sky. They continued to throw up countermeasures to confuse the incoming fire. The Kylnnar had put up portable shields along the side of the platform facing the school. They overlapped to project a barrier that was strong enough to deflect the incoming pulse rifle and pulse cannon fire. It did little against incoming missiles, which could go over it, but the countermeasures were making them largely ineffective. Helen suspected electronic jamming systems were being used in addition to metallic mist. A token amount of fire was being sent from the school against the barrier, but Simon had given the order to conserve ammunition and power packs. The single military laser pointing up the valley towards the space port would easily cut through the barrier and the ships behind it, but Simon had so far refused to use it. She did not understand why he had not. It was as though he wanted the Kylnnar to have the platform.

"What happens if we lose the armoury?" she asked.

"We can't," he replied urgently. "We lose the armoury, we lose the shields, and they'll obliterate us from orbit. That's why I gave it to Hakeswell. If anyone can hold it, she can. Did you show them what to do?"

"As you asked," she replied.

"If we can hold the armoury, it depends what the enemy do next. I think they'll try to hit us from any direction they can – probably across the rock plain. They might even come down the valley from the landing platform at the same time. Both of those directions will be open killing fields for us. Then it will just be about the numbers. Can we kill them in large enough amounts?" he finished, his tone business-like.

"The mountains above the armoury?" she asked.

"That's why I've put Travis up there," explained Simon. "If the Kylnnar got over the mountains without us knowing, they could drop on the academy from above and surprise us. As long as we know they're coming we should be okay, as the reptiles will find themselves rappelling down those cliffs into a sea of pulse fire."

Neither of them even thought about the mountains to the south of the valley. There, the geology was forbidding. The rock had been formed by some sort of heat and pressure to make a field of razor-sharp glass. A small crevice ran down from the southern mountains to the astro-hockey field and gym. It had often been mistaken as a path by some younger and stupider students, no matter how much they were warned. Helen had patched up numerous cuts and slashes that had been inflicted on those foolish and unwary enough to run up it. There was no chance the Kylnnar could get pass the crystalline rocks to the south.

"Simon," she said quietly. "You're doing a good job."

"Thank you," he said, giving her a surprised smile.

"I'm going back to the dining hall to get ready for the fight to come, but when you doubt yourself, remember what I said," she commanded.

"What?"

"That you're doing a good job," she explained.

He was confused. He knew she was driving at something, but could not work out what it was.

"And Simon, get an hour's sleep."

"Sure," he nodded.

She slipped out of the door. She looked at the young lieutenant, who was back staring at the map. He did not see her go.

CHAPTER 10

Location: Wolfsreach Armoury, Wolfstar III
Date: 19 December 2196 CE, Earth Standard Calendar
Time: 04.52 Local Time 26.5-hour clock

There were ten of them. They stood in silence, pinned to the right-hand side of the escalator. They dropped slowly into the cavernous depths of the station of Wolfsreach Academy – nine fourteen-year-old privates and a fifteen-year-old corporal. Connie Lee, an ethnic Chinese girl, had been one of the refugees from the evacuation of Talos IV, and now she was leading Tiger Squad, a group of kids she barely knew, three girls and six boys. The flak jackets were too large, the helmets wobbled precariously on heads too small for them, and pulse rifles were clutched heavily in their arms. The weapons and kit made them look younger not older; children pretending to be soldiers.

There were hints, though, that they were not complete amateurs: rifles were pointed to the floor, thumbs rested near but not on the safety switch, ready to flick the weapons live at a moment's notice. Guns were slung ready to be brought up quickly. In the harsh light and eerie quiet of the underground monorail station, war seemed to be a system away. In reality it was a station down the track.

The squad tramped onto the platform, army boots cracking and echoing on the stone floors. They took up position opposite the screen doors that shielded the monorail from the platform. Habit made them look right down the track: trains would normally sweep down from the monorail terminus service yard to the academy, then to the armoury and finally the space port. A second monorail performed the same journey in reverse. So, the group gave a start of surprise as air blew into the station from the left, heralding the incoming train. Already on edge, thumbs strayed towards safety switches and fingers towards triggers.

The blue-grey liveried train pulled into Wolfsreach Academy, hissing to a halt, before slowly chugging forward to a final stop to match the platform doors. The doors slid open with a low beeping ring. Ten soldiers disembarked, similar in age and dress to those on the platform. They pushed past their replacements, greeting them with tired upward nods of the head. The substitute squad moved into the carriage. A corporal walking from one end of the two-coach train to the other pushed through them with no apology, ignoring the disgruntled glances that he received. He stood at the end of the carriage facing out through a large glass panel that framed the end of the train. A small control panel to the right of the window was showing, normally concealed under the grey plastic of the train's interior. It allowed the train to be driven manually, overriding the automatic computer controls that routinely controlled the trains.

The corporal took a round stubby metal key from where it hung around his neck on a silver ball chain and plugged it into the panel. He hit a button and the doors purred closed. The platform doors did the same with a whine of beeps.

The train set off into the dark, back the way it had come. It juddered to a stop not long later, causing the squad, all of whom were standing, to grab for the rails or risk losing their footing. The cadets looked out through the windows either side and to the front of the train, searching for the lights of Armoury Station. They were still in the black of the tunnel, a hint of red light coming from up ahead. The train edged slowly into the platform of the station. The dull ambience of the emergency lighting spilled across the train, giving it an eerie crimson glow.

It was the first time Connie and her squad had seen what had been done to Armoury Station on Jo Hakeswell's orders. The glass of the platform doors had been smashed out and shovelled down the tunnels in the direction of the space port. The metal frame was still in place, giving a decaying industrial feel to a location which had once been a picture of slick modernity. An array of furniture, boxes and other detritus had been stripped from the armoury and its surrounding living quarters and piled up to create barricades and protective shelters for the defenders. It was doubtful they would do much against the Kylnnar equivalent of pulse weapons, but there was little else they could use. Any cover was better than no cover.

Armoury Station had a wide central platform with tracks either side of it. It tapered to a point at each end where the two monorail tracks disappeared into a single wide tunnel. A pair of escalators led upwards to the armoury buried in the cliff above them. An elevator large enough to move equipment in and out of the armoury stood beside it. Three small concrete buildings were scattered down the platforms, pumping stations for the air that circulated through the station. It had the effect of blocking out some of the lines of sight down the tunnel, but did provide some cover for the soldiers. Lieutenant Hakeswell had considered using them as blockhouses for her soldiers, but they were too packed with immovable equipment to make that practical.

The station defenders had only a single pulse cannon, sitting on its tripod pointing down the tunnel. Metallic equipment boxes stuffed with rocks and gravel had been placed protectively around it. The cannon was still exposed, but it was the only way for it to point down the tunnel in the direction of the likely incoming attack.

The train was now backing out of the station, returning in the direction from which it had come.

"Corporal Lee, get your people deployed now!" Jo roared at the hapless corporal as she strode angrily across the platform.

"This way, Connie!" barked a sixteen-year-old male corporal, waving her and her squad over to some unattended barricades.

Lieutenant Hakeswell seemed about to shout more at the unlucky girl, but her communicator beeped. It spared the retreating corporal a completely undeserved dressing down. For all Jo's calm outward demeanour, the pressure of the situation was starting to tell on her.

"Harper, that you?" she demanded.

"Yes, ma'am, coming in now," came the reply seemingly from two places.

Jo realized why. Onesie Harper was coming out of the tunnel at the far end of the platform. Two other cadets, small next to Harper's lanky frame, followed him out of the darkness. The lieutenant shut off her communicator, as Private Harper ran up the platform in great loping strides.

"We've got company coming down the tunnel," he announced.

"How many?"

"I didn't stick around to find out, lieutenant," he quavered.

Jo remembered that the tall muscular figure in front of her was in fact a fourteen-year-old boy who was as terrified as the rest of them.

"Squad Wolf and Lion intermittent fire down the tunnel. Do it now?" she shouted across the platform.

Pulse weapons started to buzz around her into the tunnel. Pockets of green light exploded as it hit the sides of the tunnel, and even larger bursts radiated out when one of them caught the metal of the rail. They cast shadows in which the defenders saw their enemy, though for now they were just shadows.

"Did you finish?" she demanded of Onesie.

"Yeah, barely, ma'am," he answered.

Pulse fire exploded across the station, purple-white globules of fire spitting out of the darkness of the tunnel and spraying across the platform.

Jo and Onesie threw themselves to the floor and commando-crawled to behind the nearest concrete air pumping station. The pulse fire coming erratically from the tunnel was gouging lumps of stone from the ceiling.

"Everyone open fire!" Jo roared the order across the station, reverberating above the increasing sound of war.

The station became a place of glaring lights and thunderous detonations. Another squad of soldiers opened up, and the pulse cannon barked down the tunnel. Forms that had been just shadows in the darkness now became very real. Jo tucked down in a half crouch, then eased her way to the edge of the blockhouse, using the wall to support her back. She loosened her sidearm and opened fire down the tunnel. The crack of bullets added to the maelstrom of pulse fire and shouting.

Harper's two shorter colleagues were running across the platform, one carrying an additional pulse rifle for Harper to use. The boy slid to a stop against the wall, using Onesie to partially cushion his landing. The cadet behind was not so lucky. A bolt of purple flame caught him in the left arm, ripping it off completely but cauterizing most of the wound in the same shot. He collapsed to the floor, screaming in pain. Harper moved to pull him to safety, but more pulse fire howled through the air and Onesie could not get to him. He slunk back against the wall, his face riven with frustration. The cadet on the floor continued to shout and sob.

Jo re-holstered her sidearm and slid down the wall until she was as flat as possible against the ground. She poked her head out, looking down the tunnel, ignoring the purple fire that blazed above her head at waist height. The shadows were now appearing from the tunnel. For the first time, Lieutenant Jo Hakeswell saw a Kylnnar in the flesh, and she was terrified. The creature was huge, nearly seven feet height, and twice the width of a grown human male. Scaly dark green skin covered his bipedal form. His lizard face had long snapping jaws that protruded forward. The Kylnnar soldier was naked to the waist, wearing only a pair of light grey shorts and a leather belt and strap across his chest. In his hand was clasped a wicked-looking double-handed sword, with a serrated curve blade. Immediately from her lessons and the news-stream, Jo knew what he was: a berserker.

It was the Confederation term for them; no human had had contact with the Kylnnar long enough to know what they might be called in the language of the reptiles. The Confederation Military officer who had chosen the term had done so with reference to the Viking warriors of old, fighters who dressed in the skins of bears and would work themselves into an uncontrolled frenzy before entering combat. The lizard creature wore no skins, nor did he froth at the mouth, which was not the reason they had been given the name. It was their sheer suicidal ferocity, their willingness to charge into a rain of pulse fire, that had resulted in the comparison. It explained why the Kylnnar were firing so high: they were seeking to avoid killing their own soldiers. Given the platforms were raised above the track, it was not really helping the defenders. The pulse cannon boomed, slamming a plasma blast through one of the oncoming berserkers and tossing him back into the darkness.

"Concentrate fire on the berserkers!" bellowed Jo, trying to keep the terror she felt creeping into her voice. "Bring them down. If they get among us, we'll be overrun."

A second pulse cannon shot smashed another berserker, sending him spiralling back along the track. There were growls of anger and rage from the blackness of the tunnel. There were obviously more Kylnnar warriors waiting behind in the dark.

What were they waiting for? Why didn't they charge? Jo wondered desperately to herself.

As if by answer, two small missiles, the size of grenades but with sharp pointed ends, spiralled out of the tunnel and into the high clearance of the station before dropping down suddenly. They slammed into the pulse cannon, as its crew threw themselves out of the explosion's way. One cadet landed on the monorail track, avoiding the explosion, which rocketed upwards in a spray of fire and shrapnel. She screamed as hot metal rained back down on her. Her colleague suffered worse: the force of the explosion rocked his prone form, throwing him forward into the side of the escalator with a sickening crunch.

Jo looked up having covered her head against the explosion: the Kylnnar berserkers were coming at them, bounding forward in a slavering, frenzied charge. She knew her orders: to hold the station as long as she could. She had to get as many Kylnnar in the tunnel before she did what needed to be done. That moment had now arrived.

"Harper, blow it!" she shouted, despite him standing next to her.

He fished out the detonator from his belt and hit the button.

Nothing happened!

He looked at it and shook it again. He was swearing now, swapping languages when he ran out of words in English.

"Harper!?" the lieutenant demanded.

97

"It's the metal in the rocks of this damn planet – you know it can mess with signals," he muttered angrily, fighting back tears.

Before she could stop him, he was up and running, heading for the tunnel, seemingly charging the Kylnnar berserkers, desperately trying to get nearer, to get a clear signal. The lead Kylnnar slashed at the teenager with his greatsword, sweeping out and down towards Onesie. The cadet jinxed around the blade, years of astro-hockey training, supplemented by a keen survival instinct, saving his life. Lack of experience meant he never saw the left uppercut coming. The Kylnnar's hammer-like fist sent the youth spiralling into the air before slumping like a sack of potatoes on the platform surface.

Onesie gasped for breath in the oxygen-poor environment; the air had been knocked from him. He rolled over and tried to crawl for the detonator, which had fallen behind him, but the Kylnnar was above him. So focused was the berserker on his task that a look of genuine shock formed on his lizard face as the first pulse shot hit him.

Then there was a second.

Harper looked up to see Joanna Hakeswell advancing down the platform, pulse rifle held at the waist, firing shot after shot, heedless of the firestorm around her.

The third shot tore off the creature's sword arm.

The fourth short slammed directly into his face, and he collapsed to the floor.

Onesie crawled forward, his fingers stretching desperately to reach the detonator. A Kylnnar warrior grabbed his right leg and wrenched him back. Onesie screamed as he was dragged across the stone floor. He wriggled enough to avoid the killing strike, but the blade still plunged through his shoulder. A piteous scream tore from his lips.

Hakeswell would not stop. She continued to advance. Another shot hit the new Kylnnar attacker, then a second and a third. The berserker teetered on the edge, then fell off the platform. Now Kylnnar soldiers were appearing from the tunnels. They were similar to their frenzied brethren, but dressed in dark grey uniforms, with padded body armour on the body and legs. The Kylnnar equivalent of pulse rifles were butted on their shoulders, and their fire was spraying across the station. Many of them were targeting the lieutenant, but none hit.

She dropped down and grabbed the detonator; it was showing a signal light. She pressed the button, tossed it in the direction of the tunnel entrance, then hit the deck. The explosion reverberated out of the tunnel. White-blue light illuminated the opening and the station and then was gone; then a screaming, crashing roar rolled over them. Rock, gravel and sand exploded out of the tunnel entrance, scattering a shrapnel of burning hot stone across defenders and attackers alike.

A Kylnnar berserker climbed slowly from the track onto the platform, unsteady and half insensible, his ears ringing from the attack. He hefted his sword. Jo Hakeswell was already standing there, and unloaded her pulse rifle into the last Kylnnar survivor, driving him off the platform and back onto the track. She continued to fire, even though the creature was dead. Her rifle stopped when the plasma pack beeped dry. She unclipped it and reloaded with another pack from her belt. She started firing into the creature again until that pack too indicated that it was dry.

"You okay, lieutenant?"

She looked up. It was Sergeant Reynolds, her second in command, a happy-go-lucky redhead. His eyes held genuine concern.

"Yeah, I'm done," she said quietly.

She walked over to Onesie Harper.

"You think two packs of plasma were enough?" asked Reynolds jokingly.

"Two plasma packs were all I had," she shot back.

"Medics!" she hollered.

Four of the medical orderlies ran forward, two carrying a stretcher.

"Get him to the hospital," Jo said, indicating Onesie. "Triage first." She realized the teenager was bleeding out slowly on the station platform.

She looked down the station at the destroyed tunnel that led in the direction of the space port. The dust was settling, coating a thin film across the station and its defenders. She coughed some out of her throat and wondered what collection of chemicals and toxic metals she had just effectively swallowed. She doubted it would matter in the long run. She was not really expecting there to be a long run.

A pulse shot rang out. She looked up. Three of her soldiers were stalking across the pile of rubble that had flowed out of the tunnel entrance, executing any Kylnnar warriors still showing signs of life. The vast majority had been killed outright in the collapse. It had been Simon's idea to mine the tunnel. She had to grudgingly concede he had been one step ahead of the reptiles up to now. Helen Murphy, the woman who would not touch a gun but knew more about them than any of the cadets, had helped too. She had instructed Harper and his team on how to set the mines to ensure a collapse. They had placed two rings of mines in circles around the whole tunnel. Luckily, they had drone mines. These were essentially a drone with an explosive charge that could be used either individually or in a swarm to take out concentrations of infantry or armour. Helen had shown them how to attach an adhesive pad that allowed them to fly the drone up and stick it to the wall. She had refused to place the explosives herself. Helen seemed determined to walk a peculiar moral line between helping them fight and refusing to participate herself.

Another pulse shot rang out. Moral considerations did not matter very much in the Kylnnar War. The Kylnnar's attack on the Gaia-Martian Confederation had been genocidal from the start, and humanity had responded in kind. At least, that had been the official line. There was of course chat from some that humanity had started it. Jo did not know. Frankly, stuck underground in a smashed-up station with her dead and injured colleagues around her, she did not much care. There were no rules of war; no prisoners were taken on either side. As far as she was aware, the closest the two sides had got to communication was hand-to-hand combat.

The tunnel was blocked. There was a small gap at the top, but how deep it went was impossible to see from down here. If it went all the way through to the other side, there was a risk of Kylnnar warriors crawling through and catching them unawares.

Reynolds appeared before her; his normally cheerful freckled face seemed sad.

"What's the count?" she asked.

"Three dead, eight injured, scrapes and bruises on the rest of us," he reported.

"How bad are the injured?"

"Five walking wounded – well, hopping wounded in one case," he said, his smile returning. "Three serious; one probably won't make it."

"Harper?" she asked.

"No, the medics reckon he has a chance."

She nodded in response.

She looked around, assessing who was left. Tiger squad had suffered particularly badly. It had been her idea to name the squads after predators, to give each of them a sense of camaraderie.

"Disband Leopard Squad and redistribute to Wolf, Tiger and Lion," she ordered.

"But Leopard wasn't on the line – they cycled back to the school before the attack," explained the sergeant.

"Precisely; they have no battle honour to forgo. The other squads fought; they keep their names. The Kylnnar won't be coming through here in numbers now," she stated, pointing up at the tunnel collapse. "But there is still the risk a few try to get through that gap at the top. I'm putting you in command: your three squads must hold the armoury. Rest one squad, but do it in the barracks of the armoury, not back at the school. And tell them to sleep with one eye open."

"Yes, ma'am," he replied.

"Good. I'm going back to the school to talk with the commander. I suspect he will want me to help command the defence of the school, as that will now be the focus of the Kylnnar attack. I am placing you in command of Armoury Station until relieved. Under no circumstances can we lose the armoury. If we do, we lose the shields; then we're all dead."

"Thank you, ma'am, understood." Reynolds replied, feeling the weight falling on his shoulders.

As the lieutenant turned to leave, she looked down, and eyes met hers. They stared at her unblinking from the corpse of the cadet at her feet. The student's heart had been blown out by a pulse rifle shot. It was a perfect shot; the hole itself had been cauterized by the pulse blast.

"Get the medics to clear these bodies away. They shouldn't be left like this," she ordered.

Connie Lee's dead eyes continued to stare accusingly as Joanna Hakeswell walked away.

CHAPTER 11

Location: Wolfsreach Academy, Wolfstar III
Date: 19 December 2196 CE, Earth Standard Calendar
Time: 06.19 Local Time 26.5-hour clock

Simon looked up at the knock on the door.

"Come," he answered.

Lieutenant Joanna Hakeswell slipped into the room; the pulse rifle slung on her shoulder cracked against the door. She hefted it back into position and saluted. Simon returned the salute. He looked at his old adversary and felt a great swell of sympathy for her and anger at the Kylnnar. She looked hot and tired, her face and uniform encrusted with dirt and dust. It was the weariness that struck him, though. Not the physical exhaustion that she was no doubt experiencing, but an emotional toll that could not be measured. He remembered Jo's eyes, sometimes querying, sometimes amused, most often, at least when dealing with him, flashing with anger. The eyes that looked at him now were empty of all emotion, just the cold focus of a warrior. He wondered if his own would look the same soon. He wanted to give her a hug, though he knew it would do no good.

"Report," he barked, a touch more harshly than he had planned. His frustration at their situation was coming through.

"We have held Armoury Station," she said. Her tone was matter of fact, not even noticing his harshness. "The Kylnnar came down the tunnel as you predicted; we waited as long as possible before we blew it. The tunnel is almost entirely blocked. There is a small gap at the top of the rubble pile, but we have that covered. In terms of casualties…"

Simon held up his hand to stop her.

"Flex has informed me of our losses and the estimated deaths on the Kylnnar side," he replied. "I've instructed him to take over the count from you. Now the battle has joined you will be too busy commanding to deal with administrative tasks."

"Our fellow dead cadets are an administrative task?" she asked, her tone neutral.

"You know what I mean?" Simon muttered back.

"You've called this right so far, sir. So, what should we expect next?" she queried.

Lieutenant Kim looked back to the map spread out on the table in front of him. It was covered with so many pencil squiggles and scrawls it was teetering on illegible.

"They won't come down the valley: it's a kill box; the south hills are impassable. So that leaves a cautious attack across the north hills using the troops they have landed at the platform or an all-out assault across the rock plain," he replied.

"Our opponent has been cautious up to now," she offered.

"I know." Simon stared at the map, searching for an answer that was not there. "Is he cautious out of habit or will that change? We're costing him time and troops now."

"He? The Kylnnar leader? Could be a she?" Jo smiled for the first time.

"Could be a she," he said, returning her smile.

"I don't mean just that it could be a female. I'm not explaining it well." Jo was serious now. "You're making them a

104

person, not a thing. That's not what they do on the news. The Kylnnar is always described as an it."

"I don't know, Jo. I just think it's easier to fight someone when you treat them as an equal, not as some alien thing."

She nodded. Simon was not sure if it was in understanding or in agreement. Since the beginning of the war, the Confederation Government had sought to portray the Kylnnar as other, avoiding any attempt to see them as another intelligent species despite their obvious sentience. To discover you were not alone in the universe had been exciting at first, then it was shocking to realize that the alien you had found was a cold reptilian species seemingly bent on genocide. Simon and Jo were both too young to remember the early days of the war except as childhood memories. Back then there had been advocates of negotiation, proponents of understanding, talking heads trying to see it from the Kylnnar point of view. The destruction of several outlying Confederation colonies had ended that. Their human populations were wiped out, down to the last babe in arms.

Simon's communicator beeped. He flipped it open and hit the speaker button.

"What is it, Flex?" he demanded.

"We've got incoming, lieutenant?" Corporal Lynch's voice crackled out of the speaker.

"What and where?"

"A dozen landing barges. Not sure where they're going – they're flying erratically to make it hard for us, but my best guess is the rock plain," came the reply.

Simon quickly grabbed up his sidearm from the table and clipped it to his belt. He pushed past Hakeswell and out of the door of the Principal's office.

"Come on," he instructed as an afterthought and set off down the corridor.

She jogged after him, following him out of the door that led to the astro-hockey court. Its surrounding mesh fence had been cut down so as not to inhibit movement, and only the metal pylons that surrounded the court were still standing. Simon stopped his own run at the edge of the court, slowing to a walk and staring up into the air. The blue shimmer of the shield was just visible against the grey of the morning sky. Dawn had broken, but the sun had not fully risen, throwing up strange moments of shadow and darkness across the school yard.

He unclipped the small pair of field glasses from his belt and scanned the sky. The other cadets distributed on roofs and at windows across the school were doing the same, using their helmet visors to scrutinize the sky. Less powerful than the field glasses, they were yet to pick out anything.

Simon continued to walk across the sports field as he scrutinized the airspace, occasionally looking down to ensure he did not trip. Frustrated at not seeing anything, he pulled his glasses down and set off at a jog towards the gym. He ran through the gap between the building and the razor-sharp rock face of the southern cliffs that ran right down to the school at this point.

He stared out across the rock plain in front of him. Bringing his field glasses to his eyes again, he scanned the wide-open expanse of stony territory before him. He could see movement, indistinct among the light grey stone, maybe two miles out. He looked up to the sky to see that twelve landing barges had broken atmosphere and were dropping almost vertically to the rock plain. He guessed they would land within half a mile of the school. Except they would not land: the barges were too heavy and flat to settle on the uneven rock-scarred surface of the plain. They would have to drop their infantry from maybe fifty feet up. His cautious opponent had suddenly become aggressive, he mused. He was thankful that the shield meant that the Kylnnar could not drop their soldiers directly onto the academy.

The lieutenant dropped his field glasses to his chest and surveyed his defence lines. The hard surface of the planet had made digging trenches impractical, and shortage of time and equipment had made it impossible. Instead, they had used explosives to blow three foxholes in front of the gym building and the officers' mess. Each had five cadets clustered in them. Behind them, more squads of rifle-armed teenagers squatted on the edge of the pitched roof of the gym and the flat roof of the main school building. More soldiers poked out from the smashed windows of the officers' mess, the main school building, and the infirmary.

This would be their thin line of defence, he lamented.

He still had his secret: the military lasers, two of which had been hidden away, pointing out across the rock plain. One was in the shadow of the officers' mess and the other was inside the gym itself. He just had to hope his opponent did not know he had them. The combination of the shields and the odd geology of the surrounding mountains should have made scanning difficult, if not impossible, for the fleet above them. If the Kylnnar knew he had such weapons, then their assault had gone from being cautious to outright reckless in one step.

Heavy pulse fire started to roar from behind him, and he ducked involuntarily.

"What's that, Flex?" he demanded over the comm.

"They are firing down the valley from the landing platform," came Flex's fizzing response.

"Any sign of troop movements down the valley?" the lieutenant demanded.

"Negative. It's weird; they seem to be firing really poorly. It's all just popping along the ground in front of the dormitories. It's not even hitting the buildings. Maybe the trainees have taken them over?" chuckled Private Lynch.

Simon clicked off the communicator and went back to looking at the sky in front of him.

"What's going on?" asked Lieutenant Hakeswell.

"Just the Kylnnar trying to keep our troops pinned down in the dormitories ahead of their landing," he replied almost dismissively.

Hakeswell nodded. If the Kylnnar on the platform fired too high, they risked their ordnance overshooting the school and hitting their own landing.

"Missile launchers, open fire," commanded Lieutenant Kim quietly over his communicator.

Fire spat into the sky, tracking the path of the incoming Kylnnar assault barges. It was greeted by a series of pops. Grey-silver metallic smoke filled the air above the rock plain, partly obscuring the incoming vessels, but more importantly throwing off the missile launchers' targeting systems. The missiles exploded around the vessels, but it was not obvious any had taken a direct hit, and they continued their steady descent.

"Simon?" queried Joanna.

"What?"

"The lasers?" she asked.

"Wait, it's too early," he insisted.

"If they all make landfall, we'll be overwhelmed for sure," she said, her tone insistent.

"You point has been noted, Lieutenant Hakeswell," he barked. "Now shut up."

He ignored the angry look that he could feel burning into his back. The landing barges needed to be lower; it was the only way this was going to work.

"Open fire, pulse weapons, all stations open fire on incoming Kylnnar transports," he ordered through his communicator.

Plasma fire exploded upwards from the roof of buildings and the windows of those nearest the rock plain. It seemed desperate and pointless: the barges were too well armoured to sustain much damage from a pulse rifle, though if it were persistent enough, it would eventually punch through. There was also the chance they could get lucky and catch an engine or a stabilization module. The three pulse cannons pointing across the plain would be more effective; a good shot might penetrate the armour.

The barges were at one hundred feet now.

"All three laser squads, open fire," Simon ordered into his communicator.

Three lines of turquoise light sprung up into the air, two out across the rock plain and one from near the dormitory out towards the landing platform. They passed seamlessly through the shields above the school, calibrated to phase in line with the barrier; an old navy trick. The line of light carved across the smoke-shrouded sky. It ionized the metallic dust within the cloud as it passed through it, creating flashes of green fire. The laser moved like a rapier, cutting a swift slash through the closest of the barges. Metal boiled instantaneously on contact as the beam cut through the ship like butter. Slicing laterally, it slowed only slightly as it met resistance. Then it was through the Kylnnar lander. It collapsed in two halves, falling out of the sky in a cascading plume of fire. It appeared from the smoke as its two parts crash-landed on the rock plain. The rear half with the fuel tanks exploded, forcing the defenders to take cover as hot metal spewed across the academy. Some caught on the shield above the school in a rainbow of fireworks. The other half landed in a crumbled mess of broken metal before being covered in the same burning shrapnel as the academy.

The laser from beside the officers' mess hit a second barge, catching its engines and stabilizing system, sending it spiralling out of control. It spun across the rock plain, its pilot clearly desperate, trying to regain control as it dropped precariously below the ridge at the end of the open expanse. It slammed into the ground a couple of miles distant from the school. The lieutenants looked for signs of an explosion, but there was nothing. The Kylnnar landing barges were dropping fast now, hoping to angle themselves out of the way of the sword-like rays of light.

As they reached a low enough point, the large rear doors of each barge started to open, moving fast in a hiss of hydraulic fluid. The pulse fire from the school switched from random targeting, instead searching for the opening portals, and pouring fire in their direction. They were still obscured by smoke and the metallic dust that prevented targeting, but suddenly there were too many targets for it to matter. Kylnnar soldiers wearing body armour and drop packs, rifles grasped in hands, poured from the rear of the transports. Some Kylnnar warriors were caught by pulse fire in the entrance of their transports, but more were making it out and hitting the ground.

At least the fire from the landing platform had diminished as the remaining laser slashed outwards across the valley. It cut along the edge of the platform, a carving knife cutting through the meat and bone of Kylnnar ships and warriors. Explosions of orange fire rocked the space port, setting out great spouts of flame as plasma fuel went up in a sheet of incandescence. Simon did not even bother to look; he was too worried about the incoming Kylnnar drop infantry, which was now sweeping across the rock plain towards the school.

Joanna hoisted her rifle to her shoulder and moved forward, aiming to join the foxhole in front of the gym.

"Stand fast, lieutenant!" Simon shouted over the bedlam.

She turned, half incredulous, half angry.

"You are an officer, Lieutenant Hakeswell: act like one. You are here to command," he explained harshly.

Jo wanted to shout at him, but her military training held.

"Yes, sir!" she barked back.

The cadets in the foxholes met the first charge of the Kylnnar assault. They opened up on the incoming tide of hulking dark green reptiles, desperate to ensure they cut them down with pulse fire before it came to close-combat fighting, in which the Kylnnar would have the overwhelming advantage.

Simon quietly signalled to Jo and the pair pulled back from their vantage point next to the gym and went to the open space of the astro-hockey court, where they had a better view of the overall battle. A squad of ten cadets had run into the gap between the gym and the rocky cliff face to its south. The Kylnnar had reached the foxhole and were leaping into it. One unslung a curved blade – a smaller version of the one carried by the Kylnnar berserkers, more a short sword than a knife. It slashed down as one cadet futilely brought up his pulse rifle in an attempt to stop the blade. The attacker was too wily, though; he thrust the defender's rifle down and inflicted a killing blow across the face.

The reptiles were now attacking across the entire width of the school facing the rock plain. The squad nearest the gym were having the best time of it, as the gym building and the rock cliff created a funnel that prevented the reptiles from bringing large numbers to bear. The squad of ten were in two lines of five, one kneeling, the other standing. They were stood as if forming a firing squad or a musket regiment on an archaic battlefield. Their constant stream of firing was holding back the incoming Kylnnar.

The ships had disgorged their soldiers: perhaps seven hundred Kylnnar had made it to the ground. Now the vessels were trying to get clear, but the military lasers continued to do their devastating work. The laser nearest the officers' mess caught another barge as it tried to escape to orbit. It scythed through the engines and then the fuel tank, and the barge vaporized in a flash of flaming metal and burning dust. The explosion rocked the vessel next to it. It teetered in the air before it began to drop, slowly but certainly to the rocky surface below. Landing flaps rotated and flexed as the pilots desperately sought to regain control. It dropped like a stone as it lost all upward thrust. Gravity accelerated it into the rocky surface, crushing Kylnnar troopers under its considerable bulk as it landed with a thunderous crash.

Simon and Jo had reached the astro-hockey court, but their view was still partly blocked by the gym and the officers' mess. Simon bobbed from one foot to the other to get a better view of events, his frustration obvious. In Lieutenant Hakeswell's case, her frustration was close to boiling over. The blood was thundering in her ears, and she could barely hear the battle, so consumed was she by the desire to get into the fight. It took a moment for her to realize that Simon was giving her an order.

"Lieutenant Hakeswell, pull two squads from the dormitories," he commanded, indicating the buildings behind them facing the valley. "Plug the gap between the gym and the dining hall. Otherwise, we'll be overrun."

"Yes, sir!" she roared.

Something to focus on. She was running for the dorms. Shouting into her communicator, ordering a pair of squads to quit their position in dormitory blocks one and three. The two bands came out of their buildings as she arrived in front of them. Some excitable ones pushed to the front, keen to join the fight, too young and callow to know what they were about to get themselves into. Some more sensible held back; others were just struck by terror. The camaraderie and the uniforms dragged them through. They were young, the youngest of the squads, eighteen fourteen-year-old orphans led by two fifteen-year-old corporals. The school was a sea of noise, periodic explosions, the burning hiss of lasers sweeping the sky, the cracking snap of pulse weaponry.

"On me!" screamed Lieutenant Hakeswell, thrusting her arm in the direction of the gap to the left of the gym.

She set off at trot, pulse rifle held at her hip. The others followed her – not that she looked to check.

The Kylnnar had overwhelmed the cadets in the foxhole in front of the gym, leaving no survivors, but now found themselves sandwiched against the solid wall of the building as the defenders fired from the roof above. They surged round the gym towards the foxhole between the gym and the officers' mess. The defenders already under close assault broke and ran, the fast-moving Kylnnar in hot pursuit. Then Jo Hakeswell and her two squads were there.

Her pulse rifle purred as she unloaded a clip into the oncoming charge. Clicking it free, she swapped in another and continued to fire. That ran out, so she slung her rifle behind her back, unclipped her sidearm, and continued to advance, bullet after bullet thudding into the Kylnnar warriors in front of her. Her cadets were with her, frightened and dazed by the noise and smoke of battle, but their leader inspired them.

On the roof above the gym, teams of cadets were throwing grenades at the rear of the advancing Kylnnar, which popped before spewing shrapnel across the reptiles.

The Kylnnar attack started to waver. The left prong of the reptilian assault in the gap between the cliff and the gym had been held by the tactical geography and the bravery of one squad. The central prong through the gap between the gym and the dining hall was being held for now by Hakeswell's counter-charge. The right prong was going for the officers' mess, and had already overwhelmed the foxhole in front of it. Kylnnar soldiers had made it to the roof of the single-storey building, which rested low to the ground as the structure was part dug into the rock of the planet. The five cadets on the roof had already made a break for it, realizing their position was undefendable. They raced along the roof of the covered corridor between the officers' mess and the main school building, slipping and skidding on the dusty plastic surface. They threw themselves through the windows of the second storey of the main school building.

The Kylnnar let them go, seemingly unconcerned by their escape. They had other priorities. They tossed grenades in through the broken windows of the officers' mess, to screams of panic. The pops of detonation reverberated in the enclosed space, then there was silence from the inside.

The remaining Kylnnar soldiers flowed around the officers' mess into a wide space to the north of the school. They set upon the military laser that had been positioned there in the shadow of the officers' mess. The reptiles attacked its crew, tearing the hapless cadets away from their machine and slaughtering them mercilessly. They then attached explosives to the generator of the laser. It erupted in a volcanic pillar of fire, sending both sides ducking to the ground.

A Kylnnar warrior was shouting to his soldiers. The humans did not speak the hissing language of the reptiles, but it was clear he was an officer gesticulating to his soldiers to surround the school and attack the unused infirmary building ahead of them. The bullet took him through the right eye, blowing out the back of his head. He slumped to the ground. A mile away, high up in the northern mountains, cadet sniper Julia Williams quietly reloaded her Mark VII sniper-grade pulse rifle and focused on the next Kylnnar officer she could see.

The advance around to the north of the school stuttered as another officer was shot down. Cadets were firing non-stop from the roof and windows of the main school building and the infirmary. The Kylnnar were brave and violent, bigger and tougher than the young cadets they were attacking, but they simply could not cope with the volume of pulse fire being poured into them. They did their best to return the favour, but the defenders were well entrenched in the buildings, which had been designed to resist both severe dust storms and a potential military assault.

A sound like a giant electronic horn thundered across the battlefield.

"What the hell was that?" demanded Simon to Flex through his communicator.

"No idea, sir, but we've got incoming," came the terse response.

"What incoming?" Simon tried to keep panic out of his voice.

"Fighters, I think?"

Lieutenant Kim scanned the sky with his glasses. Four fighters were coming in fast in two groups of two. They were dropping in a spiral, spinning as they went, trying to make it difficult for the lasers or missile launchers to get a lock on them.

Simon needed to give no order: they were already being targeted; the sky was alive with ordnance. He heard a supersonic boom from behind him. His glasses scanned the sky again. Two bombers had come over the landing platform. Moving fast and dropping low, they raced down the valley towards the academy.

The four fighters pulled to a sharp stop, hovering over the rock plain in front of the school. Remorseless fire cascaded through the school across the roof tops. They were not targeting anything in particular, just trying to keep the cadets pinned down. They were covering the Kylnnar infantry on the ground, who had broken combat and were making a jogging retreat from the school towards the rock plain.

"Gym laser team, bring down those fighters!" Simon screamed into his comm.

"What the hell do you think we're trying to do?" came the insubordinate reply.

Now holding position, the fighters were vulnerable. The military laser sprung out, carving a blue-green line in the sky it slashed through the first fighter and then a second. The other two did not wait around. They dropped as low as possible, skimming the surface in a frantic effort to stay below the shimmering line that meant death. They stayed low all the way to the ridge at the end of the rock plain, before dropping out of sight completely.

The explosion reverberated across the academy. Simon was knocked flat. Suddenly he struggled to breathe as the planet's limited oxygen was sucked from the air. He coughed and spluttered, feeling like he was drowning, trying to clear his lungs.

There was no water in them, so it did little good. He was gasping for air. Suddenly the oxygen was back, and he drank it in as he gasped for breath, his throat raw.

He looked up. The west side of the school facing the landing platform was a wall of fire. The bombers had dropped incendiaries just short of the school, for fear of them hitting the shield and being rendered useless. They had created a sheet of liquid flame that had jetted across the walls of the three dormitory blocks. All three were now burning. Cadets were rushing to use the school's sand blowers in an attempt to douse the flames, but they would do little good against the chemical propellant that had been used to create the fire.

Simon pushed himself to his feet and staggered exhausted to the gap between the gym and the officers' mess. Jo was standing there, her pulse rifle slung over her shoulder, her face covered in dirt and blood.

"You okay?" she asked him.

"You're asking me, but you're the one who's been fighting?" he said with a smile.

"You're bleeding from your right ear," she replied.

He reached up and touched his ear, feeling the wetness there. It was then he realized his hearing was foggy.

"What's the situation?" he demanded, ignoring his injury.

"The Kylnnar have retreated back across the plain," replied Jo.

"Casualties?"

"I don't know yet, but it's going to be a big number," she said sadly.

"Tell me when you have an accurate count?" Simon ordered. "I'll be in my office."

She nodded and he turned to leave.

"And sir," she said.

He glanced back.

"Go via the hospital and get that checked out on the way back."

"Thanks for the concern, lieutenant."

Chapter 12

Location: Wolfsreach Academy, Wolfstar III
Date: 19 December 2196 CE, Earth Standard Calendar
Time: 07.03 Local Time 26.5-hour clock

Simon stopped just outside the dining hall that was doubling as a makeshift hospital. He fished a handkerchief out of his pocket and used it to clear off the blood from around his ear and his face. He then rattled down the steps into the hospital. The room was quieter than he expected. Not in terms of numbers: three dozen injured were being cared for in the room by Helen and her ten assistants. There were more arriving, injured cadets carried on stretchers or between the shoulders of two colleagues. The quiet was in the muted atmosphere; the near silence of the room.

Normally that many people should have created a buzz of noise. Even if they were making an effort there would still be that low hum from everyone whispering. Instead, the eerie silence was broken by the clink of medical equipment and the occasional groan or scream from one of the occupants. Most of the injured were sat up perched on the edge of makeshift camp beds or on chairs around the room. Dirt-covered faces, scraped, and bloodied. Arms hanging in slings, bandages across arms, legs, and foreheads. Visages were hollowed out, gaunt and shadowed.

At the far end of the hall Helen was quietly working away, the occasional tinkle of metal on metal as she operated. She was wearing green scrubs, face mask in place, hair covered with a green plastic shower cap, only hints of her luxurious red locks sticking out.

On the table was the slumped form of a female cadet. To Simon she looked more childlike in her repose than her fifteen years would suggest. Helen pulled out a piece of metal using magnetic pincers, dropping it into a metal medical bowl. She then pulled out her cauterizer and started to seal the wound with the heated tool. A small hint of burning flesh filled the air, though maybe Simon imagined it. The cadet, heavily sedated, did not move. Helen put down her cauterizer and sighed heavily. Simon felt a moment of deep sympathy for the medical auxiliary. It was hard for him leading these cadets to injury and death. It must be so much harder for someone to clear up the mess that resulted.

Helen nodded to a pair of her assistants, who gingerly transferred the injured girl to a stretcher before carrying her down the room to a camp bed halfway down the hall. They shooed a lightly injured cadet out of the way. He stood up and almost absentmindedly wandered off out of the dining room, still under the effect of the painkillers he had been given.

"You injured?" Helen's voice pierced the air.

She was not shouting, just projecting a little to cover the distance, but it sounded thunderous in the quiet of the room. She turned to a temporary water station and started to scrub the blood from her hands.

"No, I'm fine," he lied, crossing the room.

"Come to see your handiwork then," she asked nastily, turning back to face him.

A shadow crossed his visage. Suddenly the hard look on Helen's face softened as she took in the young man in front of her.

"Sorry, lieutenant, that was uncalled for," she apologized.

"No problem," he answered.

In truth, Simon was less concerned by her jibe than the fact it sounded like she was talking to him from underwater. He changed positioned slightly so the sound of her voice was coming predominantly to his good ear.

"You sure you're okay?" she asked, her nose wrinkling suspiciously.

"I said I'm fine." A hint of annoyance crept into his voice. "What's the situation?"

"What you see?" she replied with a weary wave of her hand. "Mostly lightly injured. They'll be back to their position soon enough. They're just waiting for the painkillers to work and for us to check there aren't any internal injuries we can't see at first. A few concussions waiting to be cleared before we let them back on the line. We have four with more severe injuries: a broken leg, two with serious but non-fatal pulse wounds, and the girl you just saw with the shrapnel wounds. Then we have two that are touch and go." She indicated a pair of students lying in nearby beds surrounded by beeping and hissing equipment. Simon recognized the lanky form of Onesie Harper as one of them. "There'll be more coming in," she concluded.

"And the dead?"

"We've lost two that made it here, but died on the table. They've been taken to the infirmary block. It has a basement with a mortuary," she explained.

"A mortuary? I didn't know that!" Simon was incredulous.

"Well, it's not something you really share with school kids," she observed, a touch of amusement creeping onto her lips.

120

"Half of you want to break in and see it; the other half get freaked out and have to see the school counsellor. We are out here at the fringes of the universe and students and teachers occasionally die from disease or accidents. We have to put them somewhere before we ship them back to a more civilized planet. No one wants to be buried, burned or excarnated here. There are eight berths. If they're not full by now, they will be very soon. We can double up, then stack the rest on the mortuary floor. It will still be cooler in there than the rest of the school."

"So, what do you want to be: buried, burned, excar-, excan-, or whatever the last one was?" he asked.

She laughed, a deep warm laugh as she remembered that the man in front her was still a student.

"Excarnated. It means put on the top of a high platform to have your body devoured by birds," she explained.

"People do that? That's awesome," he said with a large grin.

"I think you, lieutenant, would have been one of the students breaking into the mortuary had you known about it," she observed. Her tone was all disapproving parent, but her eyes crinkled with amusement. "I think buried; take me back to Earth."

Earth was the old name for the planet Gaia, the capital world of the Gaia-Martian Confederacy. Simon had never seen it; his grandparents were the most recent ancestors of his who had been born on humanity's home world.

"Well, I suspect none of us will have much choice. We'll end up on some Kylnnar's dinner plate."

"I'm fairly sure it's a myth that the Kylnnar eat human flesh. I think it's just a way of making them seem more of a threat," Helen replied.

"Look out the window: I'm not sure they need to seem much more of a threat," he shot back.

"I don't think the propaganda, if that is what it is, is designed for us out here on the border – more for those sitting safely back in the inner systems."

"They'll know about the Kylnnar soon enough at the rate we're retreating. Though chances are they'll never know what happened here."

"I thought Flex Lynch was broadcasting a distress call asking for help," she said, concerned.

Simon looked around him. He did not want people to lose hope of rescue, though he knew most of them knew it to be forlorn. He had regretted getting annoyed with Flex and telling him there would be no evacuation ships from pretty much the moment he had said it. Such short-temperedness was of no use in their situation. Hope was one of the few things they had to grasp onto. He was just glad that Flex, being the introvert he was, would be unlikely to talk to anyone.

"He is, and as far as we can tell it is getting through," he told her quietly.

"As far as we can tell?"

"Well, as far as we can tell, the reptiles aren't blocking it. The only problem is we can't be sure we would be able to tell," Simon explained.

Helen chuckled at that.

"When we first started sending it, we were also picking up similar broadcasts from perhaps half a dozen other Confederacy outposts. Mostly mining colonies, a long-range scientific research station, that kind of thing. As of four hours ago, we were the last one broadcasting. So maybe they were evacuated, but maybe the Kylnnar are blocking the signals," he finished with a shrug.

"Maybe they're dead," Helen countered.

"Maybe," Simon nodded quietly.

"You are doing well, lieutenant," she observed, a look of concern on her face.

She wanted to hug the young man, try somehow to make the pressure he was under go away. That was not an option; they were not that close, and he needed her respect more than her affection.

"Glad to hear you don't regret putting me in charge," he smiled.

"Not my decision," she laughed. "Just following the regs."

"You heard about Joanna in Armoury Station?" he asked. She gave a smile and a nod.

"Now, that is bravery," he observed.

"Different types of bravery, lieutenant," Helen replied. "For some, it's the heat of the fighting; for others, it's giving the orders and making the decisions that will send soldiers to the death. We will need both if we are to survive this."

"I am trying to decide if her striding across an open space firing from the hip, heedless of the risk, is a sign of bravery or that she's losing it."

"Losing it?" Helen arched an eyebrow. "Is that the correct medical term?"

"Sorry, I don't know the right way to put it. There's a fine line between courage and having snapped."

"Snapped?" Helen's eyebrow rose further, as she smiled involuntarily.

"Cut me a break, will you?" the young lieutenant demanded, his frustration clear. "I'm asking if my second in command is okay?"

"Sorry, lieutenant, just yanking your chain; it's been one of those days. Yeah, Jo Hakeswell is fine – at least in the way you mean it. I reckon she's from a military family; an old one, would be my guess. I've seen it before: the expectations weigh on you; you see it in their actions day to day. They either become all polished boots and salutes or they rebel against the whole thing."

"I didn't know she was from a military family?" the lieutenant commented.

"Neither do I for sure," the matron replied. "But she has all the signs. It's when they're on the battlefield that the weight of expectations really shows."

"How so?" asked Simon.

"Well, they either use their background as an excuse to sit at the back and give out orders, or they rush to the front in a bid to emulate their ancestors. I suspect that Jo grew up under the picture of some old war hero and heard stories of fearless bravery. It's a little different when you get to the reality and are hit with the flames, the blood, and the roar of the battlefield," Helen explained.

"You sound like you speak from experience?"

"A little, perhaps," she replied with a smile. "Different class. My ancestors were all gunners, privates – conscripts, not volunteers. Or if they did volunteer it was because they needed the money."

"And Hakeswell?" he asked.

"My guess is officers, probably a colonel or something similar; maybe even a general," Helen responded with a grin tinged with a hint of sadness.

"Then what is she doing here among us orphans?" he wondered.

"Posh people lose their parents too," she observed.

"You know what I mean?"

"I don't know; maybe I'm imagining this all and her mum was actually a plumber," Helen shrugged.

Simon let out a laugh at that loud enough to raise a look from the other people in the room. He covered his smile, his merriment feeling inappropriate in this place.

"I'm just saying she shouldn't be here," he explained.

"None of us should be here," she grunted.

"The Confederation has left a bunch of teenagers to defend a planet. We're kids; we should not have to do this," he muttered angrily, trying to keep his voice down.

"No, you shouldn't, but that doesn't mean you can't," the matron replied.

"We're too young," Simon said, his voice filled with doubt. It was the first time he had given into it since being put in command.

"How old are you, Simon?" she asked.

"Seventeen."

"A year older than Alexander the Great at his first battle."

"Thanks, Miss Murphy; you got an example more current than two and a half millennia ago?" Simon asked sarcastically.

"Roman legionaries were recruited at seventeen," she offered.

"Better; a bit over two millennia ago," came his biting response. "Besides, I'm among the oldest; we have fourteen-year-olds standing on the barricades."

"Napoleonic wars, teenagers that age saw battle. The British Admiral Nelson was twelve when he joined the Navy."

"Four hundred years ago; getting closer." Simon was smiling now.

"The World Wars, the Martian Civil War and a hundred wars in between. Is it right that you have to do this? No, it isn't. Can you, do it? Yes!"

"Thank you, Miss Murphy," Simon said, smiling broadly. "I needed the pep talk."

"No problem, lieutenant. Now get back to keeping us alive."

CHAPTER 13

Location: Northern Hills, Wolfsreach Valley, Wolfstar III
Date: 19 December 2196 CE, Earth Standard Calendar
Time: 07.06 Local Time 26.5-hour clock

Julia watched through her sniper scope as the Kylnnar pulled back from the school buildings, scattering back across the rock plain. She briefly considered taking a pot shot or two at the fleeing reptiles, but with all the fighters flying around decided it was too big a risk. From her vantage point in the hills above the school, she could see out across the rock plain to where it dropped away below a low ridge. It was hard to make out what was going on there, but there seemed to be large groups of Kylnnar troops preparing for something, out of sight of the school buildings. She thought about spotting in a missile strike, but her angle was not great, and chances are it would just be a waste of ordnance.

A red light flashed on the communicator lying in front of her. To prevent inadvertent discovery, they had switched to silent communications in the mountains: a simple flash of an LED to tell when they were being called. She settled her Mark VII rifle on the ground and, not leaving her prone position, picked up the unit and put it to her face.

"It's Julia, what is it?" she muttered quietly into the comm.

"We need you at peak N11," Travis's voice crackled back, barely audible; she had turned the volume to a low setting.

"Understood," she whispered and clicked off.

She placed the communicator to the side of the fabric sheet on which she was lying. She carefully moved her Mark VII off the sheet, placing it like a baby on the rocky ground to her right. She then pushed up from the sheet and skipped her back legs in, so she was sitting in a deep squat. She slowly started to roll up the fabric sheeting from the front, doing little bouncing jumps backwards as the roll approached her. She jumped back one last time, hearing gravel scrunch under her feet, and finished rolling up the remainder of her sheet. Not leaving the squat, she pulled over the rucksack next to her and clipped the sheet into position at the bottom of the pack. She pushed herself up from the squat and hoisted the pack onto her shoulders. It looked too large on her petite frame.

She crouched down again and picked up her sniper rifle. She checked it, making sure the safety was off. Knowing the weapon was live, she pointed it down. She flipped the button that shortened the stock of the rifle, making it more comfortable for her to rest in the crock of her arm with the butt resting against her shoulder. She turned the weapon to see the power pack and its barely visible gauge – the plasma pack was seventy-five percent full. *No need to change it*, she thought. She quickly scanned the area around her feet and cursed. She had almost left her communicator. She squatted down again, resting her weapon by its butt on the ground, the still warm barrel clutched in her right hand. She snatched up the communicator, clipping it to her belt. She stood up and checked the rifle again, dusting off the butt.

Julia rested the butt of the rifle against her shoulder, looping the strap around her head and arm, with the barrel pointing downward. Happy that it was sitting comfortably and safely, she then set off in the direction of peak N11. The rocky escarpment that sat to the north of Wolfsreach Academy lacked the razor-sharp danger of the one that lay to the south, but that did not mean it was safe. Gravel-strewn, dusty paths led through the peaks. They were narrow and slippery from loose rocks and thin films of sand. The paths also tended to give way to sudden sharp falls, some down into the wide valley below, others down to hidden caves where no one would find the hapless victim.

Peak N11 was the third tallest of the protruding hills that stabbed out of the rocky escarpment, though they would be called mountains as measured from sea level – not that the planet had any bodies of water large enough to call a sea. Erosion by rock storms had created odd fingers of stone pointing out at different heights. The valley of Wolfsreach stretched out before her, seeming far below, though in truth the whole area stood at quite an altitude.

Why had the Confederation engineers decided to build their base so high up in an already oxygen-deprived environment? Julia speculated it must be for its obvious defensive merits – but what had they been defending against back then other than rock storms? The valley itself looked as though it had been weathered by water; it was easy to imagine a waterfall crashing over the landing platform and down the valley towards the school. If that had indeed caused the odd geography, it must have been eons ago. No river ran here, not even on the very rare occasions when it did rain. Instead, rain would run off the mountains, streaming into the valley below before sinking into the sandy ground of its surface and dropping into natural aquifers below the surface. The Confederation Engineers had taken advantage of this to create their own underground reservoirs beneath the valley to feed the whole Wolfsreach Base.

Julia had been jogging for ten minutes when she stopped to take a swig of water from her canteen. The lack of water up here above the valley meant that they had to carry their own fluids with them, though recently as part of the plans for the defence, stashes of water and food supplies had been hidden in small caves or under rocky shelfs, so they did not have to carry all of it with them when on patrol. There was the option of returning to the armoury through a small hidden hatch from which they had initially exited the underground facility onto the rock escarpment above. That had been when Simon had first sent them into these hills. It had been designed as an emergency escape route from the armoury, involving a long climb up a metal ladder to where it entered the rock, where it continued as a series of metal rungs hammered into the tunnelled stone. At the top was a heavy metal hatch, with both an electronic release or, if that failed, a wheel-like manual handle. It opened out into an open patch of flat stone in the mountains above.

It had clearly been designed as a last resort, as it was a very dangerous way to evacuate the staff in the armoury when compared with evacuating through the monorail station or via flyer through the great metal doors. Originally Travis had planned to use it to supply his squad in the northern mountains, but quickly realized it was too small and too precarious to be practical. After the attack on Armoury Station, Lieutenant Hakeswell had ordered explosives be attached to the hatch, which could be triggered if the Kylnnar discovered the entrance. While still usable, the cadets in the rocks above the armoury had no desire to test the theory. The defenders of the armoury had become noticeably paranoid since the assault on the station. After all, everyone was aware that if they lost the armoury, they lost the power plant, and then they were all dead.

Julia finished sipping her water and fished out a blue pill from the pouch at her belt. She swallowed it and chugged back some more water to keep it down. The other problem with Wolfstar III was the low oxygen atmosphere, at least compared with what was comfortable for humans, and this was further exacerbated by the altitude of the valley and its surrounding mountains. The cadets had chosen not to carry oxygen tanks. When they were laden down with kit, weapons, food, and water, even a light oxygen tank would have been too much additional weight, especially when stealth was required. Miss Murphy had instead issued them with tablets designed to deal with altitude sickness. In the low-oxygen environment of the planet, combined with the additional altitude of the mountains, they barely took the edge off the pressure on the cadets' lungs. Julia checked the time on her watch, noting when she could take another pill. She knew her lungs would be screaming by then.

She looked up at peak N11, which loomed over her as if she were standing under it. In reality, it was still twenty minutes' jog and climb to where she knew Travis was located.

She set off again using the winding rocky paths, which took her up gradually towards the peak. In a couple of places she had to sling her weapon behind her and scrabble across rocky surfaces, slipping and sliding on the smooth rock covered with a thin layer of grey sand. The dust got in her boots; she felt it rubbing between her toes. She cursed at that but was happy when it rubbed off on her standard-issue black uniform, giving it an impromptu camouflage look. Lack of camouflage was a major problem for her and the rest of Travis's soldiers. There had been none in the armoury; at least, none that fitted. The school cadets had been issued some long before the arrival of the Kylnnar for the purposes of the exercises, but it was green and brown camo more suitable for forest or jungle warfare. In the grey dust and stone of Wolfstar III it was not just useless, but positively dangerous. The cadets instead decided to stick with their black student uniforms. When teamed with grey flak jackets and black webbing and supplemented with dust and dirt they at least approached something that would blend in with the planet's environment.

As she neared where Travis was camped, she slowed to a stop to avoid being mistaken for an attacker. She fished out her communicator and tapped a button three times, causing a small red LED to flash on the top of it – the agreed signal for a friendly coming into camp. She waited for about thirty seconds, then her communicator flashed red three times – the indication that her presence had been acknowledged and was expected. She took a breath, although it did little good as her lungs were already hurting. She set off on the final leg.

The camp was set in a small, protective circle of rocks that prodded up out of the ground, forming a natural barricade. The mountain loomed above it, careering off at an odd angle to create a stone shelter above two thirds of the camp and disguising their presence from enemy drones. Julia slipped between two rocks into the rest area. There were five people present, half of the one squad under Travis's command. They sat, backs against the protective stones, rifles clutched in their hands. They all looked weary: lack of sleep and an unrelenting atmosphere was enough to exhaust you even before you did any fighting.

"Hey, corp," she chirped quietly to Corporal Mo Abdi.

Corporal Abdi looked her up and down without replying. Then the fifteen-year-old uncurled his lanky frame from where he was sitting and stood up without using his hands. Mo was of East African ancestry and his dark skin seemed to merge with the colour of his uniform. He stalked over to a pile of meal packs stacked in one corner of the camp and picked one up.

"You hungry?" his voice was a soft whisper. It sounded like a question, but he did not wait for an answer before throwing it to her.

Julia caught it, releasing her weapon to reach round and clutch the meal pack. "Thanks."

She shoved it in her webbing before dropping her backpack and weapon to the floor. That done, she pulled the meal pack out again and squeezed its heating chemical. It snapped with an audible crack, then a bubbling sound came from the soft matt grey container. She ripped open the packet at the top, and steam

131

rose from the contents. Waiting only a moment for it to dissipate, she held the pack to her mouth and squeezed the food in. She registered the flavours of tomato, beef and pasta. It burnt her tongue slightly, but she did not care as she was so famished.

"Took your time, private," Travis observed as he entered the camp, accompanied by another two squad members.

She could not decide if it was a statement or a question, so she carried on wolfing down her meal.

"I said, what took you so long?" demanded Sergeant Travis.

Okay, so it was a question, she realized. She found him quite annoying, but he was so damn handsome, which frankly made her angrier.

"It's a long way, sir," she offered, her mouth full. She hoped the 'sir' would placate him.

"Don't call me, sir," the sergeant muttered. "I work for a living."

It was an old army joke, and it sounded very strange coming from a teenager. Julia let it go. She could see the pressure he was under.

"You wanted me for something?" she asked, trying to change the subject.

"Yes; come with me," he ordered. "Mo, if we're not back in an hour, pull what is left of the squad back to the secondary location. You are to take command if we don't make it back."

That sounded serious. Julia sucked at her mouth. She wasn't worried; she just wanted to get the last of the pasta sauce off her teeth. She was still hungry.

Mo simply nodded his understanding at Travis.

"Follow me," Travis barked, his tone sharp but hushed.

He strode off the way he had come, followed by the two privates who had arrived with him. Julia shrugged, forcing herself not to check out Travis's disappearing rear. Mo helped her sling her pack over her shoulders. She gave him a smile of thanks. He returned it with a flash of white teeth against his dark face. She picked up her rifle and set off after the sergeant.

It was a ten-minute trudge, wending through paths in the rocky surface, like naturally occurring trenches, two thirds the height of a human male. As she was shorter than that, Julia's head barely stuck above the edge. Still, she crouched, trying to stay out of sight. The sergeant strode along, heedless of his safety.

The path gave way to a flat smooth rock surface that dropped away at an angle. Travis slid across the rock, disappearing out of sight where the stone surface dropped away. The two other cadets followed him, also disappearing out of sight. Trusting that they knew what they were doing, Julia slid after them. For a moment she regretted it as she dropped over the edge, fearing she was about to fall to her death to the stone platform spread out some forty feet underneath her. Before she could screech in terror, she saw the ledge below and thanked all the gods available for her life. She slid down onto what was a natural balcony ringed by a low barrier of rocks. The others were crouched down, trying to stay hidden behind the barrier. The other two members of the squad were there too, making it a squash when all six of them were compressed on the ledge. Luckily, the stones prevented any of them being pushed out to their death.

"You could have warned me," she muttered angrily.

Travis shot her a smirk and the rest smiled at her. They all went back to staring out through gaps in the rock to the open space below.

Julia crawled forward, pushing between members of the squad to reach the barrier of rocks. She brought herself up to a crouch next to Travis. She moved to unlock her scope from the rifle, but he motioned to her and proffered the set of field glasses he was holding. She scanned the landscape from her vantage point, realizing that had this small ledge not been here she would indeed have plunged to her death. To her left the mountains spread off into the distance. She knew the space port lay behind those peaks. In front, more than thirty feet below her vantage point, a wide expanse of rock spread off towards the horizon. To the right, the craggy surface dropped away in a gradual sweep, reaching the rock plain that lay before Wolfsreach Academy. From the ledge she could again appreciate that whoever had built the base at Wolfsreach, long before it had become a military school, had done so with defence in mind.

Travis tapped Julia on the shoulder and pointed out across the plain. She could make out figures off in the distance. She handed back the glasses and looked across the plain with the naked eye. The hulking figures of the reptiles looked tiny and unthreatening from this distance. It made her appreciate that the pebbles that scattered the rocky plain were in fact boulders. She watched the Kylnnar pick their way between them. She counted four squads' worth of reptile soldiers, moving methodically towards the higher ground she and Travis's squad were hidden on. She wondered where they had landed. She could see no landers; maybe they had come from the space port, or perhaps the reptiles had landed them elsewhere. There were enough rocky outcrops obscuring the landscape to hide a host of landers, but the uneven terrain was not at all accommodating for landing larger transports. So, either they had been dropped and the landers had returned to space, or they had come from the space sport and were sweeping around in a flanking manoeuvre.

She raised her rifle, using the scope to scan across the soldiers. She could see no packs and harnesses, so she guessed they had come from the space port.

"Can you hit them?" Travis whispered.

She respected his caution; at this distance there was negligible risk of being overheard, but as these mountains could create strange echoes it was better to be careful.

"A little closer would be easier, but yes. They are over a mile out currently."

"Aim for the officers," he ordered.

"Is that allowed?" she asked, not really caring.

She knew the traditions of war; targeting officers exclusively was disapproved of. She also knew that snipers did that very thing. Travis shot her a frown.

"No problem, sir; just checking. Just thinking of you in case they return the favour," she said with a grin.

"I'm a sergeant, not an officer," he observed.

"Well, here's hoping the reptiles will make that distinction," she offered with a raised eyebrow.

She flipped down the small tripod of her weapon, resting it on the rock in front of her, nudging aside one of the other cadets to give her the space. It was not her favoured firing position; she preferred to be lying down. She was lightly built, and it would be a struggle to control the recoil of the Mark VII against her shoulder. Between the narrowness of the ledge and the height of the rock shelf that was the only option. She calmed her breathing and felt the light waft of air coming from the east across her right cheek.

"Load with a tracker round," Travis ordered quietly in her ear.

A look of annoyance crept across her face; she would have to start her preparations again.

"Yes, sergeant," she acknowledged.

She moved the rifle off her shoulder and flipped a setting on the stock of her weapon. A small electronic tracker would be injected into the plasma shot as it fired. It was specially shielded so that it would, in most cases, survive the plasma shot's contact with its target, leaving an exact geolocation that could be tracked.

She reshouldered the weapon and again took slow, measured breaths. She rested her eye near the sight, not touching, aware of the recoil. She judged the wind, and her scope started to play across the approaching Kylnnar figures. They were closer now; about a mile out.

The Kylnnar were wearing full helmets, with tinted visors pulled down across their lizard-like faces. Perhaps they did not like the sun on this arid world, or maybe they were struggling with its lack of oxygen even more than the cadets. She scanned down, looking for an oxygen tank on the belts, but could not see any. *Pity*, she thought; that would have turned a plasma shot into a small explosion. *Maybe it was built into the suit*, she speculated. She looked for rank markings, but there was little sign of any. She noted a small number with what looked like white claw marks against the blue-grey of their helmets. Stylized like an animal's claw slash, it went down across the top of the headgear and the side of the visor in three stripes. It could just be a bravery mark or something else, but Julia's best guess was that these were the officers.

Her scope played across another figure so quickly that she almost missed him as she moved to the next grey-armoured Kylnnar.

The figure had not stood out from the Kylnnar because of his height; he was north of six feet and comparable to one of the reptiles. It was his rangy form that contrasted so markedly with the Kylnnar. Long limbs sprouted from a thin frame. A wide cavernous chest narrowed almost like a triangle to a tiny waist. Robes the colour of the grey sand were thrown over loose-fitting white trousers that whipped gently in the wind. The clothes and body were perfectly adapted to the environment of Wolfstar III. He was human, but barely: one of the Colonials who had long made this planet their home. She looked for signs of coercion: a leash, a chain, discomfort in the man's walk or face. She saw none. This human was acting as a scout for the reptiles, against his own people, she surmised, and anger filled her.

She made a decision and disobeyed her orders. A mile out, the plasma shot took the Colonial through his narrow face. She watched the figure drop to the ground. She immediately sighted on the nearest Kylnnar officer and shot him through the chest. She sighted a third, and the plasma shot missed, grazing his armoured arm.

The cliff top was lit up with fire as the advancing Kylnnar took cover and unleashed a storm of pulse shots up against the cadets. Luckily, they had not seen the location from which the sniper's discharge had come and were just firing to suppress the incoming attack. Julia hoisted down her Mark VII and took cover behind the rocks to avoid the sporadic attacks. The other students in the squad were crouched as low as they could as they sheltered. Travis was almost flat on his belly.

"I said officers first," he hissed at Julia.

"They have a Colonial; a human scouting for them," she retorted.

A look of surprise crossed the sergeant's face, but he dismissed it from his thoughts. This attack was the priority.

"Team two, this is team one!" he shouted into the communicator over the noise of the incoming plasma explosions.

"Yes, sir," Mo replied softly.

"Give me the code," Travis demanded to Julia.

She looked down at the rifle.

"Alpha, Charlie, One, Three, Nine, Six, Foxtrot, Zulu," she read out.

Travis repeated it down the communicator.

"Acknowledged," came Mo's response.

"Fire on that mark," Travis ordered.

There was a pop in the distance. A mortar shell sailed over the heads of the cadets of squad one and exploded a mile away among the Kylnnar. It threw up a cloud of earth and fire, devouring Kylnnar soldiers in its embrace. A second shell was already in the air. It slammed into the ground nearly on top of the first, spraying more destruction in its wake. The Kylnnar were moving back now, and the fire at the cliffs had dropped to a few isolated blasts.

"Time to move," instructed Travis.

A third mortar shell spiralled over them and detonated out on the plain with a thunderous roar. The Kylnnar were pulling back now so it did little but distract them.

Travis boosted Julia up onto the slippery rock and she scrabbled across the flat surface until she got back to the path above. The others followed her, with Travis bringing up the rear. The Kylnnar must have spotted them. A few plasma bolts smashed into the rocks. One caught a member of the squad, a fifteen-year-old girl, who screamed as she slipped down the rocks, spiralling past the ledge and out into the void beyond. Travis grabbed for her, but she was too far away. He just hoped the plasma blast had killed her before she hit the ground.

CHAPTER 14

"What was her name?" Julia asked.

"Zoe," Travis replied, his face riven with sadness.

The group sat in a loose circle in their camp in the shadow of peak N11. They might have looked like scouts gathered around a campfire, except there was no fire, not even a jumbled circle of stones to contain one. Instead, a pile of used military meal packs created a dull silver-grey focus point at the centre.

"Zoe Green?" Julia's voice, while low, held a hint of incredulity.

Travis looked at her, confused. The group had sat mainly in silence for the brief period of time since they had got back to the camp. There had been some hushed comments about food, but no substantive conversation. Travis was surprised that it was the usually taciturn sniper who had started the conversation.

"Yes, Zoe Green," Travis confirmed.

"Didn't recognize her without the hair," Julia shrugged.

That prompted a low chirp of laughter from the female members of the squad. Travis just looked more confused.

"I mean, I guess going to war with all that hairspray on would be a risk. It would be an explosion hazard for starters," the sniper continued.

"What are you talking about?"

"Just didn't realize it was her, not without the big hair, face all squished in an infantry helmet, that was all."

Laughter rippled through the group; not just the females this time.

"Bit dark, Jules," Mo said.

Julia searched his face – it sounded like a criticism, but she couldn't tell. She felt exhausted and she knew her mouth had run ahead of her.

"Sorry, just thinking out loud," she apologized.

Travis scrutinized her; she had been the one doing the killing, so it was only to be expected it would have some dehumanizing impact. He would have berated her in a normal situation, but this was so far from a normal situation he had nothing to offer. She seemed more affected this time around than after her actions against the Kylnnar on the platform. Maybe it was cumulative; maybe it was the loss of Zoe. He suspected it was her decision to shoot down one of the Colonials. In his mind at least it was easy to separate the Kylnnar from humanity. The reptiles were different and animal-like; something that could be killed without regret. Their genocidal nature made them something different; something other. That was not true of the Colonial. Killing another human must be harder, he supposed. He did not know as he had never done it. The Colonials may have been off-putting in their behaviour and traditions – at least they had been on the rare occasions one of them had come to Wolfsreach – and they may have been odd-looking, but they were still demonstrably human. He did not understand why they were helping the Kylnnar against their own kind. He also struggled to comprehend why the Kylnnar had not killed the Colonial outright. Every newscast he had watched, everything he had read, told him that the Kylnnar slaughtered Confederation citizens on contact. Why were the Colonials being treated differently?

"The Colonial," Travis asked Julia. "Was he being coerced?"

"I don't know; it did not feel like that," the sniper replied.

"What does that mean?" he demanded.

"There was no leash, no chains, no shock collar, nothing I could see," she replied with a shrug.

"So, it could have been a gun at his back," the sergeant offered.

"Maybe. I don't know," she shrugged again.

"But you said he was scouting. You shot him because he was scouting for them?"

Travis's urgency felt unpleasant to Julia. She wanted him to back off. He had turned in her direction, and he looked as though he wanted to grab her and shake the answer out of her.

"It's just a feeling, sergeant; I can't be sure," she tried to explain.

"You want to cut her some slack, Travis?" Mo said, his tone low but concerned.

The sergeant slumped angrily back against the rock and gave the pile of empty meal packs a frustrated kick.

"A *feeling*," he said, his tone dismissive. "What can you *feel* a mile away down a sniper scope?"

"You'd be surprised: there's something about seeing someone in the cross hairs that gives you an insight. It's hard to explain," Julia offered lamely.

"Why would the Kylnnar need a scout? I reckon you just shot a prisoner," Travis observed with a hint of nastiness.

If Julia heard the barb, she did not react. Instead, her eyebrows were posed in thought.

"Say that again?" she asked.

"I said, I reckon you just shot…"

"No! the first bit," she interrupted him.

"Why would the Kylnnar need a scout?" he replied.

"Why would the Kylnnar need a scout?" she muttered a couple of times under her breath.

She pushed herself to her feet and looked like she might start pacing – not that there was enough room in the camp for that. Instead, she stared up at peak N11, which loomed over their camp.

"Why did Lieutenant Kim put us here?" she asked.

"To protect the school's northern flank. Stop anyone coming up into the mountains and down towards the school," he replied.

"So, we figured they would come from the landing platform. That's why we mined that route, blew up ledges and overhangs, did everything to make that difficult or impossible. Those paths are obvious if now arduous, but they didn't come that way: they came over the plain with a Colonial," Julia summarized.

"Is there a point?" asked Travis, though he was now fascinated not frustrated.

"How were they going to get up here?" Julia swung her arm around for emphasis.

"Climb, I guess?" supplied the sergeant.

"What, thirty or forty feet in full kit?" she queried.

"Why not?" replied Travis. "We climbed more than three times that to get up here. Sure, we did it up the armoury ladder not up a rock face, but we still did it."

"Why would they need a Colonial for that?" Julia queried.

"I don't know?"

"Could there be a path up?" she asked.

A look of alarm crossed Travis's face; he knew where she was going with this.

"I don't know. I wouldn't know. This planet is hardly welcoming; we're not encouraged to go wandering. I know these hills, because Inaya and I used to come up here, but that was from the paths near the landing platform." Travis waved his hand in the direction of the space port back down the valley.

"Urgh, that's an insight into your love life I didn't need, Travis," said Mo, screwing up his face.

The sergeant shot him a look of annoyance.

"What if there is a path up? What if that is what the Colonial was showing them?" Julia continued her argument.

"It's possible," conceded Travis. "It would be a problem for us. If they could get enough soldiers up here to drive us off the mountains then they would have overwatch on the academy."

"They could assault down the cliffs into the school," Julia suggested.

"No, they can't: those cliffs are forty feet high; the cadets in the school would slaughter them as they rappelled down them," Travis countered.

"Even with them having troops firing down on the academy from up here?" the sniper asked.

"Even then, maybe they could get a pulse cannon up here, or a bunch of sharpshooters, but not anything big enough to force our heads down. At least not for long enough to allow them to get troops down the cliff without losing most of them."

"What about mortars?"

"Won't work," he grunted. "The shield."

Travis pointed off in the direction of the school. The shimmer of the barrier could be seen resting above the school. The fringe of it rested about ten feet above the rocky escarpment on which they were seated. They were outside its protection, being several hundred yards away from its edge and thirty feet or so above it. Firing a mortar on the cliff from outside the shield would result in it exploding on impact with the shield as it dropped towards the school. Firing one from the small part of the cliff that was covered by the shield would be even worse. It would explode on impact with the shield on the rising part of its arc, showering the crew and surrounding troops with their own ordnance.

"If the Colonials know a secret way up onto these hills, then maybe they know a way down into the valley?" Julia speculated.

"I may not know the other side of this rock escarpment, but I know the valley. The only path down from this side is near the space port, and they already control that. Obviously not counting the armoury ladder," Travis clarified.

"On this side..." muttered Julia. "I need to check something."

In a swift motion she picked up her pack and rifle and headed out of camp.

"Where's she going?" asked Travis.

Mo shrugged.

"Where are you going?" the sergeant whisper-shouted after her.

Julia ignored him. She circled round to the left and up a narrow shale path that would take her up towards the top of peak N11. Loose stone skittered and tumbled under her feet, but she continued her ascent. It got tougher as she got higher. Julia dropped to her hands and knees, crawling upwards to avoid slipping down to the rocks below her. She felt horribly exposed out here on the open path up to the peak. The morning light from Wolfstar shone across the crystals in the rocks, changing their colour from a greyish tinge to a sparkling yellow. Julia's black clothing and drab grey equipment was providing no camouflage, but she did not care: she had to check her hunch.

The path stopped, giving way to a flat rockface. Above was a ledge and above that the final peak of the mountain. The ledge would give her the perfect vantage point. She climbed the rockface, dragging her body up by her hands, silently regretting bringing her pack with her. She struggled onto the ledge, which was big enough to accommodate her and the kit she carried but not much else. She gasped; up here she really felt the thinness of the oxygen. She rustled in her pack for another of the blue pills. Glancing at her watch, she knew it was too soon, but she didn't care. It felt like her lungs were crushing her. She took out her canteen and swallowed another pill. A moment later she fainted.

Ten minutes later she came round, nearly rolling off the ledge as she did so. She clasped at the rocks to stop from falling to her death, and adrenaline pulsed through her. Sudden terror sent her heart thundering. She clawed her way back onto the ledge and rested against the stone of the mountain. She took several big gasps of air and realized her lungs were no longer screaming but her vision was hazy. She should not have taken two of the pills so close together. It took several minutes for her panic to subside and her vision to clear.

She pulled over her Mark VII and cushioned it against her shoulder, resting the rifle on her upraised knee. Not a great firing position, but she was not shooting: she was looking. She was over a hundred feet above the school. She could see it to her left off in the distance. The armoury was to her right; she could see the remnants of the two destroyed towers sprouting from the wall, shimmering under the protection of the shield. In the distance she could see the space port. She watched the light show as the school and landing platform exchanged pulse and laser fire. The military laser was weaving side to side up the valley, forcing the Kylnnar to keep their heads down.

She looked across the valley to the opposite side. The southern side of the valley was rocky hills like those to the north, but lower. They also dropped away quickly as they ran down the valley from the space port to the Academy, finishing in a stubby group of rocks next to the school. From this distance it did not look like it would provide much of a barrier for the Academy's defenders' southern flank. The reason it did was given away by how it looked in the sunlight: it sparkled like glass; in some places, it shone so strongly it was hard to look at. The crystals in the rock reflected the light from the sun. They also made the rock razor-sharp, lethal to anyone foolish enough to try and move over it.

Some of the more foolish students of the academy, especially recent arrivals, would not believe the warnings of teachers and even other students. They would use the path-like gulley behind the gym that led up into the southern peaks: a way to prove their bravery or their superiority, or simply to rebel against authority. They would soon be disabused of their youthful arrogance when they returned with slashed clothing and a body covered with lacerations. In the worst cases, the teachers would have to go in and retrieve a particularly precocious and hapless pupil who had made it further in than most. The teachers, wearing the heaviest body armour in the base's inventory, would go in and carry out the bloody, passed-out form of a student. The pupil would then spend the next couple of weeks in the infirmary recovering, often for part of the time with one of the teachers who had dragged them out as they recuperated from the wounds suffered during the rescue. Meanwhile, the military staff in the armoury would be busy repairing the rents and tears in the armour the teachers had used. There were, of course, legends of pupils who had never been recovered from the southern hills and whose ghosts could be heard wailing through the rocks. It was a good story to explain the odd howling sound the rocks produced when the wind blew through them a certain way.

Musing on all this, Julia was genuinely shocked by what she was seeing. There were figures moving through the rocks. She rubbed her eyes and looked back through her scope. Part of her was telling her it must be a mirage; maybe it was the after-effects of the pill she had taken. The light glinting, almost burning, off the rocks made them hard to focus on. Despite her brain trying to tell her it was impossible, her eyes told her it was

146

real: the Kylnnar were moving through the rocks of the southern hills towards the school. Their dark blue uniforms blended with the grey of the rocks; their forms disappeared completely in the shining, blinding light of the crystalline rock.

How were they doing it? she wondered. Was their armour strong enough to get through? Maybe they did not realize the task they had taken on. She quietly smiled at the thought of the reptiles being sliced up in the rocks. Then she caught sight of something else that struck dread in the pit of her stomach. It was hard to make them out at first, as their flowing grey robes merged with the rock, and their lithe forms moved quickly and confidently through the hills, but there were Colonials among the Kylnnar. They knew a way through the rocks. She could not tell how, but she was certain that the Colonials were guiding the Kylnnar along a hidden path. There was something in the way they moved through the rocks. It was not only the odd route they were taking – cutting back on themselves before moving forward again – it was the speed with which they were moving, like a person who knows how to get to the centre of a maze.

So focused was the sniper on the advancing reptiles and their human allies that she did not see or hear the Kylnnar fighter as it dropped from orbit. It spun as it banked down from space, then pulled up sharply as it disappeared out of sight behind the space port. It swept round behind the landing platform, using the mountains as cover to obscure it from the school and the valley below, careful not to expose itself to the military laser it knew was waiting for it. Its plasma engines hissed quietly as it skimmed the surface of the rocky plain below the mountains – a dangerous move for the pilot, as it potentially placed the fighter in the sights of the cadets in the hills, but less of a risk than facing the military lasers. The fighter banked higher coming off the plain, aiming for peak N11.

Distracted, Julia only heard it when the plasma engines turned from a hiss to a roar as it raced towards the mountain. She looked around as the fighter opened fire. She threw herself off her vantage point, slipping and sliding down the smooth stones to the rocky gravel of the path below. The mountain exploded in a shower of stone shrapnel, covering the sniper. She screamed in pain as shards of stone ripped through her clothing and body armour, opening up bloody welts on her arms, chest, and face. Sobbing in pain, she focused on the survival of the school. She grabbed her comm from her belt and called Travis.

"You okay?" his worried voice gargled over the comm.

"Sergeant," she ignored his question. "The Kylnnar are moving through the southern hills – they're going to flank the school!"

Travis struggled to comprehend what she was saying. His own squad had been hit with debris from the attack and two were wounded.

"Say again," he said.

"The Kylnnar are moving through the southern hills – you have to call it in!" She wondered if she should call Flex herself, but there was a chain of command.

"Understood," Travis barked back.

She heard another roar. Julia looked up. She had lost her vantage point, so craned around the rocks. Was the fighter coming back? She could see it off in the distance, heading for orbit in an upward spiral. She never saw the two bombers that had followed it in. They dropped their payload. Peak N11 exploded outwards as the bombs contacted, sending the rocks of the mountain streaming down its sides. The sniper specialist, Private Julia Williams, never had time to cry out.

CHAPTER 15

Location: Wolfsreach Academy, Wolfstar III
Date: 19 December 2196 CE, Earth Standard Calendar
Time: 08.55 Local Time 26.5-hour clock

The glass-like rocks of the southern hills sparkled in the morning sun, showering occasional prismatic rainbows across the gym wall. Mostly it shone with a burning white light that made it difficult for anyone to look at it for a sustained period. A squad of six cadets were seated between the gym building and the glassy surface of the rock, tasked with holding the gap between the rockface and the gym building. They had seen action during the Kylnnar's initial drop trooper attack. It had originally been a squad of ten. One was now in the dining hall's makeshift hospital. One was in the morgue. Another two had been pulled off to somewhere else by Lieutenant Kim, no doubt plugging a gap somewhere else in the line.

They were crouched down behind a low barrier made of metal and wood furniture dragged out of the school building to give them some protection. It was a largely illusory barrier; a pulse weapon would have blown straight through it. It had been thrown together in the two hours since the last assault. Some protection was better than none.

The squad was tired; they had been awake most of the night. Then the main assault had come. They had experienced less fighting than those further down the line, but they had still experienced casualties. Two of the squad stood staring out towards the rock plain, scanning for attack. In the far distance, figures that might be the reptiles could be seen moving around on the ridge where the rock plain dropped away, allowing the Kylnnar to remain largely out of sight. The occasional shot roared out from the school targeting the distant figures, but at this range it was largely a forlorn hope. In the imaginations of the cadets, great hordes of Kylnnar warriors in serried ranks were waiting to attack just out of sight.

The other four cadets were clustered in a circle, chattering about nothing in particular, making off-colour jokes and rude remarks to each other. None of them were watching to the rear. That was protected by the student barracks buildings, fire-scarred but still usable. The barracks were currently filled with younger, less experienced cadets, whose job it was to face any attack coming down the valley from the space port. They were even more confident about the protection that the southern hills gave them. All of them knew the stories of their razor-sharp impenetrability and the treacherous gully that ran down from the glassy hills, looking invitingly like a path for those who knew no better.

Ten armoured Kylnnar stole quietly out of the gully, moving with surprisingly imperceptible stealth for such large creatures. It was only a hundred yards to reach the weary, unaware cadets. The reptiles carried no pulse rifles. Instead, the Kylnnar grasped long daggers in their hands, looking more like a medieval falchion than a modern weapon. Their single long blade had a wickedly serrated edge. The creatures fell on the teenage cadets before they could let out a single scream. It was simple butchery.

Had the reptiles shown the patience to wait until night the surprise might have been total. At least the cadets would have been confused as to what was happening. For whatever reason, the Kylnnar seemed to be under time pressure to take the base, and that had forced their hand. The students on the gym roof heard the commotion, poking their heads over the parapet to see the battle below. They opened up with their pulse rifles, but the Kylnnar were already gone. They could be heard entering the gym below, to the alarm of the defenders.

Simon Kim's comm was a crackle of shouts and panic as he dashed down the corridor of the main school building towards the dining room. Ducking through the main door, he gave Helen the barest of nods before running across the hall. He jinxed round the prone forms on the beds and the medical staff. He used the small door that led out of the side of the hall into the kitchens. The door, the service type they used for kitchens, thumped softly as he thrust through it. It gave the squad of five cadets in the room a sudden shock. They looked back. One, a sergeant, from his insignia, raised his pulse rifle before dropping back.

Sergeant Andrei Popov was a serious, pale-skinned, blond-haired fellow, whose hangdog looks were exacerbated by his teenage gloom. He swung back to look out the narrow window at the top of the kitchen. His four colleagues were arrayed next to him, pulse rifles pushed through loops cut out in the durable transparent plastic of the windowpanes. Spurts of plasma fire were spitting out from the kitchen. The energy discharge from the power packs was heating the air in the room, giving it a cloying feeling, as if someone had left the cookers on.

The cadets had pushed the workstations, large stainless-steel affairs, up against the walls to use as makeshift platforms on which to stand and fire from. Simon clambered up next to the other students.

151

"Report, sergeant," he demanded.

"See for yourself," came the surly response.

Simon looked out from the kitchen. As with all the buildings, the first storey was half buried in the ground, so he was looking out at knee height across the flat artificial turf of the astro-hockey court. It was hard to tell what was going on from this low angle. He desperately wished he were on the roof or somewhere with a better vantage point.

The door banged behind and Simon whirled round, his pulse rifle coming up. He dropped it down as he recognized Jo Hakeswell in the doorway. She was breathing hard, a bead of sweat moving slowly down across her forehead.

"You called, sir?" she asked, bestowing a rare smile on her commanding officer.

"Yes," Simon affirmed, seeming momentarily caught in his thoughts.

Then, as if making up his mind, he clapped Sergeant Popov on his shoulder and slid off the countertop. He bent his knees to cushion himself as he landed, the metal of his pulse rifle clanking loudly against the steel of the kitchen unit.

"Stay here and keep up the fire. Be aware we will be breaking out, so don't shoot our own people," he ordered Andrei.

"Sir," came the grunted reply.

"Lieutenant Hakeswell, on me," he ordered, pushing past his number two and out into the dining hall.

Twenty fully equipped cadets stood clustered in the hall. Each grasped a pulse rifle in nervous hands, sweat dripping from fearful brows. Joanna had made her two squads run here from the barracks block, using the main school building to protect them as she had brought them round in a semicircle. She did not know why Simon wanted to attack from here as opposed to simply coming out of the barracks, but orders were orders.

"This is a hospital, not a barracks. If you are not injured, you need to leave!" Helen's commanding voice cut through Joanna's thoughts.

She looked up to see the medical orderly staring at them angrily. She was dressed in green medical scrubs marked with blood. She looked exhausted.

"We'll be on our way soon enough," Simon shot back, harsher than he intended. Ignoring her glare, he turned back to face the group of cadets. They were doing their best not to get in the way of the hospital patients and medical personnel, entirely unsuccessfully.

"The gym is under assault. Numerous Kylnnar have come out of the southern rocks, and we face being overrun," he summarized quickly.

"The southern rocks? That's impossible," blurted out one of the older cadets.

"Apparently not." Simon's voice was acid; it was unclear if his anger was at the interruption or his own error in underestimating the reptiles.

"We are going out on to the astro-hockey field. We have to hold the enemy back, or we will be overrun. It will take time for the enemy to back their attack with reserves across the rock plain. It is vital that we deal with the force that came through the southern hills before the enemy can bring up reserves. Everyone got their rifles?" he demanded.

"Sir," rang their replies.

"Combat knives?"

"Sir," the replies were less confident now.

"On me!" Simon's roar was met with an equal shout from his soldiers.

He never saw the anger and sadness on Miss Murphy's face as he pushed through the cadets towards the back door of the dining hall. He went through the exit into the sharp brightness of the morning light. The two lieutenants and their twenty cadets streamed up the steps. The gym building was directly in front of them; the astro-hockey pitch to their right. The Kylnnar had assaulted the gym; the sounds of fighting and screams of the injured could be heard emanating from the structure. The gym was a single floor, but double height. It was also the only building with a pitched roof, dull grey metal polished white in places by the planet's scouring sand. A gantry round the edge behind a low parapet provided a vantage point for a single squad of cadets to defend the building.

The reptiles seemed unconcerned by the withering fire from above and had made their way into the gym. Simon knew what they were after; the one thing that was a real threat to the invasion force: the military laser. Of the three they had, one had already been lost. He could not let them destroy this one. Kylnnar were also flooding out of the hills across the astro-hockey pitch, heedless of the fire they were taking from the main school building and the barrack blocks.

Simon cursed there was no entrance to the gym from this side of the building; they would have to go round, to the side where a pair of double doors led out up a small ramp from the gym onto the sports field. The squads dashed to the wall of the gym building and pressed themselves against it.

"We've got movement across the rock plain," Flex's voice crackled in his ear.

Simon shut off his comm. He did not have time for that now.

He edged along the side of the wall, trying to keep any cover from the fire coming across the hockey pitch. They turned the corner, ready to make the gym entrance. The double doors exploded outwards, careering up the ramp onto the hockey pitch. The cadets threw themselves flat as fire and smoke billowed out from the doorway. A Kylnnar figure, clearly injured, staggered out of the doors. Jo drew her pistol and shot him in the head.

"The laser," a stunned Simon muttered.

"Gone, is my guess," Jo observed unhelpfully.

He shot her a frown, but she was already racing towards the charging Kylnnar, her pistol cracking out round after round.

"Attack!" he screamed.

He charged in after her, his run turning into a leap, and the butt of his rifle coming up to smash into the face of the attacking Kylnnar, The pair went down in a bundle. He fumbled his pulse rifle around and pumped two shells into the prone form of the Kylnnar soldier. He smelt the horrid stench of burnt flesh. It was only for a moment, then he was suddenly lifted into the air and sent spiralling, legs flailing. He landed with an audible thump on the abrasive surface of the artificial turf, coughing as the air was knocked from him.

Then his attacker was on him. The Kylnnar was twice the lieutenant's bulk and taller. He rained down blows against the human's face. Simon did not have time to be thankful that the creature lacked a gun or a blade. He twisted his hips, bringing his legs round, and brought both his feet down on the side of the reptile's head in a powerful kick, which dazed him. Pulling his feet into his body, he kicked out straight to the face of the creature, both heels connecting with a sickening crunch. Simon clambered out from under his attacker and searched around for his pulse rifle, lying on the ground a few yards away. He crawled towards it. Suddenly he was tossed in the air again, then slammed into a Kylnnar and cadet fighting nearby. All three were sent sprawling in the dirt.

Simon pushed himself up, ducking to the right to avoid his incoming attacker. He skipped in, twisting as he did, and hook kicked the creature in the face. Without resetting, his foot dropped down and slammed sideways into the creature's leg, dropping him to his knees. He gave an audible grunt. Simon pulled his combat knife from his belt and plunged it into the gap between the neck and shoulder. It grated on armour; he pulled it out before lifting the reptile's arm and plunging the blade into the armpit,

155

then side-kicked the Kylnnar in the face. He staggered over to his pulse rifle, snatched it up and shot the Kylnnar soldier just to make sure.

Simon looked around him. Smoke was billowing out from the gym, obscuring the hockey pitch. Pulse fire continued to spray across the battlefield. More reptiles were coming out of the rocks. He picked out Jo: through the smoke, she was firing a Kylnnar pulse rifle from the hip in a desperate attempt to hold back the attacking soldiers. Where had she got the weapon? Stone exploded out from the gym wall. Simon looked around: two enemy soldiers had emerged from the rocks with handheld rocket launchers. A second missile punched through the main school building, scattering stone and plastic across the battlefield. Simon hefted his pulse rifle and took a shot at one of them, but the figure was ducking and diving and it went wide. He reached up to his ear and switched his earpiece back on.

"We've got hundreds of Kylnnar coming across the rock field!" Flex screeched in his ear.

"Shut up, Flex," Simon practically roared down the line. "Everyone on the hockey field and the gym area, pull back to the dining hall before we're overrun!"

Jo and her squad were already pushed up against the kitchen building. Another missile from a Kylnnar rocket launcher slammed into the low roof of the kitchen, sending the students sprawling. Her ears ringing, Joanna pushed herself to her feet, and dragged up the student next to her. They continued firing as the others pulled themselves up to a crouch. What was left of the other squad was already running for the dining room, the nearest entrance into the main building.

Simon, using the corner of the gym for cover, was firing his pulse rifle at the charging mass of Kylnnar, killing two and wounding others. He looked over his shoulder. Joanna had pulled her squad back to the dining room entrance. She was now lying on the steps, firing across the astro-hockey pitch towards the

156

enemy. Simon made a dash towards the dining room, the Kylnnar hot on his heels. In his imagination he could feel their searing, fetid breath on his neck, although he did not have time to look behind.

He threw himself down the steps, tumbling in a heap past Jo. He brought up his rifle and shot the Kylnnar who was looming above the steps. He crawled up the bank on one side of the step so he was lying flat next to his fellow lieutenant and opened fire.

"Thought officers weren't supposed to be fighting," she observed sardonically. Her gaze never wavered as she continued to fire at the approaching Kylnnar with a cold detachment.

A Kylnnar ran forward, grenade in hand, and Jo shot her in the throat. The reptile collapsed to the ground, and the grenade went off with a snap, sending shrapnel, earth and bits of Kylnnar spiralling into the air and over the prone humans. They thrust their faces into the sandy surface of the bank, hot metal dropping down on to their uniforms and helmets. Jo screamed in pain as burning shrapnel fell into the small gap between her neck and shoulder. Luckily, it was secondary scatter from the grenade rather than its initial fragmentation, so the damage was superficial.

"Get the hospital clear. No way we can hold them here – we need them in the buildings where their size works against them. I'll cover you!" Simon shouted his orders over the roar of battle.

Jo nodded and quickly shimmied down the sandy bank, heedless of her black uniform. She crawled through the door into the dining hall.

Lieutenant Hakeswell pulled herself to her feet, coming up to find a pulse rifle in her face.

"Do I look like a reptile, cadet?" she asked the young girl opposite her clutching the rifle. She looked fourteen. Jo could not remember her name.

"Sorry, sir, ma'am, sir," the girl jabbered.

"The gun?" asked Jo, fearful that the cadet might shoot in a state of nerves.

The weapon was lowered.

"Sorry, ma'am," the girl responded more calmly. Her eyes, though, were anything but calm. She was terrified, her whole body shaking uncontrollably.

Joanna surveyed the room. Bloodied figures of cadets were being bandaged, escapees from the gym explosion and those injured in the battle of the hockey pitch. At the far end, Helen was busy operating on a gravely injured student who lay on the makeshift operating table. Focused on the job in front of her, the medical orderly seemed uninterested in the cluster of soldiers now filling her hospital.

"Clear the hospital. Evacuate them through the main block to the science block. Grab any medicine and tech you can!" she shouted. "If you can walk, run. If they need support, help them. If not, carry them."

The stunned and injured occupants moved slowly. Jo started pushing them, grabbing up supplies and thrusting them into soldiers' arms. She pulled up the wounded, who squeaked in protest, then thrust them towards the door that led into the corridor of the main building.

"Flex, we are evacuating the hospital. We need people to cover. Flex? Flex!" she shouted into her comm. There was no reply. Where was the damn geek?

Helen Murphy ignored all the commotion, focused on the patient in front of her. The room was in pandemonium. Injured soldiers, clasping the shoulders of their comrades, limped towards the door. Medical orderlies tried to push through the door with stretchers.

There was a bang behind Jo. She whirled around. It was the slam of the kitchen door; the squad was pulling out of the room. Sergeant Popov pushed through the retreating mass towards Jo.

"Lieutenant, we've got big problem." His Slavic-accented English made it only seem worse.

"What?" Jo demanded.

The double doors at the end of the dining room exploded inwards. The form of Simon Kim was flung across the room, skittering across the smooth stone surface of the temporary hospital, scattering chairs and camp beds in his wake. Jo ran forward and squatted down next to her commander. He was bruised, battered and bleeding from several small cuts, but he was conscious.

"You okay?" she asked.

"Oh, yeah, I'm great," he answered. "Fire on the door."

Jo did not question it; she lifted her rifle and started pumping pulse shots out into the sunlight, heedless of a target. Popov joined her, followed by several others. The first Kylnnar died on his way through the door. So did the second. The third had the presence of mind to use the body of his hapless colleague as a shield from the incoming rain of plasma. Then the Kylnnar were in the room: one, then a second, then half a dozen.

Simon thrust Jo to the side, pushing her out of the way of a slashing Kylnnar falchion. He pulled out his combat knife and stabbed it repeatedly into the creature's leg. It dropped to eye level with the lieutenant. It had a cruel, angry curl to its lips, as though it would bite him. Simon used his pistol and shot it through the head. Popov was not so lucky: a Kylnnar boot crashed into his chest, crushing his ribs. He gasped for air as he dropped to the floor, and the Kylnnar emptied his own pulse weapon into the teenager.

Simon was pushing Jo towards the opposite door.

"Get them out!" he bellowed into her ear.

She nodded in recognition. She was screaming at the injured, pushing and dragging them towards the door. Helen remained, working single-mindedly on her injured charge.

Simon turned, catching a Kylnnar's long dagger on his own combat knife. He slammed his combat boot upward in a sweeping kick to the gap between the reptile's legs. On a human that would have been enough, but Kylnnar biology was different. The creature registered a look of annoyance, but it did not slow down. Simon caught another slashing movement on his knife. His muscles ached with weariness; the reptile was much stronger than him.

Jo was at the exit, and turned back. Simon was fighting off one of the Kylnnar, but another ten were advancing down the hall. Helen still stood at the table operating, seemingly unaware of the battle around her. Jo took a breath and sighted on the reptile attacking her fellow lieutenant. Simon felt the sear of plasma heat pass far too close to his face for comfort, burning his knife hand with fire. He dropped the blade with a yelp. The Kylnnar in front of him seemed to be teetering side to side in front of him. It took him a moment to realize the left side of its head and shoulder were gone. Simon thrust out both hands, pushing the Kylnnar's body into his oncoming colleagues, and made a dash for the door.

Jo was crouched down by the door, firing into the room, trying to pick off the approaching attackers. Simon rushed forward to the operating table.

"Helen, we have to go," he gasped.

She looked up at him and put down the cauterizer.

"Take him." It was an order, not a request.

Simon picked up the injured cadet in both arms, nearly staggering under the weight. Helen pushed the pair in the direction of the door.

"Ma'am, look out!" Jo screamed from the doorway.

A Kylnnar fist grabbed Helen Murphy by the shoulder and dragged her back. Simon, encumbered with the sedated cadet in his arms, was caught in indecision halfway between Helen and the door. Joanna made the decision for him. She leapt forward and forced him toward the door.

"Too late," she whispered sadly.

The Kylnnar thrust the matron up in the air and shoved his blade through her back and out through her chest.

Jo let out a scream.

All Simon noticed were Miss Murphy's eyes. He could not tell if they were relieved or accusing him. Maybe they contained nothing but shock.

Simon shouted in rage, but there was nothing he could do. Jo grabbed her commander's shoulder, pulling the pair towards the door. The three of them dashed up the small corridor from the dining room, Simon half carrying, half dragging the injured cadet, and Jo bringing up the rear, shouting at him to move faster.

The corridor joined the wide central walkway of the main school building. They were aiming to get across it and out through the matching corridor on the other side that led towards the science block. They just hoped that someone had managed to get soldiers into the corridor to shoot down their pursuers.

Simon crossed the central corridor. Glancing down it to his left, he could see a small squad of cadets at the other end. He kept running, dragging his unconscious charge, to get out of the line of fire. Jo was following fast, ten Kylnnar in pursuit. She had a moment longer to look at the squad. She picked out Flex – so that explained where he was. Then she registered what he was standing next to. She heard the whirr of it powering up and flung herself across the corridor into the passageway the other side.

A tube of blinding light blasted down the corridor, melting the plastic of the internal windows. It vaporized eight of the pursuing Kylnnar, five in the initial lance and another three when they could not stop in time and ran into it. The stench of burning flesh filled the corridor. Military lasers were used for ship-to-ship combat in space or for planetary defence. They were used to destroy armour and flyers, not target individual personnel. No one had thought to fire one down the corridor of a school –

161

not until Corporal Fletcher "Flex" Lynch did it. Usually, it emitted a single narrow beam, but Flex had recalibrated it to fire as a hollow tube. That allowed him to fire it straight without sweeping it side to side and destroying the whole school building. It also widened its field of fire so that it was effective against the reptiles when kept straight, rather than used it in a scything motion as was normally the case.

There was no stopping it, though: the laser blew through the Kylnnar and continued on. Exploding out the far wall of the school, it shot out across the rock field, carving through boulders. It culminated several miles away, where it hit the side of a mountain, the laser burning away, carving slowly into the rock, stone spitting and melting off the mountain as it turned to magma.

"They're pulling back," came an unusual voice over the comm.

Jo, who had been sprawled on the ground, sat up in the passageway where she had thrown herself. She gave her communicator a puzzled look. "Harper, that you?"

"Yes, lieutenant," Onesie confirmed, his deep voice echoing in the corridor.

"What are you doing on the comm?" she asked.

"Covering Flex; he's busy."

"Yes, I noticed: he's remodelling the school," she observed with a laugh, surveying the destruction around her. "I thought you nearly died?" she then commented.

"I did, but that was hours ago, lieutenant."

She looked at the comm and gave it a broad grin, wondering if he could feel it, if not see it.

"Welcome back, corporal," she said, then clicked off her comm and let out a big sigh.

CHAPTER 16

Location: Wolfsreach Academy, Wolfstar III
Date: 19 December 2196 CE, Earth Standard Calendar
Time: 11.47 Local Time 26.5-hour clock

The hot sun bleached the plastic green turf that covered the hockey pitch, looking like a horrible imposition on the austere grey of the barren planet. A pile of twenty-five Kylnnar corpses had been stripped of their weapons and helmets and piled up in one corner. In the centre, five figures knelt, hands held in metal bindings in front of them: four Kylnnar and one Colonial. They were all taller than the defenders; even on their knees, they were not much shorter than the dozen cadets who surrounded them, clutching their pulse rifles menacingly.

Simon Kim strode across the field, Jo Hakeswell and a full squad of soldiers trailing in his wake. The sound of the shield buzzing above them seemed louder than normal. The heat was oppressive, and a lick of sweat trickled down the young commander's face.

"Prisoners?" he asked to the group of cadets.

They nodded.

"Reynolds, what are you doing here?" Jo demanded, spotting the red-haired sergeant among the group.

"I came when Flex called. You were nearly overrun, so he called in everyone he could," he replied.

"Who is defending Armoury Station? We lose the armoury, we lose this battle," she spat angrily.

Reynolds looked nervous. "I left a squad and a pulse cannon crew. There was no attack coming through that way, ma'am," he offered lamely.

"A squad to defend the station!" she practically screeched.

"Enough, Jo," Simon intervened wearily. "We're short everywhere; we just have to take our chances."

"Pete, well done: without you we would have been overrun," Simon said politely to Sergeant Reynolds. "We'll take over here. Take your squad back to Armoury Station. Try and get some rest. I don't have the people to give you a proper break."

"No worries, sir," Reynolds replied amiably. He signalled his squad to move off.

The squad with Jo took position around the captives.

Simon scanned the southern hills, looking for any sign of movement. He knew there were Kylnnar up in the rocks, together with their Colonial allies. He could feel their eyes on him. Would one of them be foolish enough to try for a shot? It was a fair distance for even a good sharpshooter. It would also immediately reveal the shooter's position, and it wasn't easy to move quickly through the razor-sharp rocks. He was one of those foolish pupils who, when younger, had ignored the prohibition on entering the southern hills. He remembered the agony of the cuts and the frustration of lying in the infirmary waiting for them to heal fully. It had been his mistake to believe that the hills were impassable. Simon's error had cost a number of cadets their lives, and frankly it was lucky it had not got them all killed. The near calamity that his cockiness had almost inflicted on them gnawed at him.

WOLFSREACH ACADEMY

Simon took in the four Kylnnar kneeling in front of him, then the Colonial at the far end. All five had their eyes downcast to the ground. Simon moved to stand before the Colonial, his shadow playing across his fellow human. The Colonial looked up, meeting the Lieutenant's gaze. His face was impassive, but his eyes burned with anger. Simon Kim noted the man's white and grey robes, his emaciated features and odd-coloured eyes, and wondered if the creature in front of him was really human at all.

"Name and rank?" he demanded.

"Who's asking?" shot back the Colonial.

Simon had to fight down the urge to strike him. The betrayal rankled him. He disliked the Kylnnar and their genocidal war on humanity, but having faced them in battle he had too much respect for them to truly hate them. So far, for all their reputation, they had fought clean and hard. The Colonial was another matter. The creature was a traitor, to the students of Wolfsreach and to the whole of its species.

"I am Lieutenant Simon Kim, Commanding Officer of Wolfsreach Academy and Military Governor of Wolfstar III."

That elicited a dry chuckle from the Colonial. He then spoke a short series of barks and croaks. It was greeted by what sounded like a dry hard laugh from the four bound Kylnnar kneeling next to him.

"You speak Kylnnar?" asked the lieutenant.

"I speak Daoush," replied the Colonial quietly.

Simon had no idea what that was. It was not important. "Why were they laughing?"

"I told them who you were, and it amused them," responded the Colonial.

One of the Kylnnar made a series of croaks and hisses that might have been words. A pair of nervous cadets moved closer, training their guns on the reptile. Simon waved them back. He looked at the Colonial.

"He says you look young, though with your people it is hard to tell," explained the Colonial.

"You didn't answer my question. Name and rank?" Simon met the Colonial's eerie eyes again.

"Saran," supplied the kneeling human. "I'm a ranger – the closest we have to a police force."

"Why are you helping the reptiles?" Simon's lip curled up in disgust on the last word.

"You are on our world, child of the Confederation; *our* world, and you ask me that?"

"You are human?" replied the lieutenant.

"Do we look the same to you?"

The Asian Simon Kim looked at the mixed-race Lieutenant Hakeswell and then across the mixture of white, brown, black and yellow faces that made up his squad and back to the pallid features of the Colonial.

"Your DNA says you are human. We don't have to look the same to be one species," he observed.

"You have my DNA, do you?" the Colonial retorted.

"I meant your people's; you were tested by Confederation scientists," Simon countered.

"My people came to this rock before there even was a Confederation. We have traded with the Daoush for decades before your people came here. We are not you, just because our ancestors were once of you."

"You call the reptiles Daoush?" observed Simon.

"You fight a people and don't even know their name. Instead, you call them by your name for their system. You destroy and kill and burn an enemy whose name you do not even know," the Colonial enunciated with contempt.

A vague memory from a history lesson resonated with Simon. Kylnnar, a human explorer, renowned for his long space journeys seeking new planets for mankind to colonize and valuable resources to exploit. He remembered that the home system of the reptiles had been named for the adventurer. A way of honouring the great man after his death. A way of encouraging others to follow his path. That had been decades before first contact with the Kylnnar, the reptilian species that now carried the explorer's name. He wished he had paid more attention in class, for some reason it felt important, but he could not even remember the man's first name, *something Scandinavian sounding*, he thought.

Simon caught something in his peripheral vision and heard the crunch of combat boots tramping across the hockey court. He turned to see Sergeant Travis Ronin; his friend looked to be in a terrible state. His uniform was ripped and torn. His face was a mass of cuts and bruises, including a large bump protruding from his forehead. Trailing behind him was the rangy figure of Mo Abdi, looking in considerably better shape than his squad leader. Travis and Mo stopped in front of the lieutenants and the pair saluted wearily, Travis wincing as he raised his arm. The officers returned the greeting.

"We came to warn you the Kylnnar have allied with the Colonials and are coming through the southern hills," Travis reported. He looked past Simon at the kneeling forms behind the lieutenants. "Guess we're a little late," he offered sheepishly.

"You could have radioed?" observed Simon, a touch more coldly than he intended.

Travis held up his smashed communicator in his left hand by way of explanation. He dropped it on the ground. Then he pulled his earpiece out of his right ear, showing its damaged circuitry, and tossed it on the floor next to his communicator. "We got here as soon as we could dig ourselves out," the sergeant explained.

"Dig yourself out?" asked Jo, puzzled.

"Yes. The Kylnnar decided to drop a mountain on us."

"Right," she replied, wide-eyed.

"How many did you lose?" asked Simon.

"We are the only two still fully fit from the squad I took up into the mountains. A few of my troop were wounded, ranging from badly to borderline dead. They are in your new makeshift field hospital in the science block. The rest are dead," reported the sergeant.

"How many?" asked Jo quietly.

"Five of us made it off the mountain, but I doubt Rusty will make it through the day, so it will probably be four soon enough."

"Six squad members, two snipers dead," she mouthed quietly.

"We stopped them coming through the northern mountains," observed Travis. "If we hadn't, they would have overwatch on your rear when they made the attack from the southern hills. You would have been caught in a murderous crossfire."

"Thank you," said Simon, nodding. He meant it sincerely.

He turned back to the Colonial.

"You're so green, you don't know you've lost," the Colonial said, amused.

"I'm not the one kneeling in chains," Simon shot back.

That raised a chuckle from one of the Kylnnar. Dread permeated Simon's body to the depth of his stomach. The enemy could understand English. Simon sidestepped to stand in front of the amused Kylnnar. The reptile's feral eyes assessed him angrily.

"You speak our language?"

Simon got a series of croak, clicks and hisses in response.

"He says he understands it, but it is tricky to speak it, as their vocal box is different from a human's," translated the Colonial.

"Yet you speak their tongue?" Simon queried the Colonial.

"No one said biology was fair," replied Saran.

"What are your plans? What is your next attack?" the lieutenant demanded of the Kylnnar.

A series of croaks and barks came back. Simon looked to his translator.

"Very roughly, 'no idea, it's above my pay grade'," replied Saran with a chuckle.

Simon briefly considered threatening the creature, even torturing it, but he doubted he would be able to make it convincing. Besides, even if he could get information from the reptile there was no guarantee that the Colonial would render it correctly and honestly.

"What shall we do with them?" asked Jo.

"There's a small prison in the armoury barracks. Take them there and lock them in. Move them using two squads. Kill them if they try to escape," he commanded.

"You're aware of standing orders regarding the Kylnnar?" asked Jo.

Simon fixed her with a hard glare. Of course he was aware of standing orders. No Kylnnar prisoners were to be taken. All Kylnnar soldiers or civilians were to be executed on contact.

"I'm aware, but I don't really feel like killing manacled prisoners. You go for it if you want to," he replied.

Jo looked at the prisoners. Despite the loathing she felt for them, she could muster no desire to execute them.

"No, I'm good, sir."

Simon flipped open his comm with a nonchalant wave of his hand.

"Flex, you there?" he demanded of the empty air.

"No, sir – I'm on station," came Onesie Harper's deep voice.

"No matter," the lieutenant muttered. "Can you signal Corporal Hagen to bring her squad over to the hockey field?"

"Done, sir," Onesie's voice crackled in response.

"Stay on the line and set to record?" commanded Lieutenant Kim.

"Sir?" queried Onesie.

"Was my order unclear?"

"No, sir," came the comm response, "I'm recording."

"I overlooked something when I took command," Simon declared, addressing Joanna and Travis, but also continuing to speak into the comm. "I have not declared planetwide martial law."

"A bit moot: you are commander of Wolfsreach, and we are the only Confederation forces on this rock," observed Jo.

"Still best to follow the formalities. I thought you would like that, lieutenant," Simon answered with a wide, slightly mocking, smile.

Travis and a few of the others let out a chuckle at that. Corporal Hagen and her squad were jogging across the field to join them.

"I, Lieutenant Simon Kim, in my role as senior military officer and military governor, hereby declare the planet of Wolfstar III to be under full martial law with all the implications and conventions that means," Simon said with a flourish. "Lieutenant Hakeswell, as my number two, can you witness and confirm my declaration of martial law?"

Hakeswell was staring at her commander, trying to process what he was asking. She was missing something, but could not figure out what.

"Lieutenant, your confirmation, please," Simon insisted.

"Confirmed, sir," Hakeswell offered reluctantly, unsure of what she was really agreeing to.

"Sergeant Ronin, as number three in command, please can you also confirm my declaration of martial law?"

"Confirmed, sir," Travis declared firmly so the communicator picked it up.

"Excellent, Onesie. You can shut off the recording." Simon flipped his communicator closed without waiting for a response.

Hagen arrived in front of Lieutenant Kim and saluted. Simon returned it.

"Travis, you and Hagen take the prisoners to the armoury prison and lock them in. Make sure they are guarded. Don't open the door for any reason once you throw them in. You understand?"

Travis nodded his acknowledgment.

"I thought you wanted me to do it?" objected Jo.

"Hagen and Ronin can handle it," he responded.

The Kylnnar soldiers and the Colonial pushed themselves to their feet. It was slightly harder with their shackles on, but still doable. The cadets surrounded them, keeping their distance. They had seen how lethal the hulking aliens could be in close quarters.

Simon's eyes scanned the southern hills as if looking for something or someone. Jo looked at him, puzzled.

"Saran!"

The Colonial turned when Simon called his name, a look of arrogant contempt aimed at the young lieutenant.

The sidearm came up and the Colonial's expression turned to terror. Simon shot the man in the face. Saran collapsed to the floor. A pool of blood started to seep across the court. Simon stood over the body of the ranger and shot him again in the chest, through the heart. It was unnecessary: the Colonial was already dead. The four Kylnnar soldiers moved restlessly, but they did not attack; the cadet pulse rifles remained trained on them. Simon stepped past the corpse so he was standing looking at the Kylnnar who had some understanding of English.

"He was a traitor, so he needed to die. If you co-operate you will live," he instructed.

The reptile's eyes narrowed, but he made no response.

"You murdered him in cold blood," Travis said, shocked. Genuine revulsion scarred his face.

"Did I, lieutenant?" Simon addressed Joanna.

Then Jo understood; she realized what she had been missing. "No," she answered quietly. "He executed him."

Travis swung around. "That's just words," he muttered angrily.

"Under Confederation Martial Law, the planetary commander or governor has the right to serve summary justice, whether it concerns military personnel or civilians, where the planetary governor has reason to believe that the person in question is giving comfort or aid to the enemy," replied Simon Kim.

Travis looked at Jo for confirmation.

"That's not the exact wording, but the interpretation is correct," she explained. Like Travis, she was aghast, eyeing Simon with horrible fascination.

"Still doesn't make it right," grunted Travis at his commander.

"Take your prisoners away, Sergeant Ronin," ordered Simon, fixing his baleful gaze on his blond friend.

Travis did not respond: no salute, no acknowledgment. He turned on his heel and, with a largely ineffective shove in the back of one of them, herded the Kylnnar in the direction of the monorail station.

The two lieutenants watched them go. Joanna waited for them to pass out of earshot.

"Why did you do that?" she asked quietly.

"Because he was a traitor; because it needed to be done. There's a good chance that Colonial had been on the base before, even in the armoury," he replied angrily. "You would have made a different decision?"

She shook her head. "I'm just glad I don't have to."

CHAPTER 17

Location: Wolfsreach Academy, Wolfstar III
Date: 19 December 2196 CE, Earth Standard Calendar
Time: 12.02 Local Time 26.5-hour clock

Lieutenant Simon Kim trotted down the steps and pushed through the entrance into the dining hall. One door hung half off its hinges; the other was completely gone, lying flat on the floor of the hall. He winced at the memory of being thrown through it. Every inch of his back seemed to be aching. He had not taken time to look at the bruises; maybe they would not have developed yet. He knew when they did, his back would be black and blue.

The dining hall was a scene of devastation. Another pile of Kylnnar bodies had been arranged neatly next to the entrance. There were also tarpaulins wrapping body parts, those left from the reptiles that had been caught in the laser blast. The tables and camp beds were still scattered across the room. A dozen or so cadets were milling around, mostly the former medical orderlies, but a few from other squads. They were carefully sorting out the bodies of the dead students from their Kylnnar attackers and carrying them out of the room to the mortuary. Simon silently feared that they might already have run out of space in that location.

He had asked Lieutenant Hakeswell to do a count to see what they had left and more importantly who they had left. The numbers had made for worrying reading. They had lost two pulse cannons, one to enemy action and one to a malfunction that no one seemed able to fix. The four missile launchers were still operational but running low on ammunition. It was the military lasers, their most powerful weapon, which was the issue. They had only one left. Earlier he had ordered one of the pulse cannons to be moved to Armoury Station, replacing the one that had been destroyed, leaving only two to defend the school. The decision still troubled him, unsure if he had made the correct choice. The personnel situation was even worse - of the original two hundred students - thirty-eight were dead. Of the more than fifty wounded cadets, most were still capable of fighting. Walking wounded the army called them, though some would be better described as sitting wounded, leg injuries seemed to be particularly prevalent. So perhaps a hundred and ten cadets remained fully fit and even they were exhausted and battered. And then there was Helen.

Her body lay on the ground covered with a light blue tarp. A spray of red hair, marked with grey, stuck out from under one end of it. Simon squatted down next to it. He lifted his hand as if to draw back the covering, but he hesitated. Part of him wanted to look at the woman who had put him in command, but he could not bring himself to. He imagined the dead eyes staring up at him. Would they contain something? Blame, maybe; condemnation, even, or just the glassiness of death. His hand hovered above the body for a moment before dropping back to his side.

"Why did you have to die?" he whispered, knowing there was no chance of a response. "I hope you know, wherever you are, that I am trying to do the right thing."

He stared down at the covered corpse and became lost in thought – so lost in his own mind that he did not feel the ache in his thighs from the squat, so lost that it took him a moment to realize someone was screaming at him. He stood up and turned to see a petite girl raging at him. He did not know her; she must have transferred to the school recently. She was short, the top of her head barely passing his chest. Her blonde pigtails made her look even younger than she was. He guessed she was fourteen, as anyone younger than that had been evacuated, but she did not look it. So lost in his thoughts was he, it took a moment for him to focus on what she was saying.

She was screaming and swearing, blaming him for everything: the Kylnnar invasion, the destruction around them, their whole situation. It all washed over him. It was as if he were listening to it underwater. His exhaustion was chewing on him. Then he heard something that cut through the blaze of incoherent rage. She was blaming him for Helen's death. A white-hot anger consumed him. In his heart he knew he was to blame, that he should have saved her. It took all his control not to hit the fragile teenager in front of him.

"You are such a hypocrite, protecting those you like and leaving the rest us to die at the hands of these creatures," the blonde girl spat at him.

Now he was confused. Blame, anger, hate – he could suck in all that, but what she had just said made no sense.

"What are you gibbering about?" he demanded harshly.

"Inaya and your other friends, hidden safely in the roof of the school, kept away from the fight!" she screamed.

He roared with laughter at that, it was so absurd, and made the girl angrier.

"Yeah, and they're all girls," a male student in the room said. "What sort of archaic rubbish is that?"

The room was mutinous, but Simon was too taken aback by the situation to realize.

"We're not going to follow your ridiculous orders anymore," the blonde girl declared.

175

She stopped as if in mid-speech, as the barrel of the lieutenant's pistol was now pointing at her face. Panic filled her features. A trickle of hot urine passed down her right thigh.

Simon said nothing. He just stared at the cadet; his gun held calmly. The others in the room looked around nervously. None made for a weapon; they just watched in horrified silence at what was unfolding in front of them.

"Simon." His name was spoken softly from the doorway. He did not look that way, he just continued to stare at the girl who had rebuked him.

"What's going on, lieutenant?" Joanna asked, stepping through the ruined entrance into the dining hall.

"Mutiny, traitors," Simon Kim spat the words.

"She's a kid," Joanna warned softly.

"She's a *traitor*."

"No, she's not. She's a scared child, no parents, facing her death before she's even had a chance to live. Just like the rest of us. She's angry; we're all angry."

"Angry with me?" Simon's voice curled harshly as he turned to look at Jo. His pistol stayed pointing at the girl.

"Angry at all of it: angry at the Kylnnar, the Confederation, the situation, this dirty lump of rock they call a planet." Jo was speaking for herself as much as for the mutinous girl.

"So why be angry at me?"

"Because you're in command. I guess it goes with the job."

Anger was boiling through his blood vessels. He wanted to squeeze the trigger. He glanced for a moment at the corpse of Helen Murphy. Then the traitor in front of him was gone; only a little blonde teenager in pigtails was standing there. He heaved a sigh and holstered his weapon.

"She wouldn't have wanted this," he muttered.

"No, she wouldn't," Jo declared, stepping between her fellow lieutenant and the girl.

The room let out a collective breath. The blonde girl collapsed to the floor in a heap and sobbed.

Simon's eyes met Jo's. He found only disappointment in them. A few days ago, he would not have cared what she thought. Now it mattered. Every decision he had made, she had not openly disagreed with any of them; she had followed orders like the professional she was. There had been no criticism or contempt, just support. Even when he had killed the Colonial, she had understood the decision as much as she hated it. He wanted to collapse weeping right next to the kid on the floor, but that would do no one any good. He stared nastily at the girl.

"You want easy duty?" he barked. "Go join Chandra's unit. See how easy it is."

Lieutenant Hakeswell offered the girl her hand and pulled the teenager to her feet.

"You can go with her, lieutenant," Simon ordered. "Take over command from Corporal Chandra. Split the squad in two: you take command of one, Inaya can command the other."

Jo searched Simon's face, trying to work out what he was thinking. Was this a punishment or had this always been his plan?

"Yes, sir," was all she said.

The pair left the hall. The others present slowly got back to clearing up as the tense atmosphere in the room gradually dissipated. Simon stood over the body of the matron, the only adult on their side, and wondered, not for the first time, if she knew what she'd been doing when she put him in command.

CHAPTER 18

Location: Wolfsreach Academy Station, Wolfstar III
Date: 19 December 2196 CE, Earth Standard Calendar
Time: 13.12 Local Time 26.5-hour clock

Travis Ronin trudged from the platform into the underground vaulted hall that led the way out of Wolfsreach Academy Station. The escalators were located here, rising up in a gradual shallow arc towards the grey stone arch of the roof above – a route that would take him back to the dorms and perhaps a few moments of respite, if not sleep. Usually, the young athlete would stride around confidently, scanning ahead of him looking for the next beautiful girl to chat to, no matter how much such behaviour was likely to incur Inaya's annoyance. Now his confidence had been drained away by a combination of exhaustion and combat. He had just come back from the armoury, where he had been delivering the Kylnnar prisoners. He had secured the four of them one per cell, filling four of the five cells that were available. The base had been built with the expectation that there would not be much need for imprisoning personnel, so the fact that there were five cells indicated to Travis that the Confederation had once had bigger plans for the base in the Wolfsreach Valley. That, or they had an incredibly low opinion of the students and military personnel they had sent to this rock.

He had debated in his own mind Simon's decision to let the Kylnnar live. He suspected the others in the guard group had done the same, though none had done it in front of the creatures. The revelation that at least one of them could understand English had alarmed the students, but at the same time made the Kylnnar soldiers seem less other. They had been more focused on getting the truculent reptiles locked up before they turned on the smaller, weaker humans. They had pulse rifles, but the size and scale of the Kylnnar was enough to make any human nervous around them even when armed.

As they had escorted the creatures through the more confined space of the tunnels and onto the monorail, they had been nervous of an escape attempt, but the Kylnnar had made no such move. After they had locked them up securely, several of the cadets had speculated that this was some sort of strange Kylnnar plan, such was the paranoia that their situation had engendered. Maybe it was not the situation, he mused; maybe it was years of being told that the Kylnnar were monsters. They certainly fitted the bill with their hulking, scaly, slavering presence. Part of Travis wanted them dead; he just was not sure it was that simple. Was it so he did not have to worry about them coming for him as he slept, or because of some desire for revenge? His feelings were so mixed up on the matter, he was not sure what drove them. He had no desire to kill them himself, but he was willing to fight, and he was pretty sure he had shot at least two Kylnnar up on the hills. So, he had certainly injured a Kylnnar, if not killed one or two of them outright. It made him more impressed by Julia's dispassionate sniper attitude: she had gunned down faraway targets, knowing she had certainly slain them. Thinking of the deceased sniper and then the other cadets

179

under his command who had been killed and injured, he felt his hatred of the reptiles welling up again.

Lost in thought, it took him a moment to register the presence of someone in front of him. He started, reaching to swing up his pulse rifle from where it hung behind him. Instinct took over in a place he had thought to be safe. A figure was sat on the metal casing that separated the up and down escalators from each other, where the escalator flattened off as it met the ground. It was a cadet, cross-legged, with a pulse rifle resting across their knees. Corporal Fletcher Lynch stood watching the sergeant's excessive reaction with a look of detached amusement.

"Bit jumpy, aren't you?" Flex asked with a broad grin.

"If you'd ever been out of your communications bunker, getting shot at by reptiles, you might be jumpy too." Travis knew he was being unfair – without Flex they would all be dead from orbital bombardment, but he was too tired to care at this point.

Then something occurred to him.

"Hey, what are you doing out of your bunker, Flex?" he demanded.

"You got any orders?" asked the geeky cadet.

"No. You going to answer my question, corporal?" Travis coldly reminded Flex of his senior rank.

"Onesie Harper is covering me; he's more than capable. Mo not with you?"

"No, he's covering the prisoners back at the armoury. Besides, they're short of people, they'll need him if the reptiles try to take the station again," replied Travis.

"You look like you need a rest," observed Flex.

"Flex, whatever you want, can you spit it out before I decide we don't need you anymore and shoot you?" the sergeant muttered angrily.

"You've got no orders, I've got no orders. Guess we're at a loose end. Fancy a wander?" asked the corporal. He pushed himself forward, uncrossing his legs and sliding down to the floor. He staggered slightly forward before righting himself into a standing position. He slung his pulse rifle over his shoulder.

"That was supposed to look cooler," he grumped quietly.

"A wander where?" the sergeant asked.

"Come with me," instructed Flex, walking in the direction of the opposite platform from the one on which Travis had just arrived.

"You know that platform isn't in use, corporal?"

"Come on, sarge – this is me you're talking to," Flex laughed over his shoulder.

The sergeant rolled his eyes and went after Fletcher. The opposite platform sat in its own tunnel, the platform protected from the track by floor-to-ceiling screen doors. A monorail train not in use rested quietly in the platform. Travis found it surprisingly dark. He realized how much light came from the train when it was in operation, but now it sat there all dead. It made him oddly wary.

With a magician-like wave, Flex produced a small black tablet from the pocket of his equally black cargo pants. He tapped it a couple of times and the train emitted a hum from its electrical drive system. A few seconds later, the lights of the train flickered on, bathing the whole platform with light and banishing the shadows on the wall. Flex tapped the tablet a couple more times and the platform doors swished open, followed a moment later by the doors of the monorail train.

Flex stepped onto the train. "So, sarge, are you going my way?"

Travis leaned against the door, debating for a moment, then stepped onto the train.

"Way to go, sarge," Flex chuckled.

"Corporal Fletcher," Travis replied calmly. "Call me sarge one more time I'm going to shoot you in the kneecap."

Flex met Travis's cold, calm eyes. He swallowed. He could not decide if the senior cadet was joking. The look on his face suggested he wasn't.

"Sorry, sergeant." Flex's gaze dropped back down to his tablet.

Moments later, the door closed, and the train set off in the opposite direction to Armoury Station. There was only one more stop on the line: the grandly named Terminus. It made it sound a lot smarter or more important than it was. It was the end of the line, which again sounded overly grand given the line had only four stations and trains essentially shuttled back and forth on two monorails.

Soon, the train was pulling into the next station. There was a single central platform, with the track dividing each side. The track on the left ended in a buffer, while the track on the right continued on. Past the platform the track seemed to cross a circular podium, just large enough to accommodate the two-carriage train. Beyond, it widened out into a large underground cavern, where six train-size sheds were arranged in a semicircle around the far side of the podium. A short stretch of track led off the circular area into each one. Travis realized the podium was a turntable: it could rotate to allow a train carriage to be brought off the main track into one of the sheds, or for the process to be reversed. Three of the sheds appeared to hold train carriages; sparks were issuing from one of them. The railyard was dark; there was no artificial light above the sheds surrounding the podium. The only illumination came from the lamps above the platform, and a hint of daylight struggling through small window slats forty feet above them in the ceiling. Travis looked up. The sunlight was minimal; dust probably covered most of the windows, he surmised. It reminded him how much he hated this arid, dusty planet.

Flex brought the train to a stop on the platform before it reached the railyard turntable, its lights illuminating the sheds much more clearly. The doors hissed open, and the pair stepped out onto the stone of the platform. As they walked up towards the railyard, artificial lights on the roof of the cavern sprung to life. Travis looked up, staring across the ceiling, and realizing that the engineers who had built this place had taken advantage of an existing cave. The slats still admitted a limited amount of natural sunlight, but it was overwhelmed by the artificial lighting that had awoken at their presence.

A figure floated across the yard towards them. It looked like the head and torso of a human, but all carved in metal, and its mock musculature seemed odd. Its face had bug-like eyes over a thick steel mesh. It was legless; instead, an articulated cable hung down from its torso, whipping and twirling like a snake's tail, designed to balance the robot. It had disproportionately long, spindly metal arms with three pairs of claws in place of hands.

"This is a restricted area. You are ordered to withdraw." The robot's electronic voice grated at them.

Travis unslung his pulse rifle to bring it up to target the automaton.

"One second," said Flex, tapping away at his tablet again.

"This is a restricted area. You are…" the robot thudded to the floor.

Flex stared down with a slightly worried face.

"You shut it down?" asked Travis.

"Yes. It's the control robot for the whole complex," Flex replied. "So, we better hope a train doesn't fail."

"Why?"

"Because unless I can restart this thing, we won't be able to fix it." Flex gave the robot a light kick.

"Not sure that will help," observed Travis. "Why are we here?"

Flex handed the sergeant the tablet. It showed an image: the outline of a vessel. It was a sensor silhouette, not a photograph.

"What is it?" Travis asked. He adjusted the angle in the hope it would give him more clarity. It did not help.

"It's the Kylnnar ship that we couldn't identify," Flex explained. "I've worked out what it is."

Travis looked at him and handed the tablet back.

"I think it's a specialized carrier for armour," said Flex.

"Come again?"

"It's a tank carrier," Flex clarified.

Travis looked at the tablet again, trying to draw some information from the image in front of him. He had nothing of value to add. If anyone knew what it was, it would be Flex.

"You tell Simon?" he asked.

Flex nodded.

"What did he say?"

"'I hope you're wrong'," quoted Flex.

Travis grunted agreement at that.

"If they have tanks, why haven't they used them?" Travis asked.

"This environment is hardly set up for tank warfare: hills on three sides and a plain covered with boulders, some the size of a small vehicle. It's like a readymade tank trap."

The senior student nodded his agreement at Flex's assessment of the battlefield.

"So, it tells us two things," continued Flex.

The sergeant raised an eyebrow.

"Firstly, they can bring armour to bear on us if we keep resisting them."

"And second?" asked Travis.

"Secondly, they have somewhere else to be," said Flex with a smile.

"How do you figure that?"

"If you want to take this place, you aren't going to bring tanks," responded Flex. "They're not suited to the attack without battlefield shaping. Besides, the Kylnnar had no reason to believe

184

we would provide the level of resistance we have. Certainly not enough resistance to require a carrier's worth of heavy armour. They probably had orders to burn the place from space, maybe check we were all dead, and then move on."

"That's a reach, Flex," countered Travis. "They had the presence of mind to cut a deal with the Colonials; it sounds like they had this planned."

"I don't know." Flex did not enjoy hearing his theory being picked at. "Maybe they've had a relationship with the Colonials for years. Maybe the reptiles forced them. I think those tanks are the key. I think that carrier and its cargo need to be somewhere else. They can't be hung up here for too long. If we hold out long enough, they will have to move on to where they are really needed."

"And leave us behind their advance?" the sergeant countered.

"Travis, we are couple of hundred kids – fewer than that now – with no interplanetary transport. What are we going to do, fart at them from a barren rock?"

"We're doing pretty well so far," Travis replied, but he was laughing. "So why have you dragged me here?" He crouched down, poking at the robot on the floor. "These things any use?" he asked.

"Not why we're here," replied Flex, stepping over the robot and walking across the central rail of the turntable platform towards the service sheds. The sergeant set off after him.

There were six sheds, made in corrugated metal with pitched roofs reaching close to the ceiling of the cavern. It struck Travis as odd that such sheds would be built inside an enclosed facility. There was no weather to protect the carriages from, after all. Maybe it was some sort of fire prevention requirement, or the builders had simply done it out of habit without really thinking what purpose the buildings served. The sheds had only two walls along their rectangular length, with the short ends completely open aside from a strengthening bar across each entrance to support the structure.

Beyond the sheds, the cavern continued, lowering slightly into an open expanse of grey sand, which held a scattering of left-over metal components. Travis presumed these were from the trains, but they could have been from anything. The area was shadowed; its artificial lighting had not come on. At the far end some natural light seemed to be creeping in, but it was hard to tell from where. It cast odd shadows across the grey sand floor.

The track led to a shed in the centre of the six. The turntable was designed for the track to shift, connecting the main monorail with one of the spare service sheds. It could then be rotated to connect each of the sheds to the track, bringing a train into whichever shed was available. The structure in front of Travis was the one from which sparks had been emanating, although these had stopped now. A single carriage filled the shed, and was surrounded by service robots. They now stood motionless, caught in the moment of repair. Flex's decision to shut off the control robot had carried through to the service automatons.

"What are you looking at? This way!" Flex shouted; he was standing in front of a shed at the far end of the semicircle of structures.

He disappeared into the dark of the building as if to emphasize his point. An automatic light flickered on in the shed as he stepped in, its sensors apparently able to distinguish organic from mechanical life. Travis jogged over to join his fellow cadet.

When he reached the building, the scene was the same as the other sheds. An open-ended structure of corrugated metal enclosed a track. There were work benches on each side of the long walls, with carefully placed racks of tools above. Neatly categorized components were stored in plastic trays, marked with bar codes rather than by names, a system more useful to the robot servitors than to humans, none of which were present in the shed.

There was something filling most of the shed. It was hard to tell exactly what it was, as it was covered in heavy grey tarpaulins – something that felt unnecessary given it was in a shed, in a cavern, on a bone-dry area of dusty planet. Maybe it was just to protect it from the abrasive sand that seemed to get everywhere. The vehicle, whatever it was, loomed above him. It was shorter and flatter than the train, and considerably wider, pushing up against the work benches and almost bulging out of the long walls of the shed.

"What is it?" asked Travis.

"Not one hundred percent sure, but I think I know," Flex grinned. "You want to do the honours?"

Travis stepped forward and yanked at the nearest grey tarpaulin. A thin layer of sandy dust scattered into the air, causing the cadet to cough. He continued to pull. A long tube appeared, which he realized was the barrel of a gun: a very large gun. He continued to pull the heavy coverings off the front of the vehicle, while Flex did the same at the rear. Once it was cleared of its concealing tarpaulins, the pair stood in front of it and assessed the vehicle.

Its metal front rose in front of them at a shallow angle to a flat top. Resting on the top was a turret, from which was poking a long-barrelled, large-bore pulse cannon. On top of the turret rested a minigun, behind which was a closed hatch. Travis looked for tracks or wheels. There were none; the vehicle was instead resting on three heavy metal axles across its base. Then he noticed the turbines, like small jet engines: four on each side, evenly spaced, and shielded with armour. They were pointing out from underneath the vehicle at a forty-five-degree angle. It was painted dark green with irregular stripes of lighter greens and browns.

Travis could not believe what was in front of him. "Flex, that's a tank," he said in a shocked whisper.

"Even better than that: it's a grav-tank," Flex grinned. "A Windhawk, state of the art – at least it was five years ago."

Travis ran his hands over the gravitational-turbine engines, that explained why it had no tracks or wheels, it did not need them. Instead, it would hover above the battlefield at a chosen height – up to as much as ten feet above the ground, though usually much lower than that. This was a tank that could truly ignore terrain.

"Who leaves a tank in a rail repair shed?" asked Travis rhetorically.

"Confederation Army," replied Flex, missing the nature of Travis's question.

"When did you find this?" the sergeant asked the corporal. He was stroking the front of the tank now, marvelling at its clear lines.

"Same time as you. I've not been in this yard before – you saw how grumpy the control robot was," replied Flex.

"So how did you know it was here?" Travis turned to Flex, looking perplexed.

"Math!"

"Math? Huh?" asked Travis.

"It's on the manifest in the armoury computer files. Twenty grav-tanks were temporarily stored here five years ago. It was only for a matter of months before the Army moved them back out. The out manifest showed nineteen tanks being taken out of the armoury," explained Flex.

"And you didn't assume it was an error? You assumed there must be a tank somewhere," Travis laughed. "Flex, you are brilliant. How did you know it was here?"

"Well, it wasn't in the armoury; I don't think it would fit, anyway," the corporal said with a grin. "I speculated maybe it needed to be repaired and then I guessed that the only place they could do it was here in the railyard."

"So, it doesn't work?" Travis looked disappointed.

"Well, it wouldn't be here if it was in full working order. You can't have everything, sergeant. Anyway, give me a bunk up."

Travis steepled his hands to create a step and boosted Flex up onto the top of the tank. The corporal scrabbled across the metal behemoth to the hatch. He opened it and dropped in out of sight.

"Hey, there are steps at the back, you idiot!" Travis shouted after him.

Flex's head and shoulders appeared through the hatch. "Sorry," he offered with a shrug, then disappeared back inside.

Travis pushed himself up the two widely spaced steps at the back of the tank and clambered over it to the turret. He could not see Flex, so slipped down into the seat used by the tank commander. He landed in the chair, bouncing slightly as he did. It was surprisingly cramped. The thick armour and reactive covering made it look bigger than it was. There were two seats in front, both sitting lower than the commander's seat. The one on the left was for the driver, the one on the right for the gunner. Flex was in the driver's seat, muttering to himself as he ran his hands across the control console.

He pressed a large black button marked 'power' and the tank hummed, its electrical systems purring. Red lights blinked across the various consoles inside the tank. Screens flashed to life and Travis found himself looking at a view of the shed and the rail turntable beyond. A screen in front of Flex came on and demanded a four-digit identification number. Flex tapped the keyboard in front of him, the flat lines turning to stars as he entered the number.

"Access granted," the tank's electronic voice declared.

"You know the code?" asked a shocked Travis.

"I typed in four ones," said Flex with a grin.

"You're kidding?"

"Army security at its finest," Flex declared.

189

Travis rolled his eyes. "What are you doing now?"

"Running a diagnostic," Flex muttered, staring intently at the screen.

A series of lines was appearing, then a cursor would flash for a few seconds before turning into a green-coloured word: *confirmed*. The computer continued to run more diagnostic pages, stopping after the fourth page of completed data. Flex tapped a function key, and the full page of data was replaced by two lines. Instead of the green word *confirmed* these showed a red word: *error*.

"So, what's the verdict?" asked Travis.

"Well, the good news is we have enough plasma to fuel the engines for – I don't know, a decade. All the main systems appear to be working; they even left the armaments fully stocked. Pulse cannon on top is showing a full energy pack. The gun uses old-fashioned shells, and they're stocked in the rear area. We have a full complement of twenty batches."

"They left the ordnance on it?" asked Travis, surprised.

"Seems so."

"So what's the problem, Flex? Why is it in the shop?"

"Grav engines three and six aren't working and they're tripping the whole system," explained Flex.

"What does that mean in simple terms?" Travis asked exasperatedly.

"Big metal thing won't go." Flex made a buzzing noise with his lips that suddenly stopped, mimicking the sound of a plasma engine.

"Great – thanks, corporal." Travis wrinkled his face in annoyance. "Can you fix it?"

"I don't know," muttered Flex.

Chapter 19

Location: Wolfsreach Academy, Wolfstar III
Date: 19 December 2196 CE, Earth Standard Calendar
Time: 15.24 Local Time 26.5-hour clock

Joanna Hakeswell took a nervous glance out of the ruined exit from the dining hall. She marvelled that only a few hours earlier she and Lieutenant Kim had been willing to stand in the open ground ahead of her so confidently. Maybe it had been the reptiles' struggle to regroup from their failed attack or the presence of the captured Kylnnar, but then it had seemed safe. At least, as safe as the open spaces at Wolfsreach Academy could be. Since then, the attackers had regrouped in the razor-glass hills to the south of the base. They had found some advantageous positions above the hockey pitch and were taking periodic pot shots at anyone foolish enough to be caught out in the open. Sporadic fire from the main building was keeping it from becoming a real problem, but the cadets struggled to target the Kylnnar amid the gleaming crags.

She looked at the devastated gym building directly in front of her. The roof had now collapsed inward, and the metal struts of its supports pointed out at odd angles from the floor. The walls were still largely standing, though the one opposite her had crumbled so it was only at her waist height. She considered whether it would be safer for her to vault the wall into the building. She dismissed the idea – like almost all the buildings at the school, the gym was partially dug into the ground, so the drop on the other side would be a lot steeper than it looked from this angle. She also had no idea what was on the other side. Besides, the cadets remained understandably jumpy: it would be just her bad luck for someone to shoot her by accident as she made the vault.

Instead, Jo decided to run round the corner of the building to where the entrance to the gym used to be. She dashed up the steps and sprinted for the corner of the gym, sandwiching herself against it. Then she exploded outward, jinxing left and right across the small area of hockey pitch she had to cross to reach the door. Her teeth were clenched; she was expecting to feel the burning hit of a pulse shot. She threw herself into the entranceway of the gym, landing against a pile of rubble. She turned around to look the way she had come. She had not heard a shot. She let out a sigh of relief and turned around.

The pulse rifle was pointing straight into her face. Jo unconsciously raised her hands.

"Whoa, easy there," she said calmly, trying to keep the panic out of her voice.

She looked into the face of the fourteen-year-old boy in front of her and racked her memory for his name.

"Private Patel, you want to point that somewhere else," she ordered.

The boy stared back at her determinedly for a moment, then lowered his weapon.

"Sorry, lieutenant, we're all a bit on edge," Vishnu Patel explained in a clipped English accent.

"No worries, private."

"Will you stop messing about, lieutenant!" Simon's shout came from the other end of the ruined building – the side that faced the rock plain.

Jo looked for him, but could not find him; he was concealed amid the rubble. She jogged over to where she guessed he was. Crouched at two thirds of her normal height, she used what remained of the building, together with the rubble and collapsed roof struts, to hide herself from any Kylnnar in the hills above. She wondered why Simon had stationed himself out here. After all, he had lectured her on officers keeping back and commanding. Now he was hunkered down in the most open and probably most forward position their defence had.

A squad of ten were scattered through the structure, crouched behind blasted stone, using bits of half burnt furniture and anything else they could to create makeshift barriers. They were spread thinly, half facing towards the southern hills, and the remainder facing out to the rock plain.

She passed the destroyed remains of the military laser and tapped it affectionately on a smooth section of its twisted, charred metal. She felt genuinely sad at its passing despite its inanimate nature. It had done more to keep them alive than practically any other weapon.

She dropped to her knees before a section of internal wall and crawled through a narrow gap. It opened up into a square area surrounded by walls and rubble. Simon was seated in one corner, squeezing a meal out of a silver foil pack.

"You hungry?" he spat unattractively through his mouthful of food.

"What is it?" asked Jo sceptically.

"Beef bourguignon," he replied.

"You heat it?"

"Nah."

She wrinkled her nose. "That's gross. Anyway, I've already eaten, thanks, sir," she replied.

He shrugged and squeezed some more into his mouth.

"It's alright. I mean, it's veggie substitute, not the real thing, but it will do," he commented.

"You're not selling it to me," she laughed. "Anyway, you called?"

"Yeah," Simon replied, swallowing his food and putting the packet down on the floor.

He walked to the other side of the square and used the piled-up stone as a makeshift step ladder to reach the top. He popped his head above the surface before ducking back and waving to Jo to join him. She followed him gingerly up the rubble, small bits of stone scattering down in her wake. Jo positioned herself next to her commander. She glanced behind, afraid they were exposed from the rear. The mass of tangled steel work and collapsed roof largely blocked anyone trying to target the pair from the southern hills.

They were slightly above ground level. The lower part of the gym wall was still standing, and they were essentially leaning against it, looking out across the rock plain. It flowed away at a gentle gradient in front of them before dropping sharply lower about two miles from their position. It was scattered with jagged rocks ranging from pebbles to small balls, to the size of a personal transport. It provided some cover for anyone crossing it, but would also slow down anyone moving across it to attack the school.

Simon handed Jo his field glasses. She scanned the horizon. The hot sun and light breeze had created a sandy haze. She picked out a couple of Kylnnar troop transports, similar to the ones they had used to bring their infantry down to the planet, moving in the air at a very low altitude, using the hills beyond the rock plain to cover their movements. She dropped the glasses lower and picked out some figures at the edge of the plain where it dropped away.

"Some ships in the air. Maybe worth a pulse cannon shot? We might get lucky," she suggested.

"And what else?" asked her commander.

"A few soldiers down at the far end of the rock plain. Nothing different to what we've seen before," she replied.

She made to give back the glasses, but he held up his hands and indicated she should look again.

"What are we doing here, Simon?" she demanded. "There's a safer and probably clearer view of what's going on from the roof of the main building."

"You think I have a death wish?" he asked.

Jo licked her lips. "I think Helen's death has affected you," she offered carefully.

"Will you take another look, lieutenant?" he asked. His tone contained the hint of an order.

She let out a big sigh and took another look down the rock plain. Was she missing something – or was he just losing it? Despite what she had said at the beginning, she had no desire to be commanding this defence. Her respect for Simon had grown hugely, although that had been before he had shot the Colonial and threatened a teenage girl. The former she could get her head around even if she did not much like it; the latter not at all.

It was then she noticed Kylnnar soldiers scurrying between some larger rocks. They seemed to be dropping packages before moving to the next location. The defenders were taking the occasional shot at them: at this distance, without a sniper scope, it was optimistic but not impossible. She also noticed the Kylnnar were laying wires back from the packages.

A barrage of pulse fire exploded out across the rock plain, forcing the defenders in the school to take cover. Jo dropped behind the wall and covered her head. She could feel the heat of the plasma from the pulse fire as it slammed into the wall inches from her head. She silently prayed the wall was thick enough. After a few moments it subsided. She let out her breath.

"What was that?" she demanded.

"Means we got one of their sappers," Simon observed laconically. "They give us a barrage when we hit one of them. Otherwise, they don't bother."

"Sapper?" she enquired. "You think they're planting explosives?"

"That's what it looks like to me, don't you think?"

"What's with all the wires?" she asked.

"Are you serious? What's your family background?" Simon responded.

It was a matter of politeness in the academy that you did not ask about a person's family background. That had been the case even before the evacuation due to the large number of orphans in the school. So, none of them knew that much about each other's family history. The uniforms and the military discipline were further designed to remove social differences.

"Career military; why?"

Simon laughed. "That explains a lot."

"What's that supposed to mean?" she asked peevishly.

"Never mind. Your parents weren't miners is all I was trying to find out."

It was reasonable to suppose her parents were miners or connected to the mining industry. It was a common profession among the parents of the academy students. Out here, on the edge of Confederation-controlled space, mining was the primary economic activity, along with the industries that supported it: haulage lines, refinery workers, leisure activities. Everyone knew at least a little about mining; it permeated everyone's lives, feeding down to the next generation.

"I know nothing about mining," she said.

"Typical military," Simon chuckled. "My mum was a miner, and my dad worked in a bauxite refinery."

"Heart-warming story, sir," she countered sarcastically. "Is there a point in our future?"

"They're laying mining explosives," he explained. "At least, that's my guess: it's the only way I can explain the wires. Otherwise, they would use remote denotators or use their bombers."

"Maybe the Kylnnar don't have remote denotators?" Jo suggested.

"Maybe," Simon replied, unconvinced.

"Why would they need mining explosives? What are they trying to achieve?"

Simon reached into his pack and rustled out a small tablet. He tapped away at it for a few seconds and handed it to Joanna.

She looked at the picture he had brought up. It was the grey outline of the unidentified Kylnnar spacecraft, almost indistinguishable against the black background of space.

"The craft our computers could not identify?" she asked.

"Flex has a theory," Simon replied.

"Of course he does," Jo remarked drolly.

"He reckons it's a tank carrier."

A shiver went down Jo Hakeswell's spine. "A tank carrier? They have tanks? Why haven't they used them? We're screwed."

"They haven't used them because tanks are hardly ideal for attacking our location," Simon observed calmly.

Jo crawled back up the wall and peered out across the rock plain, ready to duck back down in case of another Kylnnar barrage. The reptile sappers were still scuttling from one large rock to another. She felt sick. She scooted back down from the wall until she was sitting next to Simon.

"They weren't planning on using them – at least not on us. And now they are," she muttered, trying to contain her mounting terror. "They're going to blow the largest boulders on the plain so they can bring tanks across it."

Simon nodded his agreement.

197

"We have nothing, *nothing* that can stop tanks. The one military laser we have could do some damage, but we've lost the other two. The launchers might help initially, but the tanks will soon be in under their arc. Pulse weapons will bounce off. We have no anti-tank missiles." Jo summarized their desperate situation.

Simon pulled out something from underneath his back. It was a rounded metal object painted in army green with two small wooden sticks stuck on it. Jo recognized the green metal part – it was an anti-tank mine – though she had no idea why someone had attached bits of wood to it.

"What are you going to do with that?" she demanded. "No one's going to be dumb enough to walk out on the rock plain and place it. And it's not like we can dig it in – it's solid rock out there."

"I get that," Simon said. "That's what the wooden paddles are for: they will stabilize it and we can drop it from a drone."

"That might work," she conceded grudgingly. "How many mines we got?"

"A couple of hundred," he replied with a smile.

"It really might work." She returned his grin.

"Only problem: we only have twenty drones."

"Still, it's a chance," Jo said.

"I need you to head back to your command. We'll need you when they come. You know what to do?" he asked.

She nodded, then gave a small salute in their cramped conditions. She crawled back out of the foxhole into the remnants of the gym, before jogging towards the entrance, keeping her head ducked down.

She did not look back as the rock plain behind her exploded in a sea of fire and burning rock.

Chapter 20

Location: Terminus, Wolfstar III
Date: 19 December 2196 CE, Earth Standard Calendar
Time: 15.45 Local Time 26.5-hour clock

Mo Abdi walked across the turntable track of the monorail repair yard, trying to work out where Travis was. The sergeant's orders had come over his communicator and instructed him to go to the Terminus station. Beyond that he had no detail, such as where exactly he was supposed to meet him. At least he had managed to get a train here. Initially he had been worried that he would have to walk through the dark tunnel. Flex had somehow arranged for a train to run him here, though he had to change platforms at the station under the school. The rangy East African had expected to see Flex or Travis at the Terminus station platform. Instead, he had found himself alone, unsure where to go, so he had wandered in the direction of the turntable towards the service sheds that lay beyond. He passed the disabled control robot, nudging it gingerly with his foot. *Flex's handiwork*, he speculated. He must be going in the right direction.

The whole service yard was lit up, as were all the sheds, so that did not tell him where he might find his squad leader. He listened, hoping for a noise that would give something away. He heard an intermittent clanking of metal on metal, but sounds bounced around the walls of the cavern so it was hard to tell where it was coming from. Mo took his best guess and headed for the shed to his far right. He poked his head in.

"Mo, what took you so long?" barked Travis grumpily at his friend's arrival.

"Sorry, sergeant," Mo replied, slipping smoothly into the shed. He decided it best not to berate his commander for the paucity of his orders. Instead, Mo stared open-mouthed at the huge metal object that filled the shed.

"That's a grav-tank?" he half stated, half asked.

"Obviously," came Travis's off-hand reply.

To Mo it was anything but obvious, but he restrained himself again and decided not to point it out. He just stood in the wide entrance of the shed, marvelling at the mechanical beast. The sergeant, meanwhile, was staring at the tablet clutched in his right hand.

"Have you tried bypassing the primary circuit?" Travis demanded.

Mo wondered if Travis was addressing him, then the sweating, dirty form of Flex Lynch pushed himself out from underneath the rear engines of the grav-tank.

"Of course I tried that," Flex shot back grumpily.

"It doesn't make sense," muttered Travis.

"Are you basing this on your years of experience as a mechanical engineer specializing in tanks?" asked Flex, dripping sarcasm.

"Look, Flex, get snotty with me all you like, but who builds a tank with eight engines that stops working when two of the engines break? It's a dumb design for a transport or a speeder, but for a tank it's positively ridiculous. The thing is supposed to get shot at; engines are supposed to get damaged and fail – that's why it has eight," Travis growled with frustration.

Flex knew his friend was trying to help, but he was too tired and angry to cut him any slack.

"We've been through this, Travis. You can point it out as much as you like, it still isn't fixing the damn thing."

"Maybe it's the sensor?" Mo's voice sounded nervous as he inserted himself into the conversation.

Travis looked at him with a withering glare. Mo swallowed nervously in response.

"We've checked the engine. It's obviously not starting, so it can't be the sensor," Travis grunted.

"Shut up, sergeant," Flex said peevishly. "Follow that thought, Mo."

If Travis was annoyed by his subordinate's tone it did not show.

"Well, my dad always used to say that the sensors failed before the part they were supposed to be monitoring failed," Mo replied.

"Thanks, Mo, very helpful," Travis responded sarcastically.

"Wait, Travis – maybe he's on to something." Flex's face was riven in thought.

"But we checked the sensor?" Travis asked. "We did, didn't we?"

"That's why they couldn't find it!" Flex grinned. "Give me that tester."

Travis put his tablet down, grabbed up the small grey and black tester with red and black probes from the work bench and handed it to Flex. The youngster clambered up the tank and disappeared through the hatch into the bowels of the vehicle.

"What are you thinking, Flex?" demanded Travis. He looked over at Mo, who just shrugged.

"Flex?" he shouted up in the direction of the tank turret.

All he got in reply was a series of clanking noises. "It can't be that obvious," came a muffled comment from Flex, clearly talking to himself.

Travis considered climbing up after the corporal to find out what was going on. Suddenly, an explosive blast of air burst out from under the tank and washed across the shed, and the steel monstrosity lifted into the air. Travis pinned himself to the workbench in shock, fearing he would be crushed against it as the vehicle bobbed in the air in front of him. Mo had jumped to the side of the shed at the same time. He now pushed his head round the side of the shed entrance to see the grav-tank levitating.

Travis, once confident that he was not about to be squashed, started to circle the tank, admiring its lines now it was fully alive.

"Well done, Mo – you fixed it," said Flex, popping his head out of the turret.

Mo looked back, entirely convinced he had done nothing at all to fix the hovering behemoth.

Travis looked up at Flex. "It's running on seven engines, including the two that were supposed to not be working."

"It's running; that's the main thing," said Flex with a broad smile.

"But what was wrong?" demanded Travis.

"It was the sensors, like Mo said."

"Explain what was wrong?" Travis asked exasperatedly.

"How complicated do you want it?" Flex queried.

"I'm not an idiot, Flex: explain?" Travis was getting annoyed now.

"The sensors were aligned wrong, so they were detecting the wrong engines compared to what the firmware thought should be the case. One engine had failed, but it was being detected as another engine. That was causing the computer to shut down the wrong engine. However, the engine that was broken was then not powering up, which was causing the failsafe to trip to prevent an overload in the other engines. So, it was telling the computer it was not working but the monitoring sensor was saying it was working, which the computer was resolving by shutting off all the engines. Make sense?" replied Flex.

Travis's confused look indicated that it did not.

"You got there from 'maybe it's the sensor'?" marvelled Mo.

"Yes," Flex beamed back.

"So, the sensors," observed Travis seriously.

"Yes, sir," replied Flex with mock seriousness and winked at Mo.

"Right now, can you get it running on all eight engines?" asked Travis.

"No," Flex replied, his smile dropping. "That I can't do. You would have to strip the engine down and find the failed component, for which we probably don't have the spare. If I had a couple of weeks of tinker time to teach myself grav-engine mechanics then there might be a chance, but we don't have a couple of weeks. We might not have a couple of hours."

Travis nodded his understanding. "Can we run it on seven engines?"

"No problem," replied Flex. "It will need a bit more care when driving, but not majorly so."

"It's great you've got this thing working," observed Mo. "But I've been meaning to ask: what do you need me for?"

"It needs three crew," Travis said. "A gunner," the sergeant pointed at Flex. "A commander," Travis tapped his own chest. "And a driver," he pointed at Mo with a large smile.

"I don't know how to drive a tank," Mo said, swallowing nervously.

"You can drive a speeder, can't you?" asked Travis.

"Well, yeah," Mo conceded.

"Same thing, just bigger," Travis said, trying to sound reassuring.

"Really not!" observed Mo. "Also, how do we get this thing out of here?"

"He's got a point," Travis said, turning to Flex.

Flex disappeared into the tank and shut off the engines. The tank lowered gently, resting on its metal under-rungs. His head popped out of the hatch, followed by his body, then he clambered down the tank and headed towards the back of the shed.

"You coming?" he asked to the two cadets behind him.

Flex walked over to the piled-up tarpaulins, kicking his feet free as they caught in the folds of the scattered coverings.

Travis and Mo looked at each other and with a simultaneous shrug headed off after the tech prodigy. The cave dipped down until it was around fifteen feet in height, providing enough clearance for a low-flying grav-tank, but not much. The area behind the sheds was covered in soft grey sand. Indentations in the surface indicated that this is where the grav-tanks had been stored. Deep marks showed where the three bars under the tanks had sunk into the sand – how the tanks rested on the ground when their engines were switched off. Travis absentmindedly counted them. There were at least a dozen sets of prints, indicating that this was where the tanks had originally been stored. He looked back towards the sheds and beyond that to the station. He wondered if they had been brought in on specially designed rail carriages, but that seemed unlikely given the lack of such carriages in the Terminus. There was none elsewhere on the network that he was aware of. Certainly, there were none at the armoury when he had been responsible for doing the inventory. They had used the rail maintenance carriage, which had a flat open platform covering half its length, to move the heavy weapons to the school, but that would not have been big enough to move one tank.

Then it occurred to him to wonder how they had got the monorail trains onto the network. They had certainly not been manufactured here. They must have been brought in from somewhere else, and there must be an entrance to have got them in. Even if some final assembly had been carried out within the tunnels, he doubted it would be enough to bring them in through any of the stations. The armoury, with its large external doors and landing pad, would have been large enough to bring in the tanks or trains by air, but there would have been no way to get them into the station tunnels. He had always thought of the tunnel from the station elevator to the armoury as quite wide, but he remembered getting the military lasers out of it to the school. That had been pretty snug, and the laser was perhaps two thirds the width of the grav-tank.

His right leg dropped down suddenly as the sand below gave way and his leg disappeared knee deep into the dirt.

"You okay?" asked Mo, concerned.

Travis sat down and pulled his half-buried leg out of the hole, then rubbed his bruised calf muscles.

"Careful where you walk, Flex!" he shouted after his fellow cadet, receiving a nonchalant wave in return.

The sergeant checked his leg, pulling up the trouser of his black uniform. A few scrapes but no break or laceration to worry about. He scooted around and crouched down over the small hole he had created. Pushing some sand away, he found a wooden board, baked grey by the dry atmosphere. There was another one next to it. He had fallen down the gap between the two. He cleared away more sand. Mo joined in to help, revealing a portion of silver metal track. The lack of moisture in this place meant there was no rust on it. There was a monorail track here; it had been boarded over to prevent anyone falling into it. Then, over time, it had filled up with sand, the wooden coverings obscured with grey dust to the point where the track and the boards covering it were completely hidden.

Travis pushed himself up, brushing away Mo's proffered helping hand. The pair headed off after Flex. Corporal Lynch was framed as a shadow in the low light of the cavern. As they progressed across the cave the artificial lighting, if there was any, did not come on. Initially they were disappearing further into the dark, then it slowly became brighter. A line of light at ground level was spilling out across the floor, providing minimal illumination to the chamber above. Flex was standing staring at the rock to the right of the line of light. He had fished a head torch out of his bag, which was providing enough hard white light to brighten a section of the rock. As Travis got closer, he realized that his fellow cadet was looking at a dark grey electronic panel sunk into the wall of the cave. It blinked occasionally with a pair of dull red lights.

"What's that?" demanded Travis. Flex ignored him. "Flex?"

"Uh?" replied the corporal absentmindedly.

"Corporal, can I have an answer?" The sergeant's tone was harsher than he meant, but he was losing patience.

"Oh, yeah, um, it's a control panel," Flex answered, still lost in thought.

"For what?" Travis's tone was gentler, deciding that might yield a better result.

"Well, the door, obviously!"

Travis was staring at the thin line of white light and a sinking feeling passed through him. It was sunlight spraying in from the outside. There was a door ahead of them: a really big door.

"You mean this place has a back door we didn't know about?" Travis was incredulous.

"Well, yes," Flex said, looking perplexed at his commander.

Travis raised his arm to cover his eyes against the head torch shining in his face. "And you didn't think to tell us?" Travis was angry now. "What if the Kylnnar found it? We could have been taken by surprise this entire time. They could still attack this way."

Travis was raging. Mo quietly positioned himself so he could interpose himself between the two cadets if he needed to.

"Why are you shouting at me, Travis?" Flex asked, shocked and confused.

"You knew about this all along. You put all our lives at risk, you idiot!" screamed Travis.

"What? No – I didn't know it was here; I just found it," explained a visibly frightened Flex.

"You just found it!" spat Travis, his anger cooling slightly.

"Well, they had to get the tanks in somehow – and the trains, for that matter."

"But how did you know it was here?" Travis had worked out the same thing, but only by falling into the covered rail line.

Flex took a few steps until he stood roughly in the centre of the doorway, at least as judged by the line of sunlight at its base. He jumped up and down a couple of times. A low dull sound reverberated as he bounced on the wooden boards above the partially hollow pit below.

"There's a train line under here," explained Flex.

"Yes, I know," Travis shot back peevishly.

"But he didn't have to fall into it to find it," observed Mo, grinning.

Travis shot him an angry glance. Mo only smiled wider in response.

"Why have you not opened it?" asked Travis, still annoyed.

"Because there might be reptiles on the other side," Flex said. "As it goes, you might want to keep your voice down."

Travis went to unsling his pulse rifle only to realize he had left it back at the shed.

"Does the panel work?" he whispered urgently to Flex.

The corporal nodded back.

"So, we can get through it?" Travis asked.

"We won't know until we try, but we can't try until the last moment, or we risk giving away our position to the Kylnnar," Flex explained, his tone low and level.

"You said the panel worked?" pushed the sergeant.

"Sure, but the mechanism could be jammed; there might be rocks on the other side," Flex shrugged.

"Corporal Lynch, find a way to shut the door remotely after we are through it," Travis ordered. "We don't want the Kylnnar coming through the door after we've left."

"Yes, sergeant," Flex replied.

"Right, Mo, you come with me." Travis started striding back towards the shed.

"What am I doing?" Mo shouted after him, before looking back nervously towards the door.

"You're going to learn how to three-point-turn a grav-tank in a cave!" Travis shouted back, suddenly unconcerned by his volume.

CHAPTER 21

The classroom was not small. In peacetime it could comfortably accommodate a class of twenty-five. With the chairs piled against the wall nearest the school's central corridor and the desks piled up against the windows to create a barricade, it seemed even larger. The classroom was on the second storey of the main school building, the only structure with an upper floor. Given the sunken nature of the ground floor, the building and its flat roof sat lower than was normal, but still sat higher than the rest of the academy buildings. The defenders had generally avoided the use of this floor. The roof provided better visibility for targeting, and the sunken ground floor provided a more protected area. For the cadets, whose main focus was either staying alive or killing Kylnnar, the intervening storey was just a messy compromise.

The classroom was at the far end of the main school building, furthest away from the rock plain and nearer the valley of Wolfsreach. This made it safer, with more reinforced polymer and concrete between the room and the likely direction of attack. It still showed signs of the conflict: windows were blown out and a layer of the planet's ubiquitous dust had settled across the furniture. A hatch in the corner of the room provided access to the roof via a white-painted metal ladder.

Eleven cadets, all female, sat in the room, resting their backs against the wall. They were wearing their black and red uniforms, covered with webbing but no body armour. Grey battle helmets rested in laps or lay propped on the overturned furniture. A wide variety of weapons were clasped in hands or stuffed in belts. No pulse rifles were present; instead they had combat knives and sidearms. Corporal Inaya Chandra sat in one corner, slowly sharpening a sword with a whetstone.

The door to the classroom swung open as Lieutenant Jo Hakeswell pushed into the room. The cadets made to rise.

"As you were," she ordered. The half-risen students slumped back to the ground, emitting a low grumble.

Jo strode over to the teacher's desk, which was pushed up against one wall but not overturned like the other tables. On the table rested a pair of heavy gloves and a drop pack. She took off her helmet and hefted the pack over her shoulders. It clanked as its fuel bottles knocked against each other. She tied the loops of the pack carefully, pulling them tight. They only had ten drop packs and they had already been allocated. They had found two more: one for her and one for the pigtailed blonde girl who had been sent by Simon Kim to join Inaya's unit. They had stripped them from the bodies of the dead Kylnnar jump infantry. Bloodstains marked the hard fabric of the webbing. She did not like it; it felt slightly loose – not a surprise given the creature it had been designed for was bulkier than any human. On the plus side, they were better than the human-designed drop packs that the others were wearing, assuming they had enough fuel left in the tanks. The small valves on them were marked in Kylnnar lettering that she could not translate. She pulled on the gloves, which reached all the way up her arms nearly to her elbows.

She turned and picked out the blonde-haired mutineer she had been sent here with. The girl's eyes were red-ringed from crying. Her previously perfect pigtails were ruffled and coming undone. Jo looked into the kid's eyes and felt a moment of sorrow for her.

"Stand up," she ordered the girl. "Name?"

"Siobhan," the cadet muttered, struggling to her feet, weighed down as she was by a Kylnnar jump pack.

"It's ma'am when you address me," Jo reminded her, trying to keep discipline but not be unduly harsh.

"Cadet Private Siobhan Marcus, ma'am," she said, standing to attention, fighting down the inclination to salute.

"Age?"

"Fourteen, ma'am," she replied.

"Really? You look twelve," blurted out the officer.

"If I was twelve, I would have been evacuated, ma'am," the girl replied petulantly, her chin sticking out in defiance.

"Fair point," Jo conceded. "Who tied this?" she asked, tugging experimentally at the pack.

"I did."

"They help you?" Jo asked, nodding at the seated cadets. Siobhan shook her head.

Jo busily re-strapped the pack, tightening it and readjusting its positioning. It fit better but was still clearly oversized on the tiny blonde girl.

"None of you think to help her?" the lieutenant demanded of the room.

The other cadets looked down at their feet.

"Not our problem?" Inaya chirped, not looking up from her sharpening.

Jo finished with the blonde cadet's pack then pushed her back to sitting.

"What's that supposed to mean?" said the lieutenant, standing in front of Corporal Chandra and looking down at her.

"We heard what she said about us," observed Inaya, looking up at Jo.

Jo didn't bother to berate her about her lack of respect; she took getting a response from Inaya as a victory enough.

"She will learn soon enough she was wrong; she can't do that if she falls out of the sky and breaks her neck."

Inaya grinned at that.

"What is that thing?" Hakeswell pointed at the sword.

"Cavalry sabre," replied Inaya.

"You know fencing weapons aren't designed for actual combat?"

"It's not my fencing weapon; it's a family heirloom," countered Corporal Chandra.

"It looks European to me?" Jo doubted the story.

"It is." Inaya looked up with a broad smile. "British. My ancestor took it off them during the First Indian War of Independence."

"Not really standard issue," Lieutenant Hakeswell observed.

"And your gloves are?"

Jo gave a narrow smile and nodded.

Her communicator purred. Jo flipped it on.

"Hakeswell," she answered.

"You ready?" Simon's voice crackled through the comm.

"As we'll ever be," she replied.

"Does that mean yes?" came Simon's testy reply.

"Yes, sir."

"Good. They're coming. Come when we call."

"Yes, sir," she replied, but the comm had already clicked off.

***

S imon switched off his communicator and looked out across the rock plain from his vantage point in the gym. With his field glasses he scanned the horizon, zooming in and out as they picked up what they thought might be targets. He counted them: five tanks were on the way. Five hundred Kylnnar infantry were scattered around them, moving slowly. Bombers dropped low across the plain. The bombs were not aimed at the defenders: instead they popped smoke, covering the whole area in an almost impenetrable grey haze. Pulse cannon fire roared down the valley from the landing platform. Most of it slammed into the dormitory blocks, but some passed through the gaps, hitting the surface of the astro-hockey court. Reptiles in the hills around the school kept up a withering fire of lighter pulse rifle plasma shots.

Simon heard the occasional crack of a more traditional firearm. *The Colonials were in the fight too*, he surmised. He scanned the sky, looking for fighters and air cover. There was none coming. Even the bombers were flying fast and low as they dropped smoke, before bugging out as fast as possible for the atmosphere. The Kylnnar knew the defenders had one military laser left and had no desire to lose any more aircraft. There was no messing about this time: the Kylnnar were going all out. There was one last thing they would do. His communicator hummed, and he knew that would be it.

"Sir?" Onesie's voice demanded across the comm. "Armoury Station is under heavy attack. They're asking for reinforcements. Kylnnar are pushing through the gap in the tunnel in numbers."

"There are none to spare: they will have to hold with what they've got," Simon replied calmly.

He clicked off the communicator and focused his field glasses on the rock plain. Through the smoke he could make out the flat profile of the tanks as they progressed across the stony escarpment, moving slowly so that the infantry could keep pace and prevent the tanks being taken by anti-tank teams from the side and rear. It was how things should be done. It was an unnecessary precaution, though, as the cadets had no specialized anti-tank weapons, the sort that fired a rocket which could penetrate the tank from above, where the armour was weaker. That had been the one area where the base's armoury had proved sadly lacking. The tanks stood out more than they should; they were painted in a variety of greens and browns – perfect jungle camouflage, but it only made them more obvious against the grey sand and rock of the plain. It suggested that the Kylnnar had not initially planned to use them here on Wolfstar III. The tank on the far left spat fire and the pulse shell slammed into the corner of the main school building. Rubble tumbled down, narrowly missing the final military laser team, which was now ensconced beside it.

Simon did not need to give the order to open fire. Pulse weaponry, both cannon and rifle, sprayed out from the school in a blaze of light and fire. He watched it land, wounding and killing the Kylnnar troops but having little effect on the advancing tanks. More tank fire raked the academy. Simon involuntarily ducked an incoming pulse cannon blast roaring over his head, though it was too high to be any real risk. It sailed across the ruined gym before cracking against the roof of one of the dormitory buildings and spilling flames and shrapnel across the valley beyond. The upward slope of the plain meant that it was impossible for the tanks to bring their guns to bear on the largely low-lying buildings.

"Lieutenant, it's Hagen," his communicator squawked at him. He flicked ahead.

"It's Kim. Go ahead," he ordered.

"We can't get a workable angle," she barked down the communicator. "Seeking permission to move forward."

Simon had put Corporal Hagen in charge of the last of the military lasers. She was experiencing the same problem as the Kylnnar tanks, but in reverse. Designed to be fired at incoming drop ships or strapped to a starship, it was not purposed to be used against tanks. Hidden behind the north side of the main school building near the infirmary, it rested on the artificial flat plateau of the academy, and it could not dip enough to fire at the tanks. Bringing it forward might give it the downward angle to hit the attacking armour, but it would leave it horribly exposed. Positioned where it was, it would only be of use once the tanks were practically on top of them. Simon took in a deep breath, his mind racing. "Permission denied. Hold position."

Yes, sir," came the comm reply before it went dead.

He could not afford to lose the laser. It, and the shield humming above, were the only things keeping the fighters and bombers of the Kylnnar fleet from fully supporting the attacking ground forces. Simon tapped his communicator, switching to general broadcast.

"All missile launchers open fire!" he roared into it.

A scream of rockets sprung out from the school, some heading for the landing platform, but most in the direction of the tanks. They were set to minimum range; they would get one chance at this. No attempt was made to target specific enemy. This was a barrage, plain and simple. The missiles exploded along the far end of the rock plain, sending up a rolling curtain of fire, which turned into a deep black smoke licked with orange flames. Combining with the grey cover smoke already dropped by the Kylnnar bombers, the battlefield became a blur.

Simon searched the clouds of dirty grey for some information on whether the assault had worked. The tanks pushed through the haze, all five still coming, their pulse cannons rotating left and right, spitting huge plasma blasts at the school buildings. Simon let out a stream of invective. He had hoped one of the great tracked beasts would have at least been destabilized. In all the smoke he could not see what, if any, infantry casualties had been taken.

"Launch the drones – target the two tanks on the far right," he ordered into his communicator.

He could hear fast-moving motors buzzing behind him as twenty drones, each with four small propellers, climbed into the air. Below each one hung a single anti-tank mine, already primed. Simon hoped that they wouldn't explode in the air. They climbed into the sky. Panicked shots rang out from the southern rocks as Kylnnar snipers desperately tried to down the aerial attackers. They caught one, which crashed to the ground. Its landmine struck a rock, and it exploded, spitting shrapnel across the corner of the gym and forcing its defenders to take cover. Air was sucked in before being pushed out again and a chemical stench filled the atmosphere. Simon looked back to see the small crater the explosion had created; injured cadets were struggling away from the area. He saw bodies and parts of bodies. He closed his eyes momentarily at the bloody horror. Then he turned back to watch the remaining drones racing across the rock plain. He would care later; he would rage later. He did not have the time now.

The remaining nineteen drones raced out of the school, careful not to contact the protective shield that still covered the academy. Clearing the edge of the barrier, they elevated higher and sped in the direction of the two tanks on the right side opposite the gym. Obscured by the smoke, there was little ground fire targeting them. They were running in batches of five drones – though one was now four – with four operators controlling five drones each. It would have been better for one operator per drone, to create a less predictable pattern and to make targeting more focused, but the defenders could not spare that many cadets from the barricades. Sat in the control room, the four operators viewed the battle through headsets, receiving constant updates from their attack vehicles.

Two operators and ten drones targeted the tank on the furthest right. Breaking through the smoke, they slowed almost to a stop before dropping towards the vehicle. They hovered twenty feet above the tank, keeping pace with its slow movement across the plain. They dropped their anti-tank mines, aiming for the top and rear where the armour was weakest. A landmine was not a munition designed to drop from a drone. Chances are it would just bounce off, causing some minor paint damage but little else if it could not be made to land flat directly on top of the tank. The cadets of Wolfsreach Academy had learned a lesson from an old war. On each mine had been glued two sticks, looking like small plungers, one slightly longer than the other. As the mines dropped, they bobbled in the air, the sticks offsetting the weight of the mine, then they dropped straight down, landing flat on the tank. They exploded, and metal screamed and ruptured. Ammunition inside the tank caught fire, exploding out the back of the vehicle. The turret and gun lurched sideways, flinging the tank into a nearby boulder. Secondary explosions ripped through the vehicle, leaving only a burning wreck.

The assault on the second tank was less successful: two more drones were shot out of the air before reaching their target. One operator, less experienced or less naturally talented than the others, dropped his mines early. One smashed down on the front of the vehicle, sending up a sheet of fire but doing no real damage. The other four dropped in front of the tank, just as it rolled forward. They worked as landmines should, blowing out the tracks and sending the tank lurching to the left. This caused the other drone operator to miss his targeting, dropping his mines to the side of the vehicle, further damaging the tracks, but not destroying the tank.

Simon, watching through his field glasses, pumped the air with satisfaction.

"Get the drones back, rearm, and attack again!" he ordered into his communicator.

The drones were halfway back when Simon felt rather than heard a fizz in the air. His heart sank. The drones dropped from the sky as one, crashing useless and broken to the rock-scarred surface of the plain. Moments later, the electronic buzz in the air stopped. The Kylnnar had jammed the drones.

Simon felt wretched: just when something was working, it was snatched away again. He supposed he should have been happy that they had at least destroyed one tank and damaged another before losing the drones, but he found it impossible to see the positive. He tapped his communicator.

"Travis, we need you now," he said quietly.

***

"We've got to go, Flex!" Travis popped his head out the grav-tank and shouted down to his gunner.

"I'm working as fast as I can," Flex shot back.

Flex was standing next to the door with a large can of mechanical lubricant in his hand. He was spraying at the hydraulics of the half-open portal. Sun was now blazing through the gap. The sand-filled metal of the door system continued to creak and groan as it refused to open further. Flex used up the last of the lubricant spray. He screamed in rage and flung the can at the door; it bounced off with a ring of metal on metal.

"Won't it open?" asked Travis, pointing out the obvious.

Flex ran to the back of the tank where the small ladder was and clambered up onto the top, stopping next to the turret. He found himself face to face with the normally taller Travis.

"You're in the way," he observed peevishly.

The cadet sergeant ducked back into the tank, taking up his position on the commander's seat. Flex climbed in after him, dropping down the rungs of the turret into the gunner's seat.

"Back her up, Mo," said Flex.

Mo, sat in the driver's seat, looked back at his commander and got a nod of confirmation. The grav-tank reversed twenty feet.

218

"You're not going to do what I think you are?" Travis asked Flex.

"Yes," came the reply.

"That's a military-grade door; you can't destroy–" Travis did not finish before Flex fired.

The pulse cannon roared in the confined space of the cavern. It impacted on the lower part of the door. Fire flowed out and around the door and then back across the tank. The three flinched as the monitors showed the flames rolling over the vehicle in which they sat. The door was bent at a cruel angle of twisted metal.

"Not big enough," muttered Flex. Before Travis could say anything, Flex fired again.

Fire flowed back across the tank. It was starting to feel hot inside, though that was probably more the closeness of three people in a small place than the burning outside. The flames cleared to reveal the door was bent slightly more.

"Big enough?" Flex asked Mo.

"Let's see," came his phlegmatic response.

Mo backed up further until the tank was almost against the train service sheds. Mo revved the engine to maximum and then let off the brake. The tank lurched forward.

"We're not going to fit!" screamed Travis, staring terrified at his monitor.

A moment before they hit the door, Mo shut off the engine. The vehicle dropped, lurching and bumping along the sand of the cavern floor. Its momentum carried it under the metal barrier, and a horrific sound rang through the vehicle as the tank's turret scraped against the door. Then they were through.

Mo slammed the engines back on before they lost all momentum and crashed into the rocks outside. The grav-tank purred back to life and rose into the air. Mo dragged on the controls, gaining enough height to get above the rocks. The whole tank bounced side to side as the grav-engines tried to compensate for the uneven surface.

Flex turned to Travis and tossed him up a small plastic device.

"What's this?" asked the puzzled tank commander.

"The remote you wanted for the door," observed Flex, turning back to his gunnery console.

Travis looked at the piece of plastic and then at the monitor showing the rear of the tank. The mangled remains of the door were disappearing into the distance as the armoured vehicle roared forwards.

"Thanks," he grunted, and tossed the useless remote over his shoulder.

Mo was powering ahead as the fast-moving grav-tank purred happily at its release from captivity. The tank rounded a large outcrop of rocks and drove onto the rock plain. Shocked Kylnnar soldiers who had been infiltrating round the side of the rock plain opened up with pulse rifle fire. Travis tapped his console, taking control of the minigun that sat on top of the tank. He hoped it was still there and had not been ripped off by Mo's escapade with the cavern door.

He pressed the button, and metal spat from the spiralling circular machine gun. Travis directed it across the rocks. The sergeant marvelled at the viciousness of the gun as its ordnance cut through the bodies of the surprised reptiles, which tumbled from the rocks.

Then the cadets were out into the plain. It was a place of smoke and dust and fire. Pulse fire, both light and heavy, rained across the battlefield. Travis picked out the five tanks. The furthest one away from them was a smouldering ruin, and another near it was disabled but its heavy pulse cannon was still barking shots at the school buildings. The three tanks still moving were now pressing on the school. One was approaching the ruined gym, while the other two were nearing the main school building.

"Go for the nearest one!" shouted Travis.

"Yes, sir," Mo replied eagerly.

The tank swung tightly round the outcrop of rock coming up on the rear of the nearest tank. It was one of the two that was approaching the main school building. Kylnnar soldiers shielding themselves behind the tank scattered as they heard the harsh buzz of the Confederation grav-tank approaching. Travis and his tank crew were moving fast – faster than made sense for aiming and firing, but they did not know that as it was their first time out in a tank.

"Fire at will," ordered Travis.

Flex fired; the first pulse cannon blast went wide, coursing through a group of Kylnnar infantry before exploding just in front of the gym.

"Another shot like that and Kim will be ripping us a new one," said Travis.

"I'm trying," muttered Flex.

A second shot caught their target on the rear of its tracks. They gave way, unwrapping as the vehicle tried to reverse to meet the oncoming assault. Realizing it was beached, its turret started to swing round. A third pulse shot boomed out from the grav-tank and slammed into the rear of the Kylnnar vehicle. Looking through the monitor, the three crew could see the ruptured and torn armour. It was still operating, though the turret completed its rotation, sending a shot just wide of the fast-moving Confederation grav-tank. Coming in closer, the cadets fired a fourth shot straight into the rear of the disabled tank. The shell ruptured the weak rear of the vehicle, catching the ammunition stored inside. It exploded in a gigantic pillar of flame, sending the turret and the main gun skyrocketing up into the air. It crashed down fifty yards across the rock plain on some hapless attackers.

With no air cover and no support, Travis and his team had decided to go with the element of surprise and try to inflict as much damage as they could. Had they been older and more experienced, they would have known this was suicide. But they were young, maybe a little foolish, and definitely brave. They were already one tank up, but now the Kylnnar tanks were moving. The stranded but operational tank that had lost its tracks to the drones sent a shot their way. It slammed into their side armour, but hit at a difficult angle, which kept the damage to the minimum. At least the Confederation vehicle could still manoeuvre.

The other two Kylnnar tanks were moving fast. Their experienced crews were spinning them around, turrets rotating on the turn. A shot pulsed from the one nearest the gym, crashing into the front armour of the grav-tank. Anywhere else and it would have ruptured the hull and exploded inside, but the front armour was just strong enough to withstand the hit. It rocked them all back in their seats, before throwing them forward again. Flex gasped for breath, the wind knocked out of him. He reached his hand to his nose; it came away wet with blood. He spun the main gun around. It did not have to move far; it barked at the Kylnnar tank that had just hit them. It missed, passing wide over the gym before slamming into the glass-like stone of the hills behind. A rain of razor-sharp sparkling stone showered the school and part of the rock plain.

"What we got left?" demanded Travis.

"Three more shots," Flex spat back.

"What?" Travis yelped. "There should be enough capacity for forty shots."

"Sure, if the plasma cells were at full capacity, but they weren't – they were a quarter full. I told you that!" shouted Flex.

"No, you didn't! You told me they were at full capacity earlier!" muttered Travis angrily.

"So, I misread it, I'm not a tank gunner," shouted Flex over his shoulder.

"How can you misread the difference between a quarter full and full? You're supposed to be a genius, Flex. Oh, never mind. I wasn't expecting us to last this long anyway," the sergeant replied.

"What do you mean?" Mo was incredulous. "We've been in this thing for less than ten minutes."

"I know," Travis said. "Target the disabled tank; it will be easier to knock out than the moving enemy."

"What do we do about them?" shouted Flex. His ears were muffled by the noise and heat of the metal can in which he was sitting.

"Nothing!" Travis roared above the racket. "We need to take out what we can to stop it targeting the school."

The tank plunged on, heedless of the two enemy now moving to intercept, racing towards the Kylnnar vehicle previously incapacitated by the drones.

"Destroy it, Flex," ordered Travis.

The stranded Kylnnar vehicle knew what was coming and was desperately firing at the oncoming Confederation vehicle. Pulse plasma splashed uselessly against the front armour of the grav-tank. Flex unleashed his three shots one after the other at the sitting duck in front of him. It exploded in a ball of flame, hot metal ripping outward across the plain. As the smoke cleared, Travis noted the crumpled pile of metal; the remnants of the vehicle they had destroyed.

The grav-tank shook again as a pulse shot crashed into the corner. The remaining enemy tanks were on their side and trying to get behind them where the armour was weakest.

"We've lost an engine!" shouted Mo.

"Hard right. Get us side on at least to those other two tanks," responded the sergeant.

"Another engine gone!" Mo screamed as he yanked hard right on the controls, turning back in the direction of the gym. This was impossible in a normal tank and difficult in a flying tank, especially one that had lost nearly half its engines.

Mo gunned the remaining engines, trying to get clear. Another pulse cannon blast slammed into the side, rocking the tank. Then something hit the roof of the tank where it was weakest. The metal on the rear left blew inward and exploded fragments into the confined space of the tank. The three screamed as they were fragged with burning shrapnel.

"What the hell was that?" shouted Travis. "That was on top."

Flex was staring at his rear-view screen. "They have anti-tank weapons."

"Why do they have anti-tank weapons when we're not supposed to have tanks?" shouted Travis, offended at the unfairness of the situation.

Flex was staring at his screen. Teams of Kylnnar infantry carrying anti-tank missiles were coming up the plain. They launched! The screen went black, and at the same moment the tank was lifted high in the air from the back as the missiles slammed into the ground under it. The tank pitched forward, almost somersaulting. Just before it flipped over completely, it stopped, lingering in the air for a moment, before crashing thunderously back to the ground the correct way up. The three were flung about the vehicle, slamming into the metal of the can. Flex was thrown sideways and crushed under the warped metal of his firing console. Travis watched his panel as three more engines failed. Then the panel itself burst into flames. He popped the hatch.

"Mo, Flex, get out," he ordered, his voice rasping in the hot space.

Mo leaped back and scrambled past out of the hatch.

"Flex, get a move on; this thing is on fire," Travis commanded.

"I can't, Travis, I'm stuck; the heat is horrible." Flex was weeping.

Travis reached down, but the flames from the console were beating across the lower part of the tank. Noxious black smoke had filled the whole cavity.

"Help me, Travis," Flex said, desperate.

Travis tried to push down towards the young cadet.

Suddenly arms grabbed him and lifted him bodily up through the turret. He shouted and kicked but could not get free.

"Flex, Flex, we need to save Flex!" the sergeant screamed.

Mo yanked his protesting commander through the hatch and flung him from the tank. Travis landed hard on the stone, his left arm crashing against a large rock with a sickening crunch. Mo leapt down beside him. He thrust his arm around the injured sergeant's shoulder and pushed and dragged him away from the burning vehicle.

Travis was befuddled. All he could think was that he needed to get back to save Flex. Then the tank rocketed upward into the air, snapping in half before exploding in a ball of flame as two pulse cannon blasts from the Kylnnar tanks caught it in the side. The pair of cadets were sent flying across the rocks. Bloody and grazed, they staggered back to their feet. They looked back. The grav-tank was barely there, a mass of twisted, burning metal. Black smoke billowed across the plain from the shallow crater the explosion had left. The cadets were terrified that the two tanks would hunt them down, but they had already turned away and were driving at speed back to their original target, the school.

Mo looked at Travis. "I'm sorry about Flex."

Travis said nothing. All he could hear was the dying screams of his fellow cadet – screams he could not possibly have heard over the explosions and noise of the battlefield. That would not stop him waking up in the middle of the night hearing those screams. Every night. For the rest of his life.

***

Simon Kim ducked back into his foxhole as the grav-tank perished in a series of spectacular fiery bangs. He did not know how they had done it. He had expected them to provide some flanking fire, not go charging into battle. Still, they had destroyed one tank and finished off another. He had seen figures jumping from the tank, though with all the smoke and dust he could not tell who; he just hoped all of them had made it out alive.

Now the enemy was reduced to two tanks, but they were bearing down on the school, aiming for the gap between the devastated gym building and the dining hall. The pulse cannon of the lead tank was firing, slamming plasma blast after blast into the dining hall and the adjoining main school building. The second tank was flowing in behind, using the leader as cover. Kylnnar soldiers had reached the edges of the school. Their numbers were much diminished by the fire coming from the academy, but still a substantial proportion had survived the bloody destruction of the plain, and over three hundred had reached the buildings.

The students' defensive line ran from the southern hills to the gym to the main school building to the infirmary, to the northern cliffs that framed the other side of the valley. A thin line of black-uniformed cadets was firing from behind any cover available. The ruined gym had been turned into a strong point near one end of the line. The destroyed structure of smashed-up concrete and twisted metal provided the perfect cover for two full squads of older students, together with two of the surviving pulse cannons, which were ploughing out fire across the plain. The driver of the lead Kylnnar tank was rumbling past the ruined wall of the gym. Suddenly he slammed it left, mounting the ravaged stones at the corner of the gym and sending rubble tumbling into the lowered foundation of the devastated structure.

WOLFSREACH ACADEMY

Simon, in his lead position at the front of the building, was almost crushed, and crawled swiftly to get clear of the loose building material collapsing around him. The rear of the tank disgorged ten Kylnnar soldiers into the complex. Simon turned around, throwing himself on his back, and opened fire on the exiting enemy. He cut down the third trooper out and then the fourth, but the others were out now and firing on him. He scrabbled up a bank of collapsed stone, shuffling on his backside, his feet pushing desperately to get over it. He threw himself over, heedless of what lay beyond, and landed below in a dusty pile of firing cadets. There were shouts of annoyance and surprise. Vishnu Patel pulled his commander back, helping him struggle up to his knees. The fourteen-year-old private, normally a phlegmatic individual, looked terrified.

The operators of one pulse cannon just behind them had angled it upwards and were firing non-stop at the underside of the Kylnnar tank yawning above them. It felt dark despite it being afternoon, as the metal monstrosity was blocking out the sun above the cadets. The pulse cannon continued to hum, shot after shot slamming into the same place, trying to punch through the underside of the vehicle before it pulled back. The other crew were yanking their pulse cannon backwards, trying to get some space from the tank so it could counter the Kylnnar soldiers coming over the barricades.

The second tank passed the leader before performing the same manoeuvre and turning hard left, aiming for the gap between the dining hall and the gym, trying to get through between the buildings to the astro-hockey pitch beyond. Cadets who had been lying in the gap firing out at the oncoming attack rolled and ran to get clear. Not all of them made it. The second tank careered into the corner of the dining hall. Its roof gave way and the corner of the tank dropped into the gap created by the lowered floor of the building. It tried to reverse, and metal and engines screeched and squealed as it fought the building that was trapping it.

"Get the laser round, Hagen!" screamed Simon into his communicator. "Hit the tank on the gym!"

"Way ahead of you, sir," the teenaged girl replied, as her team of four wheeled the military laser round the corner of the main school building towards the dining hall. The sunken corridor between the main school building and the officers' mess blocked her way from bringing the laser even closer.

Hagen took in the scene of carnage. She reckoned if she could just get the right angle, she could get a shot, over the top of the sunken corridor, through the back of the tank trapped in the dining hall, through to the tank mounted on the gym wall. She had only one shot: the Kylnnar soldiers were merely yards away. The military laser purred to life and sent a straight line of blazing light out towards the tanks, seconds before the trapped tank got free and roared clear of the dining hall, spilling out onto the astro-hockey pitch beyond.

The other tank was not so lucky: the laser hit the tank on the gym wall in the side, punching straight through it. Then the team moved the laser unit sharply upwards, taking the beam up and through the tank. Blue light cut up through the vehicle until the laser caught the underside of the school's protective shield, sending a shower of rainbow light exploding across the whole area. The Kylnnar tank split in half, collapsing each side of the gym wall. Hagen heard screams: she hoped they were of panic or surprise and that she had not just killed her commander. The team flung the laser to the left, cutting through the already destroyed tank, catching rubble and Kylnnar attackers in its sweep.

Then the reptiles were on them. Hagen snatched up a metal tool – some sort of spanner from the carriage of the military laser – and swung it two-handed as hard as she could. It smashed through the transparent face shield of the attacking Kylnnar's helmet, continuing into the burly beast's face. It staggered back

228

in shock. Then she slung her pulse rifle free from her back and drove three rounds through the attacking soldier. A second Kylnnar was on her. The hulking creature grabbed her, one hand forcing her rifle up, the other on her throat, and threw her over the military laser and into the wall of the building beyond. She hit it like a ragdoll and slid down it, landing in the dust. Everything hurt. She had felt bones break, and she coughed blood. She hoped she had just bitten her cheek and that a rib had not punctured her lung. She was in so much pain she could not tell. Hagen fired a couple of aimless shots over the military laser at the milling figures beyond. She tried to push herself up to standing using the wall. Pain gave way to blackness, and she collapsed unconscious to the sand.

***

Simon looked up at the destroyed tank. It had not exploded, just been cut in half. He could see the injured Kylnnar crews looking shocked and dazed in their seats. They started to struggle to get themselves free, but the cadets shot them mercilessly. Simon looked around for the last surviving tank, which had halted in the middle of the astro-hockey pitch. It was disgorging another ten Kylnnar soldiers, in inappropriate jungle camo, into the centre of the school complex. They shot down the crew of one of the pulse cannons. They used the tank as a barrier, hunkering down behind it, though with fire coming in from three sides there was little place to shelter. The officer of the group seemed to be tapping at an instrument, looking for something.

"Hakeswell!" Simon shouted into his communicator.

"We're here," his fellow lieutenant responded calmly.

"Hakeswell, we need Chandra and her team on the hockey court," Simon ordered.

"And me?" Jo asked steadily.

"Behind the main line."

229

***

Understood." Jo flicked off the communicator.

She turned to Inaya to see if she had caught the orders. The corporal was way ahead of the lieutenant. Leading her team, she was already clambering up the white metal ladder to the hatch of the roof, her squad of five tracking after her. Jo turned to her own squad of five troopers. She looked across their faces: all girls, all teenagers, all of them young-looking for their age. The lighter-weight students had been chosen so the packs would work, and that meant using younger and smaller cadets. She was looking at children. She stowed her feelings; it did not matter: fight and maybe die versus be slaughtered by the reptiles. When there was only one real option, it was an easy decision to make. The frightened but determined faces stared back at her.

"On me," she said and strode towards the ladder.

She did not look back; she knew they were behind her.

Inaya Chandra climbed through the open hatch of the roof into a sea of plasma fire and thundering explosions. She perched on the edge, squatting down and pulling her colleagues up after her. Hunkering down, they ran across the roof in a half crouch towards the edge nearest the sports field. Two cadets, the remnants of the squad on the roof, were perched on the edge of the building, sending pulse rifle shots at the Kylnnar sheltering next to the tank. The pulse fire was exploding off the reactive armour of the Kylnnar vehicle, providing little threat to the squad of reptiles. They broke from the cover of the tank, heading for the control room. Inaya could not be sure of their plan, but she could take an educated guess: they were going for the shield.

"Now!" she screamed over the rage of battle.

The six cadets, drop packs strapped on, stepped up onto the raised stone edge that ringed the flat roof of the main school building. Simon had made a bet; the lieutenant had decided if he got people who were small enough and light enough, then perhaps a drop pack could be made to work like a jump pack, if only for a moment.

The students hit the arrestor buttons on their packs. The bottles of fuel fired, sending jets of air out of two propulsion units. The six leapt twenty feet into the air, dropping down in a wide curve towards the running Kylnnar soldiers. At the top of the arc, the engines started to splutter and then stopped, and then the figures dropped from the sky. Then, as one, they hit another button: a small emergency boost of fuel. It was enough to arrest their fall for a moment.

Inaya hit the ground with a thump and rolled. She came up to her knees, her sabre slashing out through the guts of the Kylnnar leader. She dragged the blade clear of the shocked reptile and stood up, slashing backwards across the creature's rear torso. The highly sharpened sabre carved through its armour into its flesh. She was on to the next one, cutting down from right to left in a wide sweep. The soldier caught it on his rifle, and the impact reverberated through Inaya. She spun, and the Kylnnar brought his rifle across, trying to block the slash and going for her neck. Suddenly though, the swordswoman dropped to her knees, slashing hard through the creature's ligaments. The reptile toppled forward with a bellow of pain. Coming up, Inaya looked for the gap between the Kylnnar soldier's armour and helmet, and plunged her sabre down through his neck, killing him. She tried to wrestle the blade free. Then another Kylnnar was on her, but a shot rang out and the creature collapsed to the ground, having been shot through the head. Inaya looked to the roof, but she could not see who had fired.

Her squad were not faring so well: two were down, dead or injured, for five dead Kylnnar – a good return, but not enough of an advantage given that surprise had been on their side.

"Get to the tank!" she shouted, dragging her sword free and engaging two more of the enemy.

She jinxed in, slashing at one and catching the sweeping rifle butt of another on her blade as it looped back. She dragged free her small firearm from her belt and shot the first through the face. The second one took another swing with his rifle, catching her on the shoulder. She was sent sprawling to the dirt, her pistol spinning across the field. She tumbled sideways, narrowly missing being shot by a pulse blast. She rolled back and flipped up no handed, her sword coming up with her. She slammed it through the transparent front of her attacker's helmet.

Two of her team were racing for the tank, trying to keep out of sight of its visual sensors. They carried explosives, anti-tank mines. The pair sprinted forward and magnetically attached them to the rear of the vehicle. A desperate Kylnnar soldier grabbed one of the cadets and threw them clear. He dragged out a combat knife and wedged it under the mine, trying to pry it off. A teenage girl, half the creature's size, flung herself at his knees. He staggered away, more in surprise than from the mass of the fragile girl he looked down on with rage. The mines exploded the rear of the tank and the whole thing burst into flames. Inaya was thrown flat by the explosion. She crawled forward and grabbed up her pistol, turning to face the next attacker.

It was then she realized that she was the only one left on the field. Everyone else, human or reptile, was dead.

***

Joanna came out of the hatch and broke into a run. She did not see Inaya make her jump; she was too focused on her own attack. The six in her squad jogged across the roof, which ran the length of the school. They sped up as they reached the far edge, heading for the side away from the dining hall. They needed a firm surface to jump from, and the partially collapsed roof of the former temporary hospital was not that. They could not jump in the middle or they risked landing on the single-storey officers' mess building in front of it. The only option was to jump to the left into the surging mass of Kylnnar soldiers heading for the infirmary building.

Drawing sidearms as they sped, the squad hit the left-hand corner of the school at a sprint. They jumped as one, hitting the jets on their packs as they leapt, and rose in the air in a great arc. The packs cut out and they started to drop, and just before they hit the ground, the squad used the final boost on their packs to slow their descent to land safely.

Joanna dropped to one knee as she landed, a jolt coursing into her body. She was behind the Kylnnar attack. She came up firing twin pistols, twenty shots in each. It was a turkey shoot. The reptiles had not expected this move, so the six cadets had to seize the surprise or be swiftly dispatched. Joanna targeted two Kylnnar soldiers in front of her and put three bullets in the back of each. The rear of the Kylnnar infantry was turning on them. She shot down another two: four bullets into one, five bullets into another. Between their body armour and their sheer size, a single bullet was not enough to take down one of the aliens. She continued firing, and one of her guns clicked empty. She tossed it away, then was slammed to the ground by a Kylnnar, the breath whooshing from her body. Maybe she cried out, maybe she didn't: in the screaming roar of close combat, she could not hear it. She grasped her remaining pistol in two hands, firing at point-blank range through the transparent mask of the creature's helmet. The heavy body slumped over her, dead. She pushed her way out from underneath, grunting and cursing as she struggled free.

"Incendiaries!" she screamed, staggering to her feet.

The six cadets unclipped small box-like grenades from their belts and tossed them into the churning mass of the Kylnnar attack. They opened with a spray of blue light, which turned into a white sheet of incandescent flame. Each one surged with an indiscriminate spin of flaming light, vaporizing everything in its way. Mostly Kylnnar, but at least two cadets fighting near the wall of the dining hall, were caught in the blast.

"Attack!" Joanna shouted.

They drew weapons, combat knives, and makeshift metal spikes and charged at the Kylnnar rear. Joanna jinxed to the left of one of the reptiles, ducking under a sweeping strike of the butt of a pulse rifle. She stepped, fist balled, aiming for what on a human would be the solar plexus. A spike jetted out from her glove and plunged into the creature's chest. The second gloved hand came round; her left. It plunged up under the reptile's right arm into its armpit. She yanked both out and thrust them back in again and again in a frenzy of stabs. Through the reptile's helmet, she could see the female's eyes go glassy, and the Kylnnar collapsed to the ground. Another attacker was running. Joanna hit the button on her drop pack, hoping there was still a drop of fuel. She got lucky. It hiccupped and she skipped into the air, coming down on top of her attacker and plunging her spikes into the soft part of the body between neck and shoulder. The pair slumped to the ground. Joanna spread face down on the Kylnnar corpse then rolled off, coming up to see a reptile soldier above her, a large male, pointing a pulse rifle in her face.

The Kylnnar raised his left hand to his head, as if trying to check his helmet communicator. Then he pulled his gun up. Sun flowed in where the creature had been. He was gone. Joanna could not fathom what had happened, but let out the breath she had been holding.

CHAPTER 22

Location: Wolfsreach Academy, Wolfstar III
Date: 19 December 2196 CE, Earth Standard Calendar
Time: 22.47 Local Time 26.5-hour clock

Lieutenant Hakeswell and Sergeant Ronin laid the shattered body of Private Siobhan Marcus gently on the ground of the astro-hockey pitch. Her ruined face made her hard to identify, but her blonde pigtails and the ill-fitting drop pack she still wore spoke to who she was.

"Brave kid."

Jo Hakeswell looked up to see Inaya standing over them. She tried to work out if Inaya was asking a question or making a statement.

"Yes, I guess," offered Jo, standing up.

Corporal Chandra returned her a quizzical look.

"I mean, is it really bravery when you're forced into it?" she tried to explain.

"You mean by you and Simon?" asked Inaya.

"I mean by the Kylnnar," Lieutenant Hakeswell shot back angrily.

Inaya said nothing. Joanna's anger told her all she needed to know. Jo's head might blame the reptiles, but her heart would blame herself.

"The lieutenant wants you in the control room," someone said.

Jo looked, trying to place the voice. It was dark now, and while the school was lit up, as was the field, the destruction of the repeated Kylnnar attacks had left pockets of darkness. Vishnu Patel stepped out into the light.

"I'm coming," she acknowledged.

"Both of you," Vishnu indicated Travis.

The sergeant nodded.

"You want to come?" he asked his girlfriend.

"Nothing much else to do," she observed with a smile.

The four set off for the control room.

Simon Kim did not look at the group as they entered and made no complaint at Inaya's uninvited presence. Instead, he continued to stare at the screen in front of him. Onesie was sat at the control panel, tapping away and intermittently bringing up different screens that Simon was studying intently.

"I thought Flex would be here?" Jo asked.

Simon looked up at that.

"You didn't tell her?" he said to Travis.

A look of pain ravaged the sergeant's face.

"How?" was all Jo asked.

"In the tank," Travis explained sadly.

Her hand moved up to cover a single tear that trickled from her eye.

Simon heaved a sigh and went back to the screen.

"That is the last run; they've not sent another?" he asked Onesie.

"Looks like. The last four times, there were landers on the way out as the other landers returned. This time it's only landers going back."

236

"What do you think: an evacuation?" Simon questioned.

Onesie gave a shrug that said 'how should I know?'

"What's going on?" Joanna demanded, stepping next to Simon to look at the screen.

"I think they are evacuating the Colonials from their homes near the pole," he replied.

"What?" Jo was staring at the screen now, as intently as Simon.

"How many Colonials are there?" he asked her.

"I have no idea: low single thousands, at a guess?" she offered.

"So, it's just possible they squeezed them all on," Simon mused.

"Maybe we could send some drones to check?" offered Onesie doubtfully.

"Too far; they'll never make it," Simon said, dismissing the idea.

"What are you thinking, lieutenant?" asked Travis.

"There has been no attack, no movement, no sign of anything near the valley for two hours," said Simon. "The Kylnnar ships cleared the landing platform about the same time, heading for the main fleet. As they were returning, further ships left from below the ridge line. In both cases they flew low, staying invisible from our weapons. We only picked them up on the screen as they came off the deck and headed for space. They started evacuating from the pole about the same time."

"What does all that mean?" Travis said.

"It means they're leaving," Jo interjected.

"So, we've won," Travis grinned. "Why not just say that?"

"Because…" Jo paused, "there's a risk they do something to us when they leave."

"Like what?"

"A chemical attack, a germ weapon, I don't know: something the shield can't stop," Simon stated calmly.

"But that's not fair," Inaya said. "That's not fair; we beat them, that's not fair."

Travis put his arm round her shoulder.

Simon watched the screen. The transport ships returning from the pole were small green dots approaching the much larger blocky outlines of the capital ships in space above. They disappeared as if merging with the large green blocks.

"Docking?" Simon looked at Jo.

She nodded; her breath held in.

Then one of the Kylnnar destroyers winked off the screen, followed moments later by the second. The six transport vessels disappeared, the tank carrier the last to go. Finally, the heavy cruiser disappeared from the screen.

The cadets stood staring at the screen as if they could not believe it. The Kylnnar had gone.

CHAPTER 23

Mo stuck out his arm, blocking Travis's path. The sergeant stopped and gave his fellow cadet a questioning look. Mo crouched down on the trail, pulled out a small canister and shook it. He sprayed it across the path at ankle height. A red laser beam sparkled for a moment in the early-morning sunlight, then disappeared again. Travis hunkered down next to his fellow student.

"Trip line?" he asked, knowing the answer, simply happy his friend had spotted it.

Mo nodded.

Travis looked to his right; he could see the laser generator tucked neatly almost out of sight behind a rock. The claymore mine planted next to it had been obscured with sand and gravel. He looked across to the other side of the trail, seeing the receiver that was picking up the laser signal. Another step and the laser would have been broken; the mine would have sprayed explosive and ball bearings across the path, ripping the pair apart. He took a breath and scooted back from the trap before standing up.

Travis pulled out his field glasses and surveyed the scene. Lieutenant Kim had sent the pair on a scouting mission that morning. Just the two of them: they had taken so many casualties, the cadets could no longer spare a full squad from the defence of the academy simply to reconnoitre. Only fifty-six cadets had survived uninjured and that was a relative term, most of them were covered with cuts and bruises. Slightly more cadets were classed as walking wounded, capable of defending the school maybe, but not hiking across rocky terrain. They had been sent to survey the northern mountains all the way up to the landing platform, looking for the presence of the Kylnnar. Starting out just after dawn, the pair had taken the exit from the roof of the armoury and then trekked up the side of the valley towards the landing platform. Avoiding their own planted explosives and now those left by the reptiles had made it a torturous, nerve-wracking journey. Until now they had seen no sign of the Kylnnar or their Colonial allies.

The landing platform was carved out of a mountain that stood at one end of the valley, flattened and asphalted by the might of the Confederation Military's Corps of Engineers. The path they were on led down to the platform, winding through the grey windswept rock. It was the only way to access the space port from the northern mountain range. Travis's gaze, augmented by his field glasses, swept across the damaged landing area. He could see the wrecked lander that Tom had crippled with his only shot from his pulse sniper rifle, and what he suspected was the exploded remains of the pulse cannon that Julia had destroyed. A wave of sadness flowed through him at the thought of the brave young snipers, both now dead. The remains of another ship lay scattered across the opposite side of the platform. Great holes had been gouged in its surface, he presumed by missile fire from the school. The Kylnnar who had been up here had not had it all their own way.

The sergeant could see no sign of any of the reptiles. No figures moved across the area, and all the dead had been taken away. It seemed that the Kylnnar had truly left. He could see the fat round shapes of mines scattered across the surface. He focused on the wrecked landers and the holes in the platform, picking out the shape of packages – packages that should not be there. More high explosives, he guessed. He also expected there to be further tripwires and anti-personnel mines similar to the one blocking the path, though at this distance he could not see any, even with his glasses on maximum focus.

"Lieutenant Kim, it's Sergeant Travis," he said into his communicator.

"It's Kim, what can you see?" Simon asked urgently.

"We've made it to the landing platform. We moved slow to check for Kylnnar. We've seen no evidence of them in the northern mountains or on the landing platform."

"So, the landing platform is clear?" Kim demanded.

"Sort of," Travis offered up with a shrug.

"What the hell does that mean?" came the angry response.

Travis looked at Mo still crouched down by the laser tripwire. The cadet gave him a shrug.

"There are no Kylnnar alive or dead visible; no Kylnnar ships; no weapon systems obvious," he relayed carefully. "But…"

"But what?" barked the lieutenant.

"It's wired to blow," Travis stated blandly.

"How bad?" came the crackled response.

"What does he mean, 'how bad'?" mouthed Travis at Mo.

The crouching student gave another shrug and a wide smile.

"Thanks!" mouthed Travis, before raising his voice into his comm. "Bad!" he stated.

There was a momentary pause and Travis wondered if his commander had clicked off.

"How long to disarm?" the lieutenant asked through the communicator.

Travis rolled his eyes at Mo. "I don't know: a couple of days if you have three specialist bomb disposal teams to hand," Travis shot back sarcastically.

He instantly regretted it. He was tired; he had struggled to sleep the previous night and trekking up here in the mountains, where the already oxygen-thin air was at its thinnest, made it harder. Also, the departure of the Kylnnar had removed with it some of the pressure for military discipline, and old school behaviours had slipped back into use very quickly. Travis stared at his communicator like a venomous serpent waiting for the inevitable attack.

"Understood," came the calm reply from his commander. "Return to base."

The comm went dead.

Travis signalled to Mo, who came up from his crouch. The pair set off back the way they had come.

***

Simon clicked off the comm and stared out across the rock plain. Shattered tanks and blasted rocks filled the view from where he stood next to the ruined gym building. On his orders they had started collecting the corpses of both sides. He could not bear for them to lie together. He did not know why. It was just a feeling. So, he had ordered the dead cadets and Miss Murphy's body to be carefully laid out on the astro-hockey pitch in neat rows. Seeing the rows of bodies had hit him hard. A great wrenching anger with life and with the reptiles filled him.

242

He had ordered the Kylnnar bodies to be dumped out on the plain away from those of the students. Oddly, to him at least, the cadets seem to have treated the enemy with broadly the same respect they had shown their own kind. They had taken all the dead attackers and brought them here, those slain in the underground station and in the centre of the school. Four students each grasped one of the slain creatures, such was their bulk compared to humans. They had laid them out in the same neat lines as they had the cadets – at least as much as the rocky surface would permit.

Joanna Hakeswell strode up to him from the rocky plain. She saluted and he realized it was the first time he had seen her that morning. She looked tired; they all did. Few had slept well the previous night, the first night since the Kylnnar had apparently withdrawn. None had really believed it; all had been waiting for some sort of night-time surprise attack. The anticipation had left them more frayed than the battles themselves, if that were possible.

"What do you want us to do with the bits?" she asked.

"The bits?" he repeated, confused.

"You know; the *bits*." She looked as though she were willing him to understand.

"What bits?"

"The body parts," she sighed, keen to avoid elucidating her point. "Some were caught up in explosions. Sometimes it's tough to separate who is who, especially on the Kylnnar side."

"Oh, the bits," he grunted, suddenly desperate to get back to a euphemism. "Wrap them up, I guess?" he offered helplessly.

"Good, that's what we are doing. Just checking we were doing it right. Any luck on the platform?"

Simon looked thankful for the change in subject. "It's a no go: it's wired to blow."

She nodded her understanding. "You've told the teams at Armoury Station?"

He looked confused.

"What if they decide to try to go down the tunnel to the landing platform?" she queried.

Simon looked at her confused again, then comprehension dawned.

"Reynolds," he demanded into his communicator.

"Yes, sir," came the Armoury Station commander's voice.

"On no account are you to progress down the tunnel towards the space port," ordered Simon quickly.

"Sure, sir," came the easy-going sergeant's response. "Any reason why?"

"It's possible it's wired to blow."

"Understood, sir," came the sergeant's unruffled reply.

The communicator clicked off and Simon turned back to Jo. Before he could say anything, it buzzed again. He swore and clicked it on.

"Kim," he answered.

"Get to the control room now, lieutenant," Onesie demanded down the link.

Simon looked at Jo and the pair loped off towards the control room. The pair pushed through the door to see Onesie staring intently at the monitor in the half dark, the green light from the screen playing across his face.

"What is it?" Hakeswell beat Simon to the question.

"Look!" Onesie shouted in panic, prodding the screen.

The lieutenants looked at the monitor and a sinking feeling washed through both. The unmistakable outline of the Kylnnar heavy cruiser had appeared in the atmosphere above the planet. Smaller specks surrounded it.

"What are the specks?" Jo asked.

"Fighters," Onesie said.

"They're sending a communication," Onesie said, flicking on the unit's speakers. A garbled hissing and clicking spat out of the system. It sounded like the same few words repeated again and again.

"What are they saying?" asked Simon.

The other two look at him perplexed.

"You know no-one in the Confederation has translated the Kylnnar language, right?" asked Jo.

"Never really thought about it, to be honest," Simon said with a grin. In the green half-light it looked more like a leer.

Jo rolled her eyes. Simon ignored it and switched on his communicator.

"Reynolds," he said into it.

"Sir," came the sergeant's reply.

"Send a full squad to bring the reptiles up to the school. Tell them to bring the one who speaks English to the control room," ordered Simon.

"Which one is that?" asked the sergeant.

Jo laughed behind him. Simon squeezed his eyes shut trying to remember some sort of distinguishing mark.

"The older-looking one with the officer markings on his armour," he clarified and clicked off.

"What are you thinking?" she asked her commander.

"Not sure," he muttered.

"Shame you shot the Colonial; he'd be useful now," she observed acidly.

Simon gave her a glare and went back to staring at the screen.

Three smaller green blobs had broken off from the cruiser; bigger than the fighters but much smaller than the cruiser. They seemed to be heading down to the planet.

"Landers?" Simon asked Onesie.

Harper tapped away at the computer. He nodded confirmation.

"Put me on general broadcast," Simon ordered Onesie.

"All cadets, this is Lieutenant Simon Kim. We have Kylnnar in orbit and three landers coming in. Everyone take position and track the incoming. Under no circumstances are you to open fire without my or Lieutenant Hakeswell's express command."

Hakeswell raised an eyebrow.

"What happens now?" she asked.

"We wait."

The group watched in grim fascination as they studied the landers progressing slowly down towards the surface.

"Where are they heading?" demanded Kim.

"The rock plain if they stay on course," Onesie replied.

"Have the fighters moved?" he asked, trying to stow his nervousness.

"No, sir," replied Onesie.

"The landers, are they running an evasion path or firing countermeasures?"

"No, sir."

"What are you thinking?" Hakeswell demanded, but received no response.

They continued to watch for ten minutes. The three flyers were presenting perfect targets: no attempt at evasion, no fighter support. To Hakeswell it made no sense, but Simon seemed to understand something she did not.

"Shields?" Simon asked Onesie.

"Running as normal," he answered.

"How many on one of those landers?" Simon asked Jo.

She looked at the specification on the screen.

"If they're carrying troops, twenty to twenty-five at a push. These are not the big landers they used when they dropped infantry last time," she offered with a shrug.

"So, seventy-five maximum across the three?" Simon declared, his question clearly rhetorical.

There was commotion at the door. Two cadets armed with pulse rifles pushed their way in before turning to face the door. A Kylnnar followed them in, with another two cadets coming in behind. All four students kept their pulse rifles pointed at the reptile.

"Put the sound on again," ordered Simon.

Kylnnar speech hissed out of the speaker, repeating the same sounds again and again.

Simon looked at the Kylnnar. "What is it saying?" he asked.

The Kylnnar looked at him for a moment, then glanced at the screen. He looked back to Simon.

"Ratriv," the creature hissed out of his mouth, the speech sounding forced and unpleasant.

"Retrieve?" Simon tried to clarify.

The reptile nodded slowly.

Simon nodded back.

"Take him and the other prisoners out to the rock plain," he ordered.

Jo watched him go, before looking back to Simon.

"What's going on, commander?" she demanded.

"Follow me," he smiled. "I'll show you."

The pair walked out into the glaring sunlight, which burnt across the grey sand of the inhospitable planet. They were followed by the four captured Kylnnar, surrounded by cadets, pulse rifles at the ready. They watched the three Kylnnar landers come out of the sky, dropping low over the rock plain. *Horrible boxy things*, thought Jo; all practical design, no beauty, no aesthetic.

They came to a stop just short of the shield, then hovered in the air for a moment before using their landing thrusters to lower themselves gingerly to the ground. They scraped on the rocks of the plain with a grinding, crunching sound, which made the cadets wince. The Kylnnar's flattening of the plain to let through their tanks had not been that successful.

"We can take them anytime," observed Jo.

Simon looked to her. She was not asking to do it, just stating the obvious. He gave a small shake of his head. He could feel the tension in the air, across the ruins and roofs of the nearby buildings. Only yesterday they would have been firing without mercy. It was a palpable effort for them to restrain themselves.

The three landers rested lightly on the ground, in the area cleared for the tanks, and let down their forward ramps. No mass of Kylnnar came charging out. There was no explosion of hidden weaponry. A pair of the reptiles progressed out of each lander, followed a few moments later by another pair. They walked slowly up the plain, arms held wide. There were no signs of any weapons being carried. Each pair stopped before a Kylnnar body and hoisted it between them. There had been no injured Kylnnar. The students may have baulked at killing those they captured, despite standing orders, but had been less moralistic when it had come to dispatching the severely wounded that the reptiles had left behind.

Simon turned to the Kylnnar officer. "You may join your comrades." He hoped he understood; he pointed out in the direction of the plain to make his point.

The Kylnnar looked at Simon; his alien face was impossible for the lieutenant to read. He brought up his hands to the chest and thumped it. He then spread his fists out before him. The other three Kylnnar soldiers followed suit. They then pushed through the cadets surrounding them and walked down towards the landers. When they reached the bodies, they picked up one corpse between each pair and walked it in silence towards the transports.

"Onesie," Simon asked through his comm. "The fighters; have they moved?"

"No, sir," came the response.

"The cruiser; has it powered weapons?"

"No."

"If the fighters so much as blip, or the cruiser does anything, tell me straightaway."

"Yes, lieutenant."

Simon went back to watching the rock plain. The Kylnnar were moving slowly, almost reverently, bringing the bodies into the landers. Sometimes they stumbled around the rocky surface, but they always did what they could to treat the bodies they carried with respect. It took them more than an hour to load sixty bodies across the three landers. The landers took off for the sky and the cadets across the complex visibly relaxed.

"This will take all day," observed Jo coldly.

Simon looked at her with a raised eyebrow.

"Look how many corpses there are," she explained with a wave of her hand across the plain. "We killed a lot of them. More than five hundred all told."

He looked shocked at the number. "Really?" he demanded.

"Five hundred and nine claimed killed by my count, it will be more when you include the ones buried in the tunnels or lost on the landing platform which we never saw. There are four hundred and eleven bodies lying out there on the plain," she informed him.

"So at least that many," Simon mused sadly.

Jo Hakeswell gave him a nod of confirmation.

"They could send more landers," offered Simon.

"No," she countered. "Three is the most they can send without worrying us."

Simon nodded. For some reason, four landers felt much more threatening than three.

"Maybe they think like we do?" he said with a laugh.

She gave him a hard look of disagreement.

Lieutenant Hakeswell was right, though. The ships took slightly less than an hour to return. The process of loading bodies continued, taking another hour before the lander departed. Each time it came back the nervous students would target the ships and their crews. Each time the reptiles would load up and head back to the cruiser without incident. It was early evening, the plain slowly being swallowed in darkness, when the final landers took off for space. The cadets watched them go and collectively gave a huge sigh of relief.

"They took them all," Jo observed quietly.

Simon ignored her, clicking on his communicator.

"What's going on?" he asked Onesie.

"One second, lieutenant," came the response. "Yeah, just docking now."

There was a pause.

"Oh no!" Onesie screeched down the line.

"What?" shouted Simon, turning in the direction of the control room.

"The cruiser; it's powering weapons!" came his panicked response.

"Traitorous scum!" roared Simon. "We do them a favour and they treat us like the cold-blooded reptiles they are. Where are they targeting? Make sure the shields are full."

"The shields are full; they're always on full," Onesie replied.

After a while he reported back. "They're firing on the upper atmosphere," he said, confused.

"What?" Simon shouted into his communicator. "Check for chemicals and biologicals."

"How do I do that?" Onesie squeaked.

Simon had no answer; he did not know himself.

"Simon." Jo's voice was calm, and a comforting hand reached his shoulder. "Look up!"

Simon looked at his fellow lieutenant and then up into the night sky. A spray of blue and green light spiralled across the sky, twisting and turning like writhing snakes, turning white and teal, back to a darker blue, and then to green.

"They're gone. The cruiser, the fighters, they've jumped," Onesie chirped through the comm.

Simon made no reply; he just stared up at the sky, watching patterns in blues and greens writhe across the blackness of night.

"What is it?" he asked Jo.

"I don't know," she offered. "I think they might be saluting us."

"Saluting us?" he queried.

"Lighting up the sky," Jo said, gazing up in wonder.

CHAPTER 24

Location: Wolfsreach Academy, Wolfstar III
Date: 21 December 2196 CE, Earth Standard Calendar
Time: 17.23 Local Time 26.5-hour clock

The planet hopper broke atmosphere and dropped in a slow sweeping angle towards Wolfsreach Military Academy. It aimed for the far end of the valley nearest to the school. They had been told there was no point trying to use the devastated and heavily mined landing platform at the other end. That was one of the reasons they had brought a planet hopper – a lander they could put down almost anywhere – rather than a transport barge. They did not trust the assurances from the Academy that the rock plain had been largely cleared of bigger boulders. What did a bunch of teenagers know about landers anyway?

The pilot was staring out of his view window, assessing his descent, when the control panel in front of him lit up like a firework display. Alarms blared and an electronic voice buzzed in the cabin.

"Weapons track detected," it droned.

The pilot looked at the panel and hit a couple of buttons. It showed the planet hopper was subject to multiple weapon locks.

"Weapons track detected," the computer complained again.

He shut off the voice warning, but the panel continued to flash in alarm. He switched on the comm.

"Wolfsreach Academy, we are a Confederation Army Planet Hopper, callsign CA1359LD. We are tracking four ground-based heavy weapons with target lock on us," the pilot announced, trying to keep the panic out of his voice.

"And?" a voice crackled back through the comm.

"Can you stop tracking us; we're friendly?" the incredulous pilot demanded.

"No. This is an active war zone; we track everything," came the reply.

"What the hell? What if you fire by accident?" the pilot demanded.

"If we fire on you, it won't be an accident. Continue your descent," came the terse reply, before the comm went dead.

The pilot looked back to the major seated behind him, seeking guidance.

"You heard him: continue the descent," said the major with a smile.

The pilot bit back his anger and went back to staring through his view screen.

The planet hopper came to a rest on the rocky grey sloping plain in front of the school. The five legs of its landing gear gave it purchase on the uneven surface. Its green-brown jungle camouflage stuck out starkly in the barren landscape. The gangway at the front of the ship dropped with a hiss of hydraulic fluid. A squad of ten soldiers spilled out of the ship, their green camo uniforms little help against the ashen surface of the planet. They carried pulse rifles and were laden with full pack. They fanned out and assumed defensive positions around the planet hopper.

The major, a tall, urbane military man, strode down the gangplank. He wore neatly pressed fatigues and carried only his sidearm. He wore his service cap rather than the sensor helmet his soldiers were wearing. That was probably for the best, as his troops were increasingly alarmed by the number of warning pings that the helmet sensors were giving. Each of them was lit up, some of them several times.

The officer scanned the devastated school. Where the gym should have stood was a burnt-out pile of blackened rubble. Much of the rest of the school was still standing, but signs of battle were obvious everywhere: the rupture from high-explosive pulse shells; the cauterized gaps from the sweep of military lasers. He took in the tangled metal of destroyed tanks, mostly Kylnnar vehicles of the latest designation. Then he noticed what might be a Confederation Army grav-tank, or at least the shattered remains of one. *What was that doing here*, he wondered? How had a bunch of teenagers taken out tanks?

As he stood staring, a woman appeared from the rubble and approached him. It was only as she got closer that he realized she was more a girl than a woman. She was exhausted and her face and hair were stained with ash and dirt. Her red and black cadet uniform was torn and soiled. She stopped in front of him and saluted smartly. She did not offer a name or rank.

"Who are you?" she demanded.

"Major Robert Burton, 9th Drop Infantry," he supplied politely.

He flipped out a breathing mask and took a hit of oxygen. He looked at the girl; she seemed unconcerned by the punishing atmosphere that was already tearing at his lungs.

"Are you in command?" he asked.

"No, sir," she replied sharply. "Lieutenant!"

Her shout ran out across the plain. Moments later, a young man appeared from the school and strode down the gentle slope to stand next to the girl. He saluted; a deal less smartly than his colleague. Major Burton took him in; *an Asian kid, not yet a man*, he thought. Then he saw the coldness of his eyes. They contained something that only those who had seen combat have. A knowing that the person had experienced things that they would never be able to let go of. He glanced at the female lieutenant next to him; her face had the same hardness. He felt a great sadness wash over him.

"Cadet Lieutenant Simon Kim, officer commanding Wolfsreach Academy," Simon supplied wearily.

"Then you must be Cadet Lieutenant Joanna Hakeswell-Smith?" Burton asked the woman. He pronounced the second surname 'Smythe'.

Simon raised an eyebrow at that but said nothing.

"Your grandmother sends her regards," continued the major.

"How is the Vice-Admiral?" asked Joanna, her tone surprisingly surly.

"Alarmed to hear her only granddaughter was trapped here on Wolfstar III."

"Is that the reason you came? Because her grandmother is an admiral?" Simon's tone was between anger and contempt.

"Not at all," the major smiled. "The press somehow got word of your situation and you have become something of a cause celebre. Though I'll admit that her grandmother's identity was probably what motivated the Navy to move a bit faster than would otherwise have been the case."

"Leaving two hundred kids to die in the deep reaches of space would play badly on the news stream?" Jo observed sarcastically.

"Something like that," Major Burton replied and smiled again. "Lieutenant Kim, my orders are to take command of

Wolfsreach Academy and arrange the evacuation of all Confederation personnel currently on the planet. Can I confirm the number requiring embarkation?"

"We have fifty-six uninjured or lightly wounded, another sixty walking wounded, though some are borderline. We have twenty-three personnel requiring full medical evacuation."

"It's twenty-one now; two died earlier today," interjected Lieutenant Hakeswell quietly.

"Apologies: twenty-one requiring medical evacuation," Simon corrected himself.

"So that leaves you with sixty-three dead?" asked the major.

"Sixty-four. Sixty-three students and one medical auxiliary," Simon explained.

Major Burton nodded. "Get everyone. We will start the evacuation immediately. My orders are that everyone is to be evacuated, both living and dead," stated the Major.

"We're taking the dead?" Jo commented, surprised.

"Those are my orders, cadet lieutenant. They are very clear."

"It's just that the standing orders are that the dead are buried where they die," she observed.

"I'm aware, but as I say, my orders are very clear."

"The press?" she asked.

"Shall we get on?" the major asked Simon, ignoring Jo.

"Yes, sir," Simon replied.

"Good. Planet hoppers will be used to evacuate. There is no space for our larger barges," explained the major.

Simon raised an eyebrow at that but said nothing. If the Kylnnar could manage it why not the Confederation Navy? He stopped thinking about it while the man was still speaking.

"They will be bringing in engineers. I have additional orders to destroy the armoury and the academy once we depart," he explained. "Lieutenant Kim, can you confirm that your gunners will refrain from targeting the incoming ships?"

"They're your gunners now, major. I consider myself relieved, but I will relay your order," Simon responded. "And it's cadet lieutenant, sir."

"That is incorrect, lieutenant. My understanding is that you turned eighteen yesterday."

Simon cocked his head as if thinking when his birthday was. The major was right; he had completely forgotten his own birthday.

"According to army regulations, as an eighteen-year-old, you cannot hold a cadet commission. So, as of yesterday, you have been gazetted full lieutenant. Normally you would go in as a second lieutenant, but the lads in the press corps were afraid that might look like a demotion to those who don't understand army regs. We have decided to promote you directly to first lieutenant. Congratulations."

"Oh my God!" Jo's shriek of exasperation came before Simon could offer any response. "I actually hate the military."

The two surprised men watched as the cadet lieutenant turned on her heel and stalked off towards the school.

"What was that about?" asked the major.

"No idea," came Simon's puzzled reply.

***

The bodies of the dead had been laid out in neat rows on the surface of the astro-hockey pitch. Armoury Specialist Felix 'Tommo' Thomas squatted down next to one of the bodies, thrusting his pulse rifle behind him as he did so. He removed his helmet and placed it on the ground next to him. A look of sadness pervaded his face.

"Hello, Gunny," he said quietly.

"You knew Helen?" came a voice from his side. He saw a hint of black and red student uniform in his peripheral vision.

"It's Miss Murphy to you, cadet," he barked unkindly.

"It's lieutenant, soldier," came the matter-of-fact reply.

The grizzled soldier placed his hands on his knees and pushed himself up. A young Asian man was standing next to him, dressed in a cadet uniform with the bar of a lieutenant on his shoulder. Tommo immediately recognized him from the briefing they had received before making planetfall. The hotshot: the kid who had commanded this defence.

Tommo's boots snapped together and, despite his missing headgear, he executed the smartest salute he had managed in many years of service.

"As you were, soldier," the young officer ordered with disquieting confidence. "So how do you know Miss Murphy?"

"I served here in the armoury. We sank a few jars over the months I was here. Did you know she used to be a marine?"

A vague look of recognition registered on Simon's face. The students had been kept away from the armoury staff, so he didn't know them well, but now he remembered the man.

"I didn't," he replied.

"Gunnery Sergeant invalided out when she lost her leg," Tommo explained.

"I didn't know, though that explains a lot. She had an odd knowledge of weapons and tactics for a medical auxiliary," said Simon with a fond smile, remembering better times. "She refused to pick up a gun, though. She hated fighting. Even at the end, when the Kylnnar cut her down, she didn't fight back."

"She told me she'd killed enough for one lifetime," observed the soldier. "I knew she'd seen action, but I only got the full story after we'd left. You remember the Samarkand?"

Simon Kim shook his head.

"I suppose you wouldn't; you're too young. It was the very early days of the war. The CSX Samarkand was a

Confederation Carrier; the pride of the Ninth Fleet. It and its carrier group came out of its wormhole right into the waiting hands of multiple Kylnnar battlefleets. Those were in the days before we knew they could jam our tracking systems, before we even knew that they were jamming them. They walked straight into a trap. The carrier lost half its starfighters to military lasers before they even made vacuum. The admiral in command made the decision to flee; it was that or die. While the carrier started to form a new wormhole, its accompanying vessels tried to protect it from the incoming firestorm. Did she tell you she was from the Isles?" asked Tommo.

"She mentioned it," Simon replied.

"There was a light cruiser, the CSLC Wellington. This was in the days when the crew would be recruited from one region, before the policy changed. The ship was all Isles people. You know what nutters that lot can be. The Wellington was tasked with covering the carrier's final escape, fighting a desperate rearguard action. The ship was burnt from stem to stern, its jump engines obliterated. Still, it kept fighting. Eventually the ship somehow grappled onto the carrier and was pulled through its wormhole as it escaped. CSLC Wellington took ninety percent fatalities. When they asked the captain how he'd managed to save his ship, he said 'we're from the Isles; we don't do last stands'."

Simon gave a laugh of recognition at that. "And Miss Murphy?" he asked.

"She was one of the rear gunners. When they got the ship to safety, they found her unconscious body strapped in her gun chair. The atmosphere had vented, the hull blown out. No one is sure how she survived. She had breathing apparatus, but her leg was blown off. She should have died from blood loss or frozen to death when the ship vented. The Admiral of the Samarkand was booted up to an office job, the Captain of the Wellington got the Navy Star, and Gunnery Sergeant Murphy got the Combined

Confederation Cluster – the highest medal for valour the Confederation can bestow."

"Not sure medals matter much," Simon observed, looking down at Helen Murphy's body.

"Try not to say that when they present one to you," laughed Tommo.

"Come again?" demanded Simon.

"Word is, lieutenant, that you'll be given the Cluster for this action, and you won't be the only one."

A pair of soldiers carrying a stretcher appeared.

"We okay to move this one, sir?" one of them asked Simon.

He gave a nod of approval.

They roughly handled Helen Murphy into a black body bag, zipping it up over her face. Simon shivered at the finality of it.

"I'll go with, if that's okay with you, sir?"

Lieutenant Kim looked at Tommo and gave another nod.

They circled around the ruined expanse of the gym and set off to the plain to where the planet hoppers had collected. Simon saw Jo standing next to the burned-out ruins, watching the ships taking off for orbit. Others were landing as people and equipment were shuttled back and forth to the ships in space.

Simon walked over to join her; it was oddly peaceful contemplating the bustle at a distance. She glanced at him without saying anything and went back to staring at the planet hoppers.

"I wanted to say one thing." Simon waited for a response, but she seemed to be ignoring him. "I couldn't have done it without you, Jo Jo."

Receiving no reply, he strode down the slope of the plain towards the evacuation site. She watched him go and then realized that was the first time he had used her hated nickname since that day in the Principal's office when he had been given command. She decided she didn't mind the nickname so much anymore.

CONFEDERATION NAVY REPORT ADDENDUM

Location: CSX Washington, Confederation Sixth Fleet
Date: 31st December 2196 CE, Earth Standard Calendar
Time: 13.00 Earth Standard Time

The following concludes the Confederation Army's report on what they are rather dramatically calling 'the defence of Wolfsreach Academy'. Given our lack of participation in the defence we have chosen not to compile our own complete report but instead provide an addendum for the Confederation Army Report. Despite the Army's attempt to appropriate credit for this action, we would note that it was our vessels that rescued the students of Wolfsreach Academy.

We have also contested the attempt by the Army to assign partial blame for the failed evacuation of all the students of Wolfsreach Academy, prior to the alien arrival, to the Navy. This was clearly an administrative failure by the Army. We have no record of being informed that two hundred students were stranded on Wolfstar III. Had we been made aware of this, every effort would have been made to evacuate them. The presence of the granddaughter of a senior naval officer at the defence has helped with the government narrative that we are all in this war equally. The Navy Press Corps has actively pushed this angle.

The Kylnnar sub-fleet is believed to be the same one that joined the Kylnnar assault on Comendan IV, in the Comendan System. This fleet was designated Kylnnar Sub-Fleet Barracuda on its arrival. Barracuda's constituent ships, and the tanks it brought to the jungle world, indicate it may be the same fleet. Certainly, the unexpected arrival of further heavy armour for the Kylnnar assault on Comendan IV has resulted in our position on the southern savannah being overrun. Initial reports indicate that this has forced the Confederation Army to begin a phased withdrawal from the area to the central belt of equatorial jungle, where the Kylnnar heavy armour is less effective. This is not the place to discuss the ongoing defence of Comendan IV, in which I continue to hope for the best. It is simply to highlight that the caution that the Kylnnar displayed with regard to their assault on Wolfsreach Academy, together with their abrupt withdrawal, likely reflected the need for their troops and equipment to be preserved to support the assault on Comendan IV, which has now taken place to our detriment. The Sixth Fleet intelligence officers surmise that Kylnnar sub-fleet Barracuda was likely tasked with destroying Wolfsreach Academy as a simple eradication operation. When the operation proved more time- and material-consuming than expected, the Kylnnar made the decision to sacrifice the smaller tactical objective of eradicating the base on

Wolfstar III for the broader strategic objective: the campaign on Comendan IV.

In terms of the students, Lieutenant Simon Kim has been deemed to have graduated the academy by the Army. He and any other students deemed to have graduated will be redeployed to full-time military duties with a yet-to-be designated unit on Comendan IV. The rest of the surviving students, including the injured, have been evacuated to the safe mining world of Altor. Five badly injured students requiring long-term care have been evacuated back to the Solar System to a specialist facility on Mars.

The Army is keen that the cadets be treated with full military honours and that those who died or who subsequently die of their wounds be interred in military cemeteries. We have contested this decision given standing orders are that casualties should lie where they die. Given the public outcry over the Wolfsreach incident we have done this quietly through channels, but we expect the Army will get their way.

The Army also intends to award medals and citations to the defenders of Wolfsreach Academy. The Navy maintains the view that what occurred during the defence has clearly been exaggerated. It is clearly implausible that a group of inexperienced, though we concede military-trained, young people could conduct such a successful defence against overwhelming odds. It will probably be one for military historians to clarify in the future, but it is clear that the extent of the Kylnnar attack has been exaggerated and was conducted with an uncharacteristic degree of caution, if not outright incompetence by the Kylnnar commander. This contrasts with the Army's approach, which is to highlight it as a textbook study in how to conduct a successful siege defence. We believe the Army is using the successful action as a way of highlighting the effectiveness of their military academy system. The Navy continues to believe the military academy system conflicts with the Navy's efforts to recruit the personnel it requires.

Given the political and media storm around events of Wolfstar III, we do not believe it would be correct to make a protest over the awarding of medals that might be subject to public scrutiny. We have protested through channels at the awarding of a medal to a civilian, most notably that her former career in the Confederation Navy somehow gives her an aura of military status. If she were indeed to be considered as a marine during the action, such a decision would be made by the Navy, not the Army. Our protest has been ignored.

Based on information gleaned from the Army, the following awards will be made for the defence of Wolfsreach Academy:

Unit Citation – Outstanding Bravery – Wolfstar III Planetary Defence Force

The Military Star Medal – The Confederation Army's highest award for bravery – this is to be awarded to eighteen members of the Wolfstar III Planetary Defence Force – names still pending at this time.

The Combined Confederation Cluster – The Confederation Combined Military's highest award for valour in the face of the enemy – nine are to be awarded, the largest ever for a single action. One is to be awarded as a comet as the recipient has previously been awarded the same medal – the names are set out below.

Cadet Private Joseph Harper

Cadet Private Fletcher Lynch – deceased

Cadet Private Julia Williams – deceased

Cadet Corporal Mohammed Abdi

Cadet Corporal Inaya Chandra

Cadet Sergeant Travis Ronin

Gunnery Sergeant Helen Murphy – Combined Confederation Cluster with Comet – deceased

Cadet Second Lieutenant Joanna Hakeswell-Smith

First Lieutenant Simon Kim, Planetary Governor of Wolfstar III and officer commanding the defence of Wolfsreach Academy.

Report Addendum compiled for the Navy by:

Commander Sonia Pandey – Sixth Fleet Confederation Navy

ABOUT THE AUTHOR

Justin Waine has been writing fantasy novels for almost as long as he has been reading them. Having spent the last two decades working in the investment industry he decided he really should get around to publishing some of them. He is the author of The Company of Slayers series and the forthcoming Kylnnar War Saga. When not writing he spends his time training and teaching martial arts.

DID YOU LIKE IT?

So, you have made it this far. Either you liked it, or you pushed through to the end. Either way I would love to hear what you think of my work. Please rate and review on Amazon, Goodreads or your platform of choice. Also don't forget to tell your family, friends, enemies and random strangers on the street about my books.

You can follow me on Amazon or on Instagram at justinwaineauthor to stay updated on forthcoming books and events. You can also keep up to date via the Epsom Fantasy Press Limited website.

www.epsomfantasypress.co.uk

Printed in Great Britain
by Amazon

46282391R00149